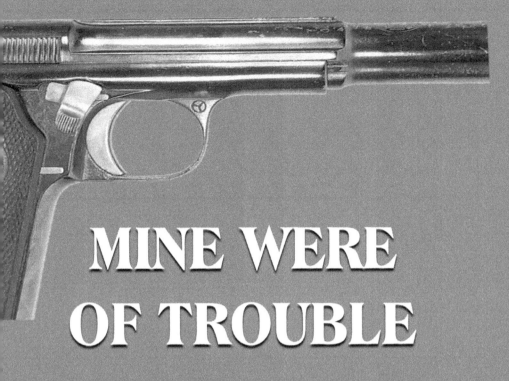

MINE WERE
OF TROUBLE

A NATIONALIST ACCOUNT OF THE
SPANISH CIVIL WAR

PETER CAMP

TO CYNTHIA

The thoughts of others
Were light and fleeting,
Of lovers' meeting
Or luck or fame.
Mine were of trouble. . . .
 A. E. Housman

In having thus complied with your wishes I only hope that your sons will support if necessary with their lives our present glorious Constitution both in Church and State, love their king and hate all republics and republicans.

Letter from Nelson to Revd Mr Priestly,

CONTENTS

PROLOGUE

It is hard now to recall the atmosphere of 1936. When I came down from Cambridge in June of that year the pattern of European politics was confused and obscure. The foundations of peace seemed in danger of collapse, but as yet few were convinced that another World War was inevitable, or could foresee the alignment of the Powers if it should happen. The bewilderment of the peoples of Europe was reflected in the mistakes and hesitations of their rulers.

Hitler had achieved supreme power in Germany, but the full horrors and dangers of his rule were not universally apparent; indeed, he was often applauded in Germany and outside for 'cleaning up the mess' of the Weimar Republic and for his suppression of Communism. But the recreation of the Wehrmacht, Germany's withdrawal from the League of Nations and her military occupation of the Rhineland gave warning of what was to come.

In a France weakened by a succession of shortlived and ineffective governments and resentful that victory in 1918 had brought neither security nor stability, the German occupation of the Rhineland induced a shock of indignation and protest. Monsieur Flandin, taken by surprise, was unable to act with the necessary decision. Having approached the British Government for assurances that Britain would support French military action against the German coup and being unable to obtain them, he acquiesced in a situation which all Frenchmen deplored, and of which most were terrified. The national disapproval was reflected in the subsequent elections, which returned to power a Front Populaire government under the nominal leadership of Monsieur Léon Blum, but with powerful, though less obvious, Communist affiliations. The national unity welded by German action was succeeded by anger and disintegration, by strikes and mass demonstrations in which supporters of the Front Populaire clashed bloodily with Anciens Combatants, Action Francaise and Croix-de-Feu. The general opinion in England was that 'the French are at loggerheads'.

The Italian people, elated by their success in Abyssinia in the face of British and French opposition, were embittered rather than discouraged by the policy of Sanctions. They become progressively and aggressively anti-British and increasingly truculent towards their French and Balkan neighbors. The Axis was being forged.

In South-eastern Europe Jugoslavia, plunged into crisis two years earlier by the murder of King Alexander, was continually disturbed by further Ustashi and

I.M.R.O. activities. The former were fomented by Italy, the latter by Bulgaria. Throughout the country Croats, Macedonians and Mussulmans were reacting against the dominance of Serbia. Albania was ruled by King Ahmed Zogu with Italian financial and economic aid. In October of 1935 King George of Greece had been restored to his throne by a plebiscite of his people.

Russian policy had been radically altered by two important events a couple of years earlier: in internal affairs the murder of Kirov in Leningrad on December 1st, 1934, put an end to all hopes that Stalin might follow a more liberal policy; there ensued a merciless repression, beginning with the trial and execution of Zinoviev and Kamenev and culminating in the virtual elimination of the Bolshevik 'Old Guard' in the great purges of 1936-38. In the words of Greta Garbo in the film, *Ninotchka*, there would be 'fewer, and better, Russians'. The other event, which had a vital effect on Soviet foreign policy and on Communist activity throughout Europe, was the inauguration, at the Seventh Congress of the Komintern in 1934, of the doctrine of the Popular Front. In the future, Communists abroad were to combine with all parties—Socialist, Liberal, Radical and even Conservative—who would join them in a 'Popular Front for Peace and against Fascism'.[1]

The control of the various Popular Fronts was to be in the firm but unobtrusive hands of the Communists. Within the next two years Popular Front governments were established in France and Spain.

The Spanish monarchy had fallen five years before in April, 1931, when King Alfonso XIII went into voluntary exile to avoid the risk of civil war; shortly afterwards Don Niceto Alcalá Zamora became President of the Spanish Republic, with Don Manuel Azaña as Prime Minister. A Socialist government controlled the country for the next two years. Its rule was interrupted briefly by an attempted coup d'état on August 10th, 1932, led by General Sanjurjo, the 'Lion of Morocco', which was quickly suppressed. Sanjurjo had commanded the Guardia Civil in 1931 and by his defeatist attitude had precipitated the departure of King Alfonso; now he declared for the King, but was captured and sentenced to death, reprieved at the last moment by Azaña and sent to prison in Spanish West Africa.

In 1933 the Socialist government was superseded by a coalition of right-wing parties under the leadership of Señor Gil Robles. In 1934 the parties of the left attempted armed revolution, which broke into civil war in Asturias among the inflammable miners of that province. After heavy fighting this revolt was suppressed, the instigators being treated with leniency. A succession of right-wing Governments continued until the elections of February 1936, which put a

Popular Front government into power, with Señor Casares Quiroga as Prime Minister.

This Government proved unable to control the extremists of the right or of the left, and preparations for civil war began on both sides throughout the country.[2]

Such was the state of Europe when I came down from Cambridge, not yet twenty-one years of age, with a Degree in Classics and Law, a restless temperament, no money, and what the Trinity College Magazine once described as a 'deplorable tendency to simper'.

---

[1] Dr. I. Deutscher, *Stalin* (Oxford, 1949) p. 419. See also Mr. Arthur Koestler in *The God that Failed* (Hamish Hamilton, 1950). pp. 70-71.

[2] See Madariaga, *Spain*, pp. 300-352 (Cape, 1942).

CHAPTER ONE

I remember very well the morning I left London. It was a cold, wet day in November 1936 and in the Temple gardens the trees, now bare of their leaves, swayed and dripped sadly in the bleak wind. I had been awake since dawn and had breakfasted lightly, for I was too excited to feel hungry; now that the one suitcase that was all my luggage stood by the door of the flat and I took a last look around. In an hour the charwoman would arrive and in the evening the two barristers with whom I shared the flat would return from their chambers; by then I should be across the Channel, on my way to Spain and the Civil War.

As I stood at my bedroom window, looking down on the puddles in King's Bench Walk, a green sports car with a long bonnet turned the corner by the library and stopped immediately beneath me. The door opened and the lanky figure of Daughleigh Hills stepped on to the pavement, making signs for me to hurry down. A year younger than myself and one of my closest friends at Cambridge, he had suggested, on hearing of my plans, that he should drive me in his new Aston Martin to the boat at Newhaven, where I would say good-bye to my mother and father. I turned from the window, took leave of my Number 2, Paper Buildings, and carried my luggage down to the waiting car.

It had taken me almost a month to make my final decision to go to this war and abandon, at least temporarily, my efforts to become a barrister. Even then I had no idea how to carry out my decision. I knew no Spanish, I had never been to Spain and I did not know anyone on the Nationalist side. Of course, if I had been willing to join the International Brigade and fight for the Republicans it would have been simple; in every country there were organizations, ably directed by the various Communist parties, for that very purpose. But the Nationalists were making no effort to recruit in England.

Luckily, at this point I received an invitation through a friend to see the Marqués del Moral, who occupied a position in the Nationalist Agency in London. Del Moral, an Englishman by birth who had distinguished himself as a young man in South Africa, received me with some reserve:

'So you want to go to Spain. Why?'

'To fight, sir.'

'Good.' He relaxed a little of his severity.

'Well now, I can give you a letter to a friend of mine in Biarritz, the Conde de los Andes. He runs a courier service across the frontier and I dare say he'd send you as far as Burgos. Better not let him know you're going to fight, though. With all this talk of Non-Intervention the French authorities wouldn't be so tolerant of his couriers if they thought he was passing through volunteers for our side—though they don't seem to mind how many go through to the Reds.' He smiled rather sourly. 'Can you get a journalist's cover? I suggest a chit from some editor saying you are authorized to send him articles and news.'

'I think I can manage that. But what do I do when I get to Burgos?'

'I'm afraid I can't help you there; you'll have to look after yourself. But it shouldn't be difficult. After all, it is the G.H.Q.'

Very soon afterwards I was in Northcliffe House, asking to see my friend, Collin Brooks, then editor of the Sunday Dispatch. At that time Lord Rothermere's newspapers were supporting the Nationalists. An accessible and genial person, Brooks listened attentively while I told him of my project and of my conversation with del Moral.

'Boy,' he said, beaming at me through the thick lenses of his glasses, 'there's anything from fifty to five hundred pounds in this! Good luck to you and send us anything you can.'

When I left his office I carried a piece of paper, signed by him, which read, as far as I can remember:

'To Whom It May Concern. Mr. Peter Kemp is authorized to collect news and transmit articles for the Sunday Dispatch from the Spanish Fronts of War.'

We were silent as the car splashed through the suburbs. I was going over in my mind the events of the past fortnight; everything seemed to have happened so quickly since I had made my decision and written, in some trepidation, to tell my father. A retired Chief Justice of the Bombay High Court, he disapproved, I knew, of many aspects of my life at Cambridge and in London—he had visions of my rowing in the University boat and getting a double First in Classics and Law, and he was justly disappointed when I gave up rowing after my first year and barely achieved an honours degree at the end of my third.

I was surprised, therefore, by his generous reaction to my letter. He came to see me in London, announced that he had told his Bank to open a monthly credit for me in Burgos, gave me a great deal of sound advice and finally took me on a tour of the Army and Navy Stores—'To see you get the right equipment for this sort of thing.' I have no idea what equipment we bought, but I remember a bulky 'medicine chest' which seemed to contain chiefly iodine, quinine and cascara and which I lost within a month of my arrival in Spain. I also bought Hugo's

Spanish in Three Months Without a Master. I rejected my father's offer of his .275 sporting Männlicher carbine as being likely to cause trouble with Customs.

The ensuring days I spent in a state of joyful excitement and in the preparations for my journey. One incident only remains in my memory. I was having tea with a friend in her house; we had often discussed the idea of my going to Spain and now, with my departure imminent, I suppose I had acquired a certain glamour in her eyes. After a while her father came into the room, an old professional soldier, now retired, with a distinguished record in the Great War and several lesser wars before it.

'Daddy!' she shouted, for he had become very deaf, 'Peter Kemp is going off to Spain!'

'Spain!' the old gentleman roared back, 'Spain! What's he want to go to Spain for?'

'He's going to fight in the war, Daddy.'

'What! What!' The Colonel turned on me. 'You're going to Spain to fight?'

'Yes, sir.'

'You damned young fool! You know what fighting means? It's hell! You bloody young idiot! Ever read Napier's Peninsular War?'—I hadn't—'You damned well read it. Icicles hanging from their noses. Icicles, frost-bite, hunger! It's hell, I tell you. You make me sick.'

* * *

We passed through East Grinstead and left the traffic behind. The wind tore across the bonnet in great gusts from the southwest, slapping viciously at the side curtains, while the rain beat in a fierce deluge on the wind-screen. Exhilarated by the roar of the engine and by our need for haste, Hills urged the car on through the Sussex countryside towards the coast. The vibration of the wheel in his hands, the hiss of the tyres on the wet tarmac and the splash of mud against the wings—all are still vivid in my memory. More vivid still is a wild moment when he took a sharp curve at close on eighty, skidded sideways towards a telegraph pole and a ditch and straightened out, apparently without effort, on the rim of disaster. I was nervous on corners since the night, a few months previously and shortly before my Tripos examinations, when I had failed to take a double bend at Melbourne, just outside Cambridge, and run a 'Speed Six' Bentley through a wire fence and a concrete wall into a telegraph pole, damaging myself only slightly but dislocating the telegraph and telephonic communications between London and Cambridge for twenty-four hours. 'Dear

Peter,' began the typewritten letter from my father a week later, 'this deplorable termination of your career at Cambridge. . . . Sometimes' he concluded, 'I think that God must have made you for a bet.'

'Peter,' said Hills suddenly, 'what the devil is this really in aid of?'

'Meaning what?'

'Well, all I know at the moment is that you're going to Spain, that you're going there to fight and that you're going to fight against the Government or the Reds or whatever you like to call them. Just why are you going? And why particularly do you choose to fight for the Insurgents? Or don't you really mind which side you fight for?'

'Certainly,' I answered tartly, 'I mind very much which side I fight for. Nothing in the world would induce me to join the other side. Moreover,' I added pompously, 'you know the interest I took in politics at Cambridge.'

'Yes, I remember you were too conservative for the Conservative Association, so you formed a splinter union of your own.' He grinned. 'I don't care about politics myself—we've had too many politicians in the family. Still, if you hold strong political views I dare say it's quite a good idea to go and fight for them.'

'My reasons aren't' entirely political—in fact, I think the political motive is about the least important, except that it determined what side I chose. You see, quite frankly this war has broken out at a particularly opportune moment for me. I've finished my time at Cambridge and taken my degree, but I haven't yet started on a career, and I have still some months to play with before I commit myself irrevocably to a job that will tie me down for the rest of my life. This war isn't likely to last more than six months; it's a splendid chance for me to go out on my own, to see a strange country and get to know its people and language, also to learn something about modern warfare—God knows that's likely to be useful enough! Above all, it's a chance to learn to look after myself in difficulty and danger. Up till now I've never really had to do anything for myself. I mean I've always known where my next meal was coming from and that, provided I look both ways before crossing the street, I'm not likely to be in any danger.

'But there's another thing, just as important: If you've read the news reports published at the beginning of this war, before the imposition of censorship, you'll know that there were appalling scenes of mob violence throughout Government territory, wherever the Reds took control. Priests and nuns were shot simply because they were priests or nuns, ordinary people murdered just because they had a little money or property. It is to fight against that sort of thing that I am going to Spain.'

I stopped for breath after this recital. Reviewing them now, I find my words embarrassingly naïve; perhaps I really was trying to justify my decision to myself, to convince myself for the last time that it was the right one. On that stormy November morning I did not know what most of us have learned since, that you do not practice to go to war for only a few months, and that it is much easier to get into a war than to get out of it.

'At least,' I finished, 'the experience is bound to be useful, and anyway I've nothing to lose.'

We must have done that drive in almost record time, but when we reached Newhaven we found that we had hurried for nothing. Owing to the gale the day service had been cancelled, and I had to wait until evening for a boat.

I found my mother and father by the jetty. They had driven from Cooden to see me off, but wisely decided to say good-bye then and there, rather than wait around the whole day. We all hated prolonged leave-takings—the forced cheerfulness, the trivial chatter and embarrassed silences with the tension mounting hour by hour. I realized that what for me was a gay adventure meant for them the start of a long period of separation and anxiety. I was deeply moved by the way they were taking everything, by my mother's cheerful and uncomplaining courage and my father's generous acceptance of a plan which must have appeared to him to be crazy. When we had said a spirited farewell, standing beside their car on the front and raising our voices above the wind and sea, I started to walk towards the hotel where I had left Hills. I turned once to look back at them. I still remember my father's broad figure in a dripping mackintosh and old fisherman's hat, standing by the open door of the car, his stern, sad face gazing intently after me. I never saw him again.

To pass the time Hills suggested a visit to friends of ours, David and Anthony Holland, who lived nearby at Balcombe. Although impatient to start my journey, I lingered gratefully by the fire in the bright, comfortable drawing-room, savouring—as I then felt for the last time—the cozy warmth of an English country house and the cheery hospitality of my friends. Truly one is never so drawn to England and things English as at moments of departure and return.

As we were leaving, their father said to me: 'Here, I would like to give you this.' He took something from his pocket. It was a small black idol about four inches long, roughly carved in wood and worn smooth and shiny with age and frequent handling. The face had an expression of unusual benevolence and charm.

'I bought him in the Congo a few years ago. He's a lucky fellow. Keep him in your pocket.'

Thereafter I always kept him in my pocket wherever I went, until the day, two and a half years later, when I was carried to the hospital on a stretcher, barely conscious and at the gate of death. In the following days of pain and oblivion he somehow disappeared.

* * *

The Conde de los Andes, seated at a heavy mahogany desk in his study, was brief and businesslike.

'I will apply for your salvoconducto to-day. It will be waiting for you at the Spanish frontier the day after to-morrow. Be here then at half past ten in the morning and one of my cars will run you to Burgos.'

I walked out into the sunshine and strolled along the cliffs, delighting in the fresh breeze on my face and the sight of the long green waves rolling in from the Atlantic and bursting in foam on the black rocks below me. I pranced with joy as I reveled in the thought of my new freedom and the adventures that lay before me.

In this mood of elation I took the bus to Bayonne that afternoon after an excellent lunch and, certainly, rather too much wine with it. After wandering round the town and the port I went into the cathedral and there, sitting in the cool, dark silence, I began to reflect on the events in Spain which had led to the explosion of civil war.

My thoughts raced across the pages of recent Spanish history as I sat with my head in my hands. Slowly a drowsiness overcame me, induced by my tiredness and the wine I had drunk at lunch. When I awoke it was night and the cathedral was deserted and in darkness, except for a few faint lights by the alter. I made my way to the door where I had entered. It was locked. So, too, were the other doors I tried. I called out, softly at first as I felt the impropriety of raising my voice in a cathedral, but louder afterwards until in the end I threw away all restraint and shouted at the top of my voice. After a time—it seemed like ages to me—I heard a shuffling and muttering and a cross little figure appeared, shaking a large bunch of keys. My French is mediocre in the best of circumstances and, feeling the fool I did, I was more tonguetied than usual. I stammered, 'Je me suis endormi' several times, grinning ingratiatingly, pressed some money into the sacristan's hand and fled.

Two days later at half past ten on a bright, clear morning I rang the bell at the Conde de los Andes's villa. Under a brown teddy bear overcoat I wore riding breeches, puttees and ammunition boots, relics of my service at the Cambridge University Officers Training Corps. I carried in my pocket my O.T.C. Certificates A and B, which I hoped might give me some prestige in the eyes of the Spanish military authorities. At half past eleven a large black touring-car drew up, driven by a well-dressed man who introduced himself to me in perfect English as the courier, Señor Pascual Vicuña. When the car had been loaded with my suitcase and a number of brief-cases, parcels and newspapers I climbed in beside him and we drove away.

We followed the coast road south to St. Jean-de-Luz and Hendaye. I sat back happily, admiring the dappled pattern of fields and woods on our left, which rolled away to the dark line of the Pyrenees that stretched eastwards in a broken contour ahead of us.

As we drove, Vicuña with great tact and courtesy questioned me on my reasons for traveling to Spain; but I had resolved to keep strictly to my journalist's cover until we were over the frontier. He told me that he often went to London, where he preferred to stay at the Dorchester, although on his last visit he stayed at that new block of flats in Piccadilly, Anthenæum Court—did I know it? I seemed to remember that he had a son and two daughters at school in England.

He was a great admirer of the English and their way of life. It was a pity that, at the present, there was so little understanding in England of the Nationalist cause—there was so much Red propaganda about. He was convinced that if the British Government really understood the issues being fought out in Spain they wouldn't hesitate to send help to the Nationalists. After all, it was really England's battle that was being fought almost as much as Spain's; because if the Reds were to win—of course this was unthinkable, but if they were to win— Communism would triumph in Spain, then France would go Communist too, then where would England be? The Reds had perpetrated appalling crimes in Spain, as I should soon find out for myself.

This theme, most of which accorded with my own views, was one which I was to hear repeated constantly and with rising vehemence by all kinds and classes of Spaniards during the next two and a half years.

While we waited at Hendaye for the French authorities to stamp our passports and examine the luggage I stood at the barrier of the International Bridge, gazing across the River Bidassoa to the green hills on the Spanish side. Two months earlier they had been the scene of some of the bitterest fighting of the year, when General Mola's Carlists, after a long and bloody assault, had stormed the dominating fort of San Marcial and secured the key town of Irun and the western gateway of the Pyrenees. A few of the defending forces—Basque Republicans and Asturian miners—escaped westwards to San Sebastian, whence they were evicted nine days later. The remainder, after burning Irun, crossed over into France to be disarmed and interned in squalor and destitution until the outbreak of the Second World War. The International Brigade was their only way out of Spain, apart from swimming the Bidassoa, and harrowing accounts were received in London of the frightened mass of refugees desperately making their way along it to safety—which I am told inspired some witty if heartless young secretary at the Foreign Office to comment: 'That's what comes of putting all your Basques in one exit.'

I could see the square fort on a hill to my left, with the red and gold colors of Nationalist Spain floating from its walls. The Nationalists had paid for their victory with some of their best blood, the gallant and devoted Carlists from Navarre and Álava who had rallied to a man to Mola's colours on the outbreak of war. Boys of fifteen and old men of seventy alike rose to defend la Fé and la Tradición, following in the steps of their ancestors who had fought under Zumalacarregui[1] in the last century. They, with no military training whatever, were taught how to load and fire a rifle as they were brought by the lorry to the front. There they were shot down in hundreds on the almost impregnable slopes around San Marcial.

The French officials, after some five minutes' delay and no awkward questions, allowed us to proceed; we passed under the barrier and across the International Bridge, alongside the railway where the trains no longer ran.

Just beyond the Spanish barrier we halted; Vicuña went into the control hut to report and to collect my salvoconducto while I studied the crowd of civilians and officials gathered around. There were the Civil Guard (*Guardia Civil*) in green uniforms, yellow belts and cross-straps and shiny black tricorn hats; *Carabineros*, or frontier guards, in lighter green and flat peaked caps; soldiers with the tasseled forage caps and soiled, ill-fitting khaki uniforms that characterized the Nationalist Army of the Peninsula in the Civil War, many of them loafing about with their round mess-tins in their hands and hunks of bread in their mouths; civilian officials with brassards and the air of busy authority common to minor functionaries in all countries. With some complacency I reflected that my last major obstacle was passed; now I was in Spain. It would not be long before I, too, should be wearing a uniform. The great adventure had begun, In my mind I could already hear the sound of gunfire and the bullets whistling past.

These ingenuous thoughts were shattered by the reappearance of a bewildered Vicuña with the news that my salvoconducto had not arrived. I had appalling visions of being returned ignominiously to France to wait until it should turn up and another courier be available to take me. However, after a quarter of an hour of shoulder-shrugging, gesticulation and excited chatter between Vicuña and the officer in charge, I was given another pass, allowing me to go as far as Burgos.

We drove through the gutted and blackened ruins of Irun and along the road to San Sebastian. We drew up at the Hotel Continental shortly after two, in excellent time for a drink before lunch according to Spanish hours. It took me a little time to accustom myself to the Spanish habit of lunching past two and dining at half past ten or later; but once I became used to them I grew to prefer these hours to the English: indication, perhaps, of a slothful nature.

After lunch with Vicuña's mother, a sweet, white-haired old lady with whom I was unable to converse because of her ignorance of English and mine of Spanish, we continued our journey towards Vitoria and Burgos. Unlike Irun, San Sebastian had suffered no damage from the war, the only signs of which, apart from the uniforms in the streets, were slogans plastered on houses and walls: the 'ALISTAOS A LA FALANGE' and 'ARRIBA ESPAÑA' of the Fascists and the Carlist 'DIOS PATRIA Y REY', the last on a red and yellow background, the former on red and black. The red and yellow was the flag of Spain under the monarchy, but the Republic had changed it to red, yellow, and purple. Red and black were the colours of the Falange, but also those of the F.A.I., or Anarchists, on the Republican side—which sometimes caused confusion in battle, since flags were carried in action by both sides. These exhortations were interspersed with others of a more practical kind: 'IPIDAN SIEMPRE DOMECQ! VINOS Y COÑAC DOMECQ' ('Always order Domecq's wines and brandy').

Our roads led inland, rising gently at first among broken, wooden hills with white, red-roofed homesteads dotted on the sides, then climbing and twisting steeply through deep gorges amid thickly forested mountains, until at length, shortly before Vitoria, we were on the Meseta, the flat plateau of central Spain. At Tolosa, Villafranca and Vitoria we were stopped by controls and made to show our passes; at Vitoria control was manned by young Requetés of fifteen or sixteen years old, very self-important but very smart in their red berets and khaki uniforms.

During the journey I told Vicuña of my true purpose in coming to Spain. His eyes lit up and he exclaimed: 'You will be very welcome with us, and I am sure we can arrange for you to join a fighting unit. In any case, I will introduce you to some friends of mine on the General Staff when we get to Burgos.'

12

We reached Burgos at seven and parked outside the Hotel Norte y Londres. The hotel was full, but I found a room in a house nearby kept by two women; like James Pigg's cupboard it smelt strongly of cheese, but was clean and comfortable. Outside, the air was bitter, a breath of ice that went right through my overcoat and clothes, and I was glad to return to the warmth of the hotel.

I stood in the lounge waiting for Vicuña to join me and watching the chattering crowd pass through the hall. There were women of all ages, most of them wearing some kind of medallion or badge attached to their dress by a red and yellow ribbon, and men in smart uniforms, or in civilian clothes with red Requeté berets or blue Falange forage caps. A tall, broad-shouldered, fair-complexioned man of about thirty-five came up and introduced himself.

'May I join you? I can see you're English. My name is Rupert Bellville. Have a drink?'

Bellville was already well-known in England as an expert on Spain, an aficionado of bullfights and a bold amateur pilot, flying his own aircraft. Finding himself in the south of Spain at the outbreak of the Civil War, he had enlisted in a Falange unit and taken part in operations at Andalusia. Horrified and disgusted by the frequent spectacles of atrocities committed by some of the anarchists and communists in the villages and countryside of that backward region, he was little less shocked when required himself to take part in firing squads to execute the criminals; eventually he left his unit. What had especially sickened him, apart from a natural revulsion at the shooting of prisoners, was that the victims went on twitching and writhing for some minutes after death and he could never believe that they were really dead. Certainly the execution of prisoners was one of the ugliest aspects of the Civil War, and both sides were guilty of it in the early months. There were two main reasons for this: first, the belief, firmly held by each side, that the others were traitors to their country and enemies of humanity who fully deserved death; secondly, the fear of each side that unless they exterminated their adversaries these would rise again and destroy them. But it is a fact, observed by me personally, that as the war developed the Nationalists tended more and more to spare their prisoners, except those of the International Brigades: so that when, in 1938, the Non-Intervention Commission began to arrange exchanges of prisoners of war, they found large numbers of Republicans held by the Nationalists, but scarcely any Nationalist soldiers in Republican prison camps.[2]

Bellville had attended the funeral of Calvo Sotelo, the Monarchist statesman whose murder by Republican police was the signal for the outbreak of the Civil War five days later. There were about eight thousand people present; the

Government had forbidden the Fascist salute, but on this occasion the feeling was so intense that, although only a few were Falangists, nearly everyone was making their salute. Shock Police (*Guardias de Asalto*) posted in side streets on motor cycles, shot up everyone they saw saluting. Bellville estimated that there must have been several hundred casualties.

'Now I have my aeroplane here,' he said, 'but I can't get permission to move nearer the front. There's nothing at all in this place except wives and sweethearts sitting around on their bottoms and discussing the latest rumours.'

At that moment we were joined by a dark-haired woman of about thirty-five, with a quiet, grave manner, whom Bellville introduced to us as the Duquesa de Lécera. She greeted me with a smile of great charm: 'And what do you want to do in Spain?'

'I want to fight,' I answered, feeling rather embarrassed.

She looked me up and down coolly: 'That is very nice of you. I don't think you will find it difficult.' She glided away.

Vicuña arrived and Bellville left us. I did not see him again for some time, but one day in the following September he sprang into prominence in the world's news. the Nationalists had launched their final assault on Santander, whose fall was expected hourly. Bellville had his aeroplane in San Sebastian when a report came through that the town had surrendered. Resolved to be the first to welcome the victorious army, he and a Spanish friend of a similar temperament, Ricardo González, of the famous sherry family, loaded his aircraft with crates of sherry and brandy, took off from San Sebastian and soon afterwards landed on the airfield at Santander. A swarm of blue-clad soldiers surrounded the aircraft and Bellville and González climbed out with glad shouts of 'Viva Franco!' and 'Arriba España!' when they realized with astonishment and dismay that these were Republican militiamen and that Santander was still in enemy hands. They were brusquely marched to prison, transferred to Gijón, in Asturias, just before the fall of Santander and for a week or two were in grave danger of summary execution. Fortunately González was able to pass as an Englishman, having been educated in England; he was released in order to arrange their exchange for two Republican prisoners held by the Nationalists. Meanwhile, Bellville stayed in prison, encouraged from time to time by his captors with stories of what was going to happen him should González fail to organize the exchange satisfactorily. In the end the Nationalists handed over two senior officers of the Republican army and he was released.

Vicuña was accompanied by a major and three captains from the Comandancia Militar, one of whom spoke English. He was Captain the Conde de Elda, and he wore, in addition to field boots and spurs, the broad blue and gold sash of the General Staff. After some curious and powerful cocktails of brandy and vermouth we dined in a small, crowded restaurant near the hotel, on river trout and the local vin rosé. Elda said:

'The military situation of the Reds is very precarious. Any day now Madrid will be in our hands.'

It was nearly two and a half years before his words came true.

---

[1] Famous Carlist commander in the First Carlist War.

[2] Statement by Mr. Hemming of the Non-Intervention Commission to the author.

CHAPTER TWO

After the initial failure of the *Movimiento*, as the Nationalists termed their rising, in large areas of the Peninsula and in the fleet, the Nationalists soon improved their position by a rapid succession of victories and, when I arrived in Spain, were at the gates of Madrid.

Indeed, when I left England I wondered whether I should be in time to see any action before the war was over.

Ever since the elections of February 1936, which established the Popular Front Government, both the extreme Right, led by the Army, and the extreme Left political parties had been preparing to seize power by force.[1] The tension increased through the spring and early summer months. Some idea of what this meant is shown in the words of Don Salvador de Madariaga, a Liberal authority by no means well disposed to the Nationalist cause:[2]

'. . . One hundred and sixty churches totally destroyed and two hundred and fifty-one set on fire or otherwise attacked;[3] two hundred and sixty-nine persons murdered and twelve hundred and eighty-seven injured; sixty-nine political premises destroyed; one hundred and thirteen general strikes and two hundred and twenty-eight partial strikes, as well as many more other cases of other forms of violence.'

On June 16th, in the Cortes, the Government was indicted for its leniency towards this crime and violence by Señor Gil Robles, leader of the Right-wing Acción Católica, and by Señor Calvo Sotelo, leader of the monarchist Renovación Española; as Calvo Sotelo sat down after speaking the Communist Dolores Ibarruri, 'La Pasionaria', shouted: 'That is your last speech!'

At noon on July 12th a certain Lieutenant Castillo of the Guardia de Asalto[4] was murdered in the street, apparently by three Fascists. In the early hours of the following morning, July 13th, Calvo Sotelo was taken from his bed by uniformed Guardias de Asalto and murdered. The Government took no action except to imprison the ninety men of Lieutenant Castillo's company.

In the afternoon of July 17th the garrison of Melilla in Spanish Morocco revolted. They were followed immediately by the entire Army of Morocco, consisting chiefly of the Spanish Foreign Legion and the Regulares or Moorish troops.

The same afternoon General Franco arrived in Morocco by air from the

Canary Islands, where he had been Governor and Commander-in-Chief. He put himself at the head of the rebels. The details of his flight had been arranged in London by a certain Major Hugh Pollard, one of those romantic Englishmen who specialize in other countries' revolutions. Pollard had taken an active part in the escape of Porfirio Diaz from Mexico in 1911, and in the revolution in Morocco of 1913 which deposed the Sultan Abdul Aziz and placed Mulay Hafid on the throne. Now on this particular operation he took an English pilot named Beeb and his own daughter, Diana, aged eighteen.

The Nationalists started with the great advantage that the most important of the fighting Services, the Army, was on their side.

Its spearhead was the Army of Morocco, of which a brief description might be helpful. The Foreign Legion, or Tercio, was founded in the early 1920s by General Millán Astray with the help of some of the ablest officers of the Spanish Army, including General (then Major) Franco. Its inspiration derived from two sources: historically and romantically from the tercios of the Duke of Alba in the 16th century, the core of the Spanish infantry in the days when 'Spanish discipline' was a byword in Europe;[5] militarily and practically from the French Foreign Legion, whose methods were studied first hand by Millán Astray and his assistants. But the Spanish Foreign Legion differed in one important respect from the French: it was composed almost entirely of Spaniards, although prior to the Civil War it was the only unit of the Spanish Army in which foreigners could enlist. Service was for a minimum of five years and was confined to Spanish possessions overseas. During the Civil War its strength increased from six banderas, or battalions, to twenty; even then about ninety per cent of the rank-and-file and nearly all of the officers were Spaniards, the remainder being Portuguese, with a few French and some Germans and White Russians.

The Regulares were Moorish troops, recruited by the Spanish Government and officered by Spaniards; although mercenaries they could show great courage and devotion. They were skilful and dangerous fighters, especially in the attack. There were also the Mehala, the troops of the Jalifa, the Viceroy in Spanish Morocco of the Sultan. They had a leavening of Spanish officers and were useful in skirmishing and mountain warfare.

Señor Madariaga states that, with few exceptions, every Army officer who was free to do so joined the Rebels. There were, however, exceptions; some of them, among the senior ranks, altered vitally the course of the war. Moreover, in the Peninsular barracks at the time there were only cadres of the regiments because the conscripts had already been dismissed. The officers of the Air Force were about equally divided in their sympathies; but, because most of the aircraft were in territory that remained in Republican hands, the Republicans had control of the air, which they retained until early in 1937. Fortunately for the Nationalists the Spanish Airforce was not strong enough to make this a decisive factor.[1]

Much more serious for them was the failure of their rising in the fleet. The Navy would have gone over to the Nationalists in its entirety but for the Communist cells which had been organized in many ships. In those ships the Communists, with their flair and training for leadership, persuaded the seamen to murder their officers and throw them into the sea. The Nationalists were left with the old battleship España, the cruiser Almirante Cervera; two new cruisers Baleares and Canarias, which were still under construction; the old cruiser República; the destroyer Velasco, and four gunboats. The difficulty was that all these ships were in El Ferrol in the north-west, except República and the gunboats, whereas the Republican fleet was based on Cartagena, able to command the vital Straits of Gibraltar and prevent the transport to Spain of the Army of Morocco. The Republicans had the old battleship Jamie Primero; the cruisers Libertad, Miguel Cervantes and Méndez Nuñez; sixteen destroyers, and twelve submarines. Their difficulty was that the crews, having murdered their officers, were unable to sail or fight the ships effectively until, later on, they were trained and officered by Russians.

On land both sides depended largely on volunteer 'paramilitary' organizations. With the Nationalists there were the traditional Requetés, or Carlists, and the Fascist Falange, the later founded by José Antonio Primo de Rivera, a son of the famous Dictator. It is worth nothing that the Falangists numbered less than five thousand in all Spain at the beginning of the war and were then of very little importance; their numbers were swelled by volunteers after July 18th, and they played an important part in the Nationalist campaign in Andalusia in the early days. Later, of course, they achieved overwhelming political power; but this was certainly not due to their fighting efficiency, which was regarded almost with derision by the various units of the Army and by the Requetés.

The Requeté movement drew its main strength from the Basque provinces, especially from Navarre, although its name originates in Catalonia. It was a product of the nineteenth century. Nominally the first Carlist War (1833-39) was fought on the issue whether King Fernando VII should be succeeded by his daughter Isabella, or by his brother, the Infante Don Carlos. Spanish law permitted women to succeed to the throne; Salic law, imported by the Bourbon Dynasty in the early eighteenth century, excluded them. Thus the Carlists, while claiming to uphold Spanish tradition, were ignoring it in this vital matter; despite this inconsistency, they believed sincerely, even fanatically, in their ideal, for which they gladly gave their lives. In reality, the war was a struggle between the Liberales, supporters of Isabella, who wished to centralize authority, reduce local rights and destroy the political power of the Church, and the Carlists, whose ideals are embodied in the words of a famous song: 'Dios, fueros, patria y Rey' (God, our rights, our country and King). It was also a war between the large towns and the countryside; the latter, especially in the Basque provinces, Old Castile and Catalonia was strongly Carlist in sympathy. It was a cruel war, ending in victory for the Liberales and in the disastrous reign of Queen Isabella.

Nevertheless the Carlist movement remained alive, almost a faith in itself. In spite of another defeat in the Second Carlist War (1870-76) it persisted in the Basque provinces and in isolated pockets of Catalonia and Old Castile, and as a political faith it still exists today.[7]

After the 1936 elections and throughout the succeeding disorders the Requetés prepared for another war. In the towns and villages and among the wooded mountains of Navarre and Álava, in country house and farmstead, in cottage and hovel the red beret and ancient rifle of a father or grandfather hung above the hearth in memory of one or other of the Carlist wars. Obsolete as they were, the weapons were taken down and cleaned, ready for instant action. Within three weeks of the outbreak of war thirty thousand Requetés rallied to General Mola in Pamplona. The women enlisted as Margaritas, as nurses for all duties short of bearing arms. Only the very young and very old remained to do work in the countryside.

Once again a Carlist song catches the spirit of those weeks:

Cálzame las alpargatas, dáme la boina, dáme el fusil,

Que voy a matar más Rojos que flores tiene el mes de Abril.[8]

Such was the shortage of troops that these had to be thrown into battle at once, without training or discipline, without adequate arms or equipment, against the fortresses around Irun and San Sebastian, and over the Guardarrama passes of Somosierra and Alto de Leon, towards Madrid. It was a glorious thing to die in defense of La Tradición and el ideal, and so they died, holding their lives cheaply and taking no care to protect themselves from the fire of the enemy. A Company in the attack was led by the captain and the chaplain, one grasping his pistol, the other his missal; all in their scarlet berets presenting a superb target.

So perished in the first few months of the war the finest flower of Spain.

Afterwards the Nationalist command, knowing the value of their courage and enthusiasm, sent the Carlists some of the best officers in their army.

The Republican paramilitary organizations were provided by the various workers' Unions. Of these the principal were the Anarchist F.A.I. (Federación Anarquista Ibérica); the Anarcho-Syndicalist C.N.T. (Confederación Nacional del Trabajo), and the Trotskyist P.O.U.M. (Partido Obrero Unificación Marxista). After the Movimiento one of the first actions of the Madrid Government was to throw open the State arsenals and distribute arms to these 'Popular Militias'. Less wisely, they opened the prisons. These, as Señor de Madariaga points out,[9] had been emptied months earlier of their political prisoners by an amnesty of President Azaña, and so could disgorge only common criminals. The latter were immediately enrolled in the various militias, and were responsible for much of the violence and horror that disgraced Republican Spain in the early months of the war.

Women, too, enlisted in the militias and fought beside their menfolk, often with even greater courage and resolution. They were also employed as jailers to guard female political prisoners, several of whom told me that they suffered much worse treatment from the *milicianos* than from the men.

Of the police forces the Civil Guard were nearly all on the Nationalist side, although in a few places, notably Barcelona, their sense of loyalty to an established Government proved stronger than their natural antipathy to mob rule. The Shock Police and Carabineros, on the other hand, joined the Republicans, whom they provided with a much needed nucleus of officers and N.C.Os.

On July 18th the Prime Minister of the Republic, Señor Casares Quiroga, resigned. President Azaña replaced him shortly afterwards with Señor Giral and a Ministry of his own friends.

But this Government, having armed the Unions, found itself at their mercy. The various militias did as they pleased, terrorizing the population. On September 4th, 1936, Señor Largo Caballero, the militant extreme Left Socialist, became Prime Minister. His Foreign Secretary was Señor Alvarez del Vayo, his Finance Minister Dr. Negrín—both of them loyal agents of Moscow.

The leader of the Nationalist rising was to have been General Sanjurjo. He was killed in an air crash on July 20th, taking off from Lisbon to fly to Spain. A Governing Junta was established in Burgos under General Cabanellas, consisting of himself, Generals Franco, Mola, Queipo de Llano and Varela, with two other senior officers. In the early days of the war 'La República honrada' was a favourite slogan of the Army, whose leaders maintained that they were in revolt, not against the Republic itself, but against the President and Government in Madrid, who were leading the country towards anarchy and communism.

Of the Army officers I knew, either personally or by repute, scarcely any had Falangist sympathies; some were Monarchists, but the majority preferred to 'leave that sort of thing to the politicians and get on with winning the war'. This also summarized the attitude of the Requetés, whose political leadership in any case was inept. The Falangists, on the other hand, never lost sight of the main chance, and schemed throughout the war to infiltrate their people into key positions of government. General Mola insisted on flying the flag of the Republic until his Requeté allies obliged him to change it for the old monarchist colours. It was only after this event that he became a legend as a 'Requeté' General.[10]

Cabanellas, although the senior General, was no more than a figurehead; after the death of Sanjurjo the choice of a leader rested between Mola and Franco; although Mola seemed to have the better claim it was Franco who, for reasons still imperfectly known, was recognized as Generalissimo and 'Chief of Operations' of the Nationalist forces. That was on October 1st, 1936; he did not become 'Head of State' until six months later.

On July 19th, 1936, the day after the revolt in Morocco, the Movimiento exploded throughout the Peninsula. The result was neither the immediate success the conspirators had expected nor the fiasco that the first Republican broadcasts proclaimed. General Cabanellas took over Zaragoza, General Mola rose in Pamplona with four hundred soldiers and General Queipo de Llano captured Seville with a hundred and eighty-five men and a prodigal use of bluff. The Basque provinces of Navarre, part of Álava, the whole of Old Castile and Léon, Galicia in the northwest, and the western region of Aragón went over to the Nationalists. But in Madrid the people's militias and Shock Police stormed the Montaña barracks and, after a bloody battle, overwhelmed the Nationalist garrison under General Fanjul. In Barcelona the Army Commander sided with the Republicans and, with the help of Civil Guards and Shock Police, suppressed the military rising, whose leaders, Generals Goded and Burriel, were captured and shot. The Republicans held all Catalonia, the eastern half of Aragón, and all of New Castile and the Mancha, the whole Mediterranean seaboard from the French frontier to Gibraltar, a large part of the province of Estremadura on the Portuguese frontier and all Andalusia, except Cadiz, Jerez, Seville, Cordova and a small pocket around Granada. In the Balearics, Majorca went over to the Nationalists; but Minorca, with the naval base of Mahón, remained in

Republican hands. In the north the remaining Basque provinces of Guipúzcoa, Vizcaya and part of Álava joined the Republicans, together with Santander and Asturias; however, Oviedo, the capital of Asturias was held for the Nationalists by General Aranda, who withstood an intensive siege until he was relieved in October, 1937.

Thus, although the Movimiento had achieved considerable initial success, it had met with some serious reserves. The most important of these were the failures in Madrid and Barcelona and in the fleet, and the loss of Catalonia and the two Basque provinces of Guipúzcoa and Vizcaya with their heavy industries and raw materials. Apart from Andalusia, where the Anarchist tradition was strong among the peasantry, it is reasonable to say that the agricultural districts were for the Nationalists, the cities and industrial areas were for the Republicans. Thus, Catalonia was lost to the Nationalists. The Basque provinces would not have gone over to the Republicans but for the attitude of the Basque Separatists. These, being deeply religious Catholics, had no sympathy with the Communist miners of Asturias, nor with the anti-clerical Unions of Santander, nor even with the industrial workers of their own provinces. But, in the belief that they could secure a more complete autonomy from the Madrid Government than from the Nationalists, they allied themselves with the former and declared and independent Basque Republic under the Presidency of Señor Aguirre. At the end of December, 1936, a young Navarrese officer with whom I was serving said: 'For me the saddest thing about this war is that not only is Spaniard fighting Spaniard, but Basque is fighting Basque.'

The loss of the fleet, and with it the command of the Straits of Gibraltar, might have proved fatal for the Nationalists but for the prompt action of General Franco in Morocco. Using six Junkers 52 transport aircraft, borrowed for him from the Germans by a certain Major Arrauz of the Spanish Air Force,[11] he immediately ferried troops across the Straits to Spain, took Algeciras and La Linea and pushed a column, under Captain Castejón of the Foreign Legion, up to Seville to secure General Queipo de Llano's hold on the city. By the end of July, after a naval action in the Straits in which the Nationalist gunboat, Dato, escorting a convoy of troops from Morocco, beat off a strong Republican squadron, the control of these waters had passed to the Nationalists; thereafter their communications between Morocco and the Peninsula were secure.

Castejón wasted no time in Seville, but sent flying columns of the Tercio and Regulares, aided by Falange auxiliaries, through Andalusia; within a very short time he had occupied the whole province as far as Málaga in the east and the Portuguese border in the west. This included the valuable mines of Rio Tinto near Huelva, and Peñarroya near Cordova. With reinforcements arriving by sea and air from Morocco Franco's forces advanced northwards to Mérida, which they captured on August 9th, and Badajoz, which fell to them on August 15th. These towns were taken by storm, with very heavy casualties on both sides. By the capture of Badajoz the Nationalists secured the whole Portuguese frontier; more important, their Southern army under Franco was able to join with Mola's forces in the north.

The latter, having secured the Guadarrama passes of Somosierra and Alto de León and held them against the sporadic attacks of the undisciplined *milicianos* from Madrid, turned to attack Irun and San Sebastian. Their object was close to the French frontier, isolating the Republican territories in the north, and secure for themselves the railway link with France. Tolosa, the capital of Guipúzcoa, fell on August 15th, Irun on September 5th, and San Sebastian eight days later. After these successes the northern front was stabilized, with most of Guipúzcoa and Álava in Nationalist hands, including the capitals of both provinces.[12]

After the capture of Mérida and Badajoz the Nationalists launched their attack up the Tagus valley against Madrid. At first it seemed as though nothing could stop it. Oropesa fell on August 29th, Talavera on 3rd September. The only opposition came from the *milicianos*, who fought with courage but without discipline or military training. They were, moreover, handicapped by the lack of any organized command; some units appointed their own commanding officers and took orders from them alone: in others there were no officers, each man acting as he pleased. It was easy for the veterans of the Tercio and Regulares to outflank them, shoot up their rear communications and drive them back in disorder upon the next defended village.

On September 22nd the Nationalists reached Maqueda, where the road to Toledo branches southward from the main road to Madrid. In the Alcázar, or citadel, of Toledo a small Nationalist force was holding out, having withstood more than two months of unremitting siege. The defenders, who numbered about a thousand men—regular officers, Civil Guard, cadets from the Toledo Military Academy and volunteers—had won the admiration of the world by their heroic resistance against repeated attacks supported by artillery and air bombardment, by mines and by ferocious reprisals against their own families. Now they were on the point of collapse, their ammunition and food running out, their medical supplies long ago exhausted.

The victorious Nationalists at Maqueda were faced with the problem whether to continue their advance on Madrid, the main military objective, and allow the garrison of the Alcázar to be overwhelmed and massacred, or to divert their effort to the relief of Toledo. Considerations of prestige and military honour impelled them to the latter course. On September 29th the 5th Bandera of the Tercio and a tabor[13] of Regulares entered Toledo, fighting their way up the steep ascent from the Puerta Visagra to the Plaza de Zocodover. The siege of the Alcázar was over. Colonel Moscardó staggered from the ruins of his fortress to greet General Franco, saluted and delivered his report, in a phrase now famous throughout Spain: 'Sin Novedad en el Alcázar' ('Nothing to report in the Alcázar.').

From Lieutenant Noel FitzPatrick and Lieutenant William Nangle, two British officers serving with the 5th Bandera, I have learnt something of that frantic advance on Toledo and the final battle. It is not a pretty story. On the eve of their assault on the city the Nationalists found the bodies of two of their airmen, shot down the day before, who had fallen alive into the hands of the *milicianos*. They were mutilated beyond description. When the Nationalist troops attacked the next day they took no prisoners. FitzPatrick told me that the gutters by the streets leading down from the Alcázar to the city gates were running with blood.

The diversion to relieve Toledo cost the Nationalists one vital week. Had they pressed on directly from Maqueda to Madrid there is little doubt that they would have taken the city without difficulty. The Republican Government, after announcing over the radio that Madrid would be defended to the last, fled to Valencia on November 7th, accompanied by the Soviet Ambassador. But already foreign help had begun to arrive for the Republicans—French Potez aircraft, supplied by M. Pierre Cot and flown by officers of the French Air Force, batteries of French '75s' and Russian tanks mounting 37 millimetre guns. The Nationalist advance was slowed, but not halted. On the 7th of November their troops held the whole bend of Manzanares, and it is said that one tabor of Regulares penetrated as far as Puerta del Sola. The next day the entire attack was thrown back in confusion. The International Brigades, volunteers from all over Europe raised by the various Communist parties and trained in Southern France, had arrived; they were sent immediately into battle with all necessary support from aircraft, artillery and tanks. Within a few days they had expelled the Nationalists, whom they outnumbered heavily, across the Manzanares into the outer suburbs of Madrid. A prompt withdrawal saved the Nationalists from envelopment and annihilation; only in the University City were they able to maintain a precarious hold across the river in the capital itself—a hold which cost both sides innumerable casualties in the next two years.

During the succeeding weeks the Nationalists, as yet ignorant of the strength that opposed them, launched a series of futile attacks against the city. These cost them casualties they could hardly spare among their best troops, but gained them no appreciable advantage. In effect the front was already stabilized when I arrived in Burgos in the middle of November.

*　　*　　*

Thus began the second phase of the Civil War—the phase of foreign intervention. To meet the threat of the International Brigades and increased French assistance to the Republicans the Nationalists invoked the help of Italy and Germany. Both supplied arms and technicians: obsolescent tanks, aircraft, anti-aircraft and anti-tank artillery, together with skeleton crews whose task was to train Spaniards in the use of their weapons; they were gradually withdrawn as Spaniards became qualified to replace them. A very few squadrons of bombers, with their fighter escorts, were flown by Germans throughout the war. Occasionally the Germans would send some new weapon to Spain for testing, after which it was withdrawn.

The Italians supplied fighting troops, maintained at a constant strength of about two divisions, with all supporting arms, including tanks, artillery and aircraft. They also provided officers for two 'Mixed Divisions', in which the rank-and-file were Spaniards, the senior officers Italians; it was not a happy arrangement. In addition, they maintained a few squadrons of Savoias in the Balearics to bomb the Republicans' Mediterranean ports. The war material they supplied was chiefly aircraft, flown by Spaniards as soon as they were trained, and small arms, especially automatic weapons.

The Russians did for the Republicans roughly what the Germans did for the Nationalists—they supplied technicians and war material of all kinds. In return they exacted a far greater measure of control over Republican policy and strategy than the Germans were able to obtain from Franco; the price of Russian co-operation was Russian direction of the war and the complete domination by the Communist Party of all Republican political and military organizations.[14]

Thus, not for the last time, Russia showed her allies her interpretation of the word 'co-operation'.

---

[1] Madariaga, *Spain*, p. 369.

[2] *Spain*, p. 351.

[3] Eye-witnesses have told me how the looters in Andalusia, at least, would in all simplicity uncover

themselves before entering the church, genuflect before the alter, and only replace their hats after leaving the building pillaged and in flames.

[4] 'Shock Police', a well armed, well trained force organized by the Popular Front Government as a possible counter to the old Guardia Civil, of whose loyalty to the government was doubtful.

[5] A Tercio in the sixteenth century was a Regiment of Spanish infantry. The Spanish Foreign Legion is also called *El Tercio*, 'The Regiment', in the same way as in the British Army the Household Calvary and Foot Guards are known as 'The Brigade'. But the Requetés in the Civil War also organized their fighting units into *tercios*, each approximately of battalion strength.

[6] But Toledo, which had declared for the Nationalists, was reduced (except for the Alcázar) in the first week, largely by Republican air attacks: the first instance in the war of the bombing of an open town.

[7] This despite the fact that the Carlists have recognized Don Juan, son of King Alfonso XIII, as rightful King of Spain, thus aligning themselves with the legitimists.

[8] 'Put on my shoes for me, give me my beret and my rifle, and I'm going to kill more Reds than there are flowers in April.'

[9] *Spain*, p. 378.

[10] H.R.H. The Infante Don Alfonso de Orléans-Borbón, a cousin of King Alfonso and a General in the Spanish Air Force, has told me that when he reported to Mola in Burgos at the beginning of August 1936, Mola refused to see him and sent him under escort to the French frontier; and that he did the same to Infante Don Juan a day or two earlier.

[11] My authority for this statement is H.R.H. the Infante Don Alfonso de Orléans-Borbón.

[12] Vitoria is the capital of *Álava*.

[13] Equal to a battalion.

[14] Dr. Isaac Deutscher (*Stalin*, pp. 422-5) states that Stalin ordered the purges of the Trotskyist P.O.U.M. and of the Anarcho-Syndicalists: 'He made their elimination from the Republic's administration a condition of the sale of Soviet munitions to the Government. He dispatched to Spain, together with military instructors, agents of his political police, experts at heresy-hunting and purging, who established their own reign of terror in the ranks of the Republicans . . . he put Antonov-Ovseenko, the hero of 1917 and the ex-Trotskyist, in charge of the purge in Catalonia, the stronghold of the "heretics" only to purge Antonov-Ovseenko himself after his return to Spain.'

CHAPTER THREE

In the course of our dinner party on the night of my arrival in Burgos I abandoned for ever my journalist's cover and asked my friends if they could help me join the Nationalist Army. They explained that the only units in which a foreigner might enlist were the Foreign Legion and the Requeté and Falange militias. I was strongly advised not to join the Legion as a private soldier—advice which I was subsequently glad I took; the politics of the Falange were not attractive to me, but the ideals of the Requetés fired my imagination. As a result, I was provided next day with letters of introduction from Elda and his friends to the Carlist leaders, Falcode and Zamanillo, in Ávila, together with a pass from the Comandancia Militar and a reservation in one of its cars leaving Burgos in the afternoon.

Burgos, the birthplace of the Cid, seemed a propitious springboard for my adventure. After a visit to the magnificent thirteenth century cathedral I spent the morning wandering through the streets in the bright sunlight and crisp, clean air, wrapped in a naïve, romantic day-dream featuring myself as a modern Campeador. At this time the town was General Franco's headquarters, General Mola having moved south to Ávila; it was also Divisional Headquarters of the 6th Division. Apart from the variety of uniforms in the streets and the posters on the walls there was no evidence of warlike activity; for that, I was told, I must go south to Ávila, Talavera de la Reina and Toledo.

I left Burgos about half past three in the afternoon in an old saloon car with two officers. We followed the Valladolid road south-westwards along the valley of the Arlanzon. The sun setting in our faces flushed the bare brown plains with gold, lit the green of the tamarisks growing beside the river on our left and outlined in sharp, dark contour the plateau rising in the distance beyond. It was dark before we came to Valladolid, the ancient capital of the kings of Castile, where we made a brief halt. At the beginning of the Civil War this was the scene of a coup by the Nationalist General, Saliquet, in which one of my companions had taken part. Saliquet was a stout and elderly officer whose enormous moustache and benign expression, giving him the look of an amiable walrus, soon became a familiar and popular sight in Nationalist territory. In July of 1936 he was living on half-pay on a friends estate near Valladolid. Although the Falangists were strong in the town, the commander of the 7th Division, stationed there, was a Republican. On July 18th Saliquet put on his uniform, collected two or three officers of the garrison and went to see the Divisional Commander, whom he found in his office with his A.D.C.

'You are,' he informed him, 'placed under arrest and relieved of your command, which you will hand over to me immediately.'

The A.D.C. drew a pistol and shot one of Saliquet's companions. The other fired back, killing the A.D.C. The Divisional Commander surrendered. Saliquet and his followers took control of the troops and arrested the Civil Governor, another Republican, who had mobilized the Shock Police. The latter thereupon declared for the Nationalists.

A similar technique was adopted by General Quiepo de Llano to gain control of the troops during Seville. On many occasions during those early days it was the courage and initiative of individual commanders that turned the scale for the Nationalists. At the end of the war, when I was in Madrid, I heard the comment of an Englishman who had witnessed both the Russian and Spanish revolutions: 'If Franco's generals hadn't had more guts than the White Russian generals, Spain would now be Communist.'

It was half past nine when we arrived beneath the battlements of Ávila and drove through a gateway in the ancient walls into the narrow cobbled streets of the town.

We went to the *Comandancia*, where we found a crowd of officers and civilians loitering around the ante-rooms. Forcing a way through, my companions introduced me to the Duty officer, an amiable old major with glasses and a sallow face as creased as a prune. Falconde and Zamanillo, he explained, were not here, but at Toledo, which was now the base for the main assault on Madrid; he would give me a *salvoconducto* at once and my companions would arrange my transport south. Five minutes later I was out of the office, the pass in my hand and his bluff shout of *'Buena suerte!'* ringing in my ears. We called at the Press Bureau, where I found Señor Melgar, the Secretary-General of the Traditionalist party, who confirmed that I should find Falconde and Zamanillo at Toledo and gave me a letter to them. He explained that they were at present engaged in forming a new *tercio* of Requetés from volunteers in the Toledo area; it was to be named the *Tercio del Alcázar* and would be commanded by a regular officer who had taken part in the defence of the Alcázar.

With Melgar I met Harold Cardozo, an old friend of Collin Brooks and the *Daily Mail* correspondent in Nationalist Spain. Cardozo had fought with distinction in the First World War, after which he joined the staff of the *Continental Daily Mail*. Brisk, tough and highly intelligent he was a great war correspondent, in the tradition of Walter Harris, Bennett Burghleigh, Gwynne and other illustrious names of the Balkan and Moroccan wars; he was also one of the kindest-hearted men I have ever known. A good Catholic, he felt a romantic as well as a religious attachment to the Requetés and was once the subject of a question in the House of Commons on his habit of wearing their scarlet beret in Spain; but he never let his sympathies affect the objectivity of his reporting, or cloud his abnormally acute perception. He seemed interested if not impressed by my plans.

'You will find the fighting conducted more or less according to text-book principles. A copy of *Field Service Regulations* should be useful to you.'

As I was leaving he added, 'What about dining with us tonight? Hotel Inglés at nine-thirty. You'll find quite a crowd of us there.'

Ávila was some twenty miles from the front line. Although the town had so far escaped damage I found the atmosphere, if not exactly warlike, at least more serious than at Burgos. A blackout was in force; there had been some air-raids, although these were directed against the airfield and had caused no casualties in the town. The hotels were full but I found a room in a house on the cathedral square. I shared it with another Englishman, James Walford, a quiet, sardonic man, by profession an artist. Through his mother, who was Spanish, he was related to Sir Basil Zaharoff. He knew the country and the language well and was on his way to the front, with the idea of compiling a book of battle sketches.

At nine-thirty I went to find Cardozo at the Hotel Inglés. It was full of British, American and French correspondents, who were trying to cover the Madrid battle from this distant spot with, they told me, very little encouragement from the Nationalist authorities. The British and American journalists were a cheerful and hospitable crowd; one of my happiest memories is the unfailing help and kindness I received from every one of them at different times during my service in Spain. Their job was not made easy for them by the attitude of the military, which seemed to be that all foreign correspondents were spies who must be kept as far as possible from the scene of operations, who were only in the country on sufferance and who ought to be more than satisfied with whatever news the Army cared to issue in the official communiques. This was in marked contrast to the attitude of the Republicans, whose Press and Propaganda services were far superior to those of the Nationalists as their fighting was inferior and who took pains to give journalists and writers all the facilities they required. Although both sides imposed a rigid censorship on all dispatches going out of the country, the Nationalist made virtually no concessions to the Press, while the Republicans laid out enormous sums on propaganda abroad. These factors account in a large measure for the poor Press which the Nationalist received—and of which they ceaselessly complained—in England and the United States.

The dinner was excellent, the wine abundant and the conversation animated everywhere except at the head of the table, where sat the Spanish Press Conducting Officer. An elegant, middle-aged cavalryman with a handsome, dissolute face, he sat through the meal in gloomy silence. 'He sees to have some secret sorrow,' I commented to the American on my right. He laughed:

'Well, in a way I should say he has. You see, he used to live in Biarritz, where he had a very glamorous girl-friend—some titled Spaniard, I forget her name; I guess she used to put the horns on him quite a bit. Anyway, about three months ago, just after this war started, she gave him the bird—finally and for good. So he came to Spain to forget his broken heart in the hell and shellholes of Ávila.' After a pause he went on: 'What got me was our friend's description of their poignant parting scene. When he asked her, "Do they mean nothing to you, those nights of love we spent together?" all she said was, "Don't be ridiculous! Sleeping with you was just like sleeping with my brother!" '

Ávila is one of the highest and coldest towns in Spain; I was reminded of this as I walked back to my lodgings and undressed in the bare stone-flagged bedroom. War in this temperature, I reckoned, was going to be no picnic.

The next morning I breakfasted in the hotel. At a neighbouring table sat a dozen German pilots in the khaki uniforms of the Condor Legion. They were operating from the airfield south of the town, flying Henschel biplane fighters of an obsolescent type. They seemed very gloomy that morning, speaking little and only in monosyllables. Later I heard that they had lost their leader over Madrid the previous day. They had cheered up by the evening, when I next saw them, and were filling the hotel with their noisy singing.

At the Press Bureau Melgar told Walford and me that a car would take us to Toledo the next day, starting at nine in the morning. The direct road, through San Martín de Valdeiglesias and Maqueda, was blocked by the Republicans, and so we should have to go by the route over the Sierra de Gredos to Talavera.

Standing on a mound in the middle of a wide plain, encircled by battlemented walls and associated for ever with the name of Saint Teresa, Ávila is renowned as *tierra de cantos y santos* (land of stones and saints). We went for a walk along the top of the famous ramparts. Built about the end of the eleventh century, they have been kept in a fine state of preservation and are, I believe, the most perfect example of medieval fortifications in existence. From the battlements we looked southward across the bare plain beyond the airfield to the horizon where the peaks of the Gredos, as yet only lightly touched with snow, gleamed in the diaphanous sunlight. Walford said:

I've been thinking I might join the Requetés with you. After all this war concerns me personally; three of my relations have already been murdered in Madrid.'

*   *   *

The Sierra de Gredos, a south-westward extension of the Guardarrama range, forms a barrier, rising to eight thousand feet, between the plains of Old Castile and the valley of the Tagus. The northern face in winter is harsh rock and bare snow, but the southern slopes are thickly covered with pine and fir. On a fine day the sun lights them with a brilliant green, picks out the sparkle of a hundred torrents, glistens from the rock and strikes blinding on the snow. The road across these mountains, with its gravel and dirt surface, its sudden ascents and declivities, its blind curves and hairpin bends flanked by unguarded precipices, might have been designed by some motor-racing enthusiast as a test track for a mountain rally. There is the extra hazard that round each corner you are liable to meet a string of mules with their cursing drivers, a heavy cart loaded with timber or a large lorry, either in the middle of the road or on your side of it. I had a Spanish friend who told me that he made it an inflexible rule on this route to drive on the wrong side round corners; thus, he affirmed, was the only way to avoid collisions—'Provided,' he added, 'that the other driver is a Spaniard. If you were to meet a foreigner you would be completely spoilt.'

Our driver on this bright morning of November 18th clearly had the same idea. A serious young man with a melancholy face and horn-rimmed glasses, who gave the impression of carrying a load of official secrets, the burden of which was intolerable to him, he had arrived at the hotel a couple hours late, picked up Walford and me and a pretty young Margarita on her way to Talavera and driven like a demon to the foot of the pass. This was the famous Puerto del Pico, which was captured for the Nationalists in the first week of September by Colonel Monasterio, who started from Ávila with two regiments of cavalry. This was one of the most brilliant actions by mounted troops during the Civil War, and a remarkable feet in such steep and broken country. We had to take the ascent slowly, with frequent stops whenever the radiator boiled. But once over the pass we picked up speed and whirled downhill, skidding round corners with the tyres screaming, swinging out over precipices, swerving sharply to avoid a cart or lorry, and braking suddenly when it seemed we had lost all control. After some forty minutes of this I noticed that the young *Margarita* sitting beside me in the back was being quietly sick into her handkerchief. We stopped to let her finish this operation in a small copse beside a stream. After further halts—for a puncture and a mechanical breakdown—we ran into Talavera in time for a very late lunch at the only hotel.

During the ensuing months I saw a good deal of this small town. Now I remember it chiefly for its dirt, its ugliness and the cloudy colour and revolting taste of its drinking water. However, it occupied a position of considerable importance to the Nationalists at the junction of their communications between the Madrid front and the north, west and south in Spain. Situated on a bend of the Tagus, it faced Republican territory across the river on the south bank. The enemy used to launch sporadic attacks on the town without achieving any success. It is a measure of their disorganization on this sector that the Republicans made no serious attempt to capture so vital a centre of communications. For the duration of the war it was the depot of the Tercio but, so far as I know, it never contained more than a very small garrison.

Darkness was falling as we left the town. On our way out we overtook a column of Requeté cavalry, wild-looking men, dark and squat, with black beards. They seemed to have come a long way and sat wearily hunched over their saddles, wrapped in their *capotes* against the icy wind from the sierra. Our road ran straight and level, but we were obliged to travel slowly, for the surface was pitted with small shell holes very roughly repaired; there were further traces of September's fighting in the frames and burnt-out lorries and cars on the side of the road. After passing through Santa Olalla we saw ahead of us the dark mass of the castle at Maqueda on its hill commanding the fork where the Madrid and Toledo roads diverged. We bore right, crossing the Madrid-Talavera railway at Torrijos and soon afterwards ran under the walls of Toledo. We turned in at the Visagra gate, climbed slowly up the narrow street and came to rest in the Plaza de Zocodover in front of the ruins of the Alcázar.

* * *

It astonishes me even today that Toledo, one of the most fascinating cities in Spain, should be so poorly furnished with hotels. In November 1936, barely two months after its occupation by the Nationalists, we thought ourselves lucky to find a room in the only one open, a draughty, ramshackle building without charm or comfort. We awoke to a raw, grey morning with overcast skies and a chilly drizzle. We set out early for the Requeté headquarters, through narrow, cobbled streets running with muddy water. Like Burgos, the town was thronged with troops—Regular Army and Foreign Legion, Moors in fezes with blue *capotes* over their thin khaki tunics, Requetés and Falange. But the difference is that here the men's faces were lined and battle-weary, their uniforms ragged and dirty; the Madrid front was barely an hour's journey by lorry, and most of them were in Toledo on twenty-four hours' leave. We found the headquarters in a two-storey building, guarded by a pair of sodden sentries in red berets and *capotes*. Inside we climbed a flight of stairs to a large room crowded with people. There was an atmosphere of bustle, even confusion; groups of men stood around in voluble discussion, clerks sat at untidy desks making out orders, passes or lists of stores, orderlies hurried in and out of ante-rooms. Nobody took any notice of us. We approached a young man, wearing the silver fleur-de-lis of a Requeté officer, who was seated at a long table. When Walford explained that we wanted to enlist and had letters for Zamanillo and Falconde he jerked a thumb over his shoulder:

'They're in there,' he said, 'they're very busy. Come back at six o'clock.' He returned to his work.

At that moment a slight, dark woman in a white hospital coat came out of one of the ante-rooms. Walford brightened:

'Blanquita!' he cried; he introduced her as his cousin, the Marquesa de San Miguel, who was working for the Spanish Red Cross in Toledo.

She was a friend of Falconde and took us in to see him at once. Without her influence I doubt if we should ever have penetrated to his office through the crowd of sentries, officers, orderlies and hangers-on that stood in our way. We found him talking with Zamanillo in a small room at the back of the house, but they broke off their conversation when they saw Doña Blanca.

It appeared that Falconde dealt with political affairs, Zamanillo with military organization; our business was therefore with the latter. He asked me about my military training and seemed impressed by my O.T.C. Certificates, which were supposed to qualify me for a commission in the event of war, in the infantry, cavalry, or artillery of the British Army.

'But,' he added, 'I do not know if we can take you as an officer when you speak no Spanish.'

I assured him that I was quite happy to enlist in the ranks. Then I remembered the cavalry we had passed in Talavera. In a war of movement, such as this had been hitherto, it was probable that the cavalry would play an important and exciting part. Now I learned that the Requetés were raising two squadrons in Seville, under a White Russian colonel named Alkon; the horsemen we had seen yesterday were the first squadron, commanded by the Requeté Captain Barrón, who was in Toledo at this moment.

Eventually it was decided that we should enlist in the Requetés immediately, after which we could make up our minds whether to join the cavalry or the infantry. The former seemed to me to offer more exhilarating opportunities, but it might be a while yet before they could come into action; whereas the infantry battalion, the *Tercio de Alcázar*, was already in the line, in the Casa de Campo sector, and fighting hard.

Afterwards we went with Doña Blanca to lunch in a little restaurant below the walls on the northern side of town, the Venta de Aires, where we had the local specialty, partridges richly cooked in olive oil and herbs. We were served by the son and daughter of the house, while the proprietress sat in the background crying quietly to herself all the time. 'She sits there weeping all day,' explained Doña Blanca. 'Before they left Toledo the Reds shot her husband. Poor man, he had never done them any harm.

Next day we reported to Don Aurelio González de Gregorio, the Requeté officer in charge of recruiting in Toledo. He gave us an enthusiastic reception, called us '*Muy bravos*', he said he was proud to have us and made us drink a bottle of dark, sweet Malaga wine with him. We were formally admitted as Requetés without, so far as I remember, the formality of signing a single document. For some reason I have never understood we were not given identity cards, nor—in those innocent pre-World War days—did it occur to us to ask for them; a fact which caused me much difficulty and embarrassment later on, whenever I wished to travel. We drew no pay and we had to buy our own uniforms for the stores had none left.[1] I bought myself a red beret, khaki shirts of very poor quality and a shaggy *cazadora*, a sort of battle dress blouse; on my left breast pocket I had the Carlist emblem embroidered, the Cross of Burgundy, red St. Andrew's Cross surmounted by the Hapsburg double eagle under the royal crown of Spain.

In the evening we saw Captain Barrón of the cavalry, a very quiet man whose age I was unable to guess because the greater part of his face was hidden beneath an enormous pointed black beard in the style of the heroes of the Carlist wars; these beards were much affected by the Requetés, both at the front and in the rear areas, giving the wearers an expression at once of dignity and extreme ferocity. Barrón told us that his squadron had moved nearer Toledo, to Santa Olalla. He suggested that we pay it a visit in a couple days' time; meanwhile he would write to the senior officer there, telling him to expect us.

The following morning we walked up to the Plaza de Zocodover to look at the ruins of the Alcázar. There was nothing but a vast pile of rubble; the cellars, even the foundations, lay bare, with twisted iron girders sticking through the broken masonry and a great pit in the middle where the Republicans had exploded a mine. From the débris rose a foul stench of ordure and decay. The houses all around the square were pocketed with bullet holes, their windows shattered. A young Carlist from Galicia told us: 'We are going to leave it like that as a monument to Marxist civilization.' In fact, no attempt has been made to rebuild the Alcázar, and when I revisited it in the spring of 1951 it looked, and smelt, exactly the same.

In the neighborhood of El Greco's house we were warned to move carefully, for the streets around were exposed to sniping from Republican positions across the river and there had been casualties. The house was supposed to be shut, but we found the custodian, a little troglodyte who reached to my waist, and persuaded him to show us round. Inside I came upon one of the strangest sights of my life: In every room, stacked against the walls like so much lumber, stood these incomparable paintings of El Greco. The Republicans had assembled them thus, intending to send them to Madrid for sale abroad, but had abandoned them in their flight from Toledo.

There were some English journalists staying in the town; George Steer of *The Times*, Christopher Holme of Reuters, Pembroke Stephens of the *Daily Telegraph* and an American called Massock. They were all disgruntled because, having come to Toledo for the express purpose of visiting the Madrid front, they had not yet been granted permission to do so, nor did their repeated protests seem to have any effect.

We collected our passes from Captain Barrón and, about four o'clock on a fine afternoon, walked down to the Visagra Gate to stop the first lorry bound for Santa Olalla. We found one soon and settled ourselves in the back, among a pile of vegetables, two furious hens and their owner, an old woman who swore at them throughout the journey with a wealth of obscenity which Walford delighted in translating. Arriving in Santa Olalla at dusk, we found Squadron Headquarters in a small house in the main street. Here we were met by a pert little clerk of about sixteen, to whom we gave our papers. A few moments later we were brought before the senior officer.

Lieutenant (Acting Captain) Carlos Llancia, Marqués de Cocuhuella, was one of the tallest and most powerfully-built men I have ever met. He seemed to flicker with nervous energy. A thin 'eyebrow moustache and cold, dark eyes gave a ruthless expression to his handsome face; but his true nature was a strange mixture of kindliness and cruelty. Although surprised to see us, which was understandable because Barrón's letter had not yet reached him, he became very friendly when Walford told him why we were there. He suggested that we spend the night with the Squadron if we did not mind sharing sleeping quarters with the men. There were two other officers with him: a tall slim lieutenant with a slight moustache, called Medina, and an ensign named Elena, a little man with a high squeaky voice, a childlike smile and the quick jerky movements of a bird. These two came from Seville; Llancia, who spoke halting English, was a Catalan. All three were officers from the Reserve. The men, it seemed, were from Andalusia, most of them over thirty, all of them volunteers. This, said Llancia, made it difficult to apply discipline—an ironic statement in view of all I witnessed later. He added that they were the simplest type of peasant, usually obedient and cheerful but easily depressed, inefficient and inclined to be lazy—on the whole little different than children.

The little clerk, Dominguez, was summoned and told to show us to the barracks and our sleeping quarters. With an authoritative air he bade us follow him and led us to the main street. On the way he told us he had studied English —I fear without much success because he pronounced each word exactly as it would be pronounced in Spanish, and so we were never able to actually converse for more than a sentence or two. The barracks was a bare stone building of two floors, at the eastern end of the village. Outside, the men were lining up for the evening meal, which seemed to consist of *alubias*—a stew of white beans which they collected in their mess tins from a great cauldron—and a mug of red wine each. Our dormitory proved to be a barn. 'I will get some straw and a couple of blankets for each of you,' laughed Dominguez, 'then you'll be quite comfortable.'

After supper with the officers we returned to the barn, where we found our bedding laid out. There were about a dozen troopers there, who greeted us with smiles and friendly chatter, not one word of which I could understand. They had lit a fire outside, which we all sat around while the men sang the high plaintive *flamenco* of their native Andalusia, passing round mugs of wine. As I drank and listened to the strangely thrilling music, watching the firelight throw flickering shadows over the dark, bearded faces, I felt a new elation. The Squadron would be in action any moment now, Llancia had told me. I made up my mind that I would join them, and in their comradeship I would cheerfully endure hardship and danger.

It was early when we went to bed but late before I found my sleep. This was due partly to the thoughts racing through my mind, partly to the strangeness of my bed but chiefly to the thunderous sounds punctuating the stillness as my companions broke wind throughout the night.

* * *

36

Back in Toledo Walford told me as he had made up his mind to join the infantry. He left the same evening for Casa del Campo, taking his sketch book with him. I have never seen him since, but I know that he acquitted himself well in the ferocious battle that raged in that sector when the *Tercio del Alcázar* was surrounded and beat off repeated attacks by Republican Infantry and Russian tanks. I owe him much, for I do not know how I should have fared during my first days in Spain without his contacts and knowledge of the language.

After saying good-bye to him I reported to Captain Barrón, who gave me a pass to take me to Santa Olalla in the morning. With him was a short stocky figure with a doughy complexion and a frog's mouth, who spoke in a deep guttural voice. He wore a beret with the two golden fleurs-de-lis of a Requeté Lieutenant-Colonel; he proved to be the White Russian, Alkon. When my Barrón told him that I was joining the Squadron he asked me my nationality; he shook his head sadly when I told him I was English. Later I heard that, like many of his countrymen, he had little love for the English. I met another like him, nearly two years later, in San Sebastian, who informed me that he was so disgusted with the British for the way they had let down his Czar that he had ceased altogether to drink whiskey.

*   *   *

Santa Olalla, never an impressive village, had been the scene of severe fighting during the march on Toledo; now it made a sad picture. A dozen private houses and two or three taverns survived intact; in one of the former was located the Squadron Office and Officers' Mess. When I reported I found Llancia talking with a fat little man of about forty, with a sallow complexion and a very gloomy expression. he turned out to be the Squadron doctor. Having been a prisoner of the Republican *milicianos* in Ronda until its capture by the Nationalists at the end of August, he could hardly believe that he was alive. He scarcely ever spoke—never about his experiences as a prisoner.

Llancia explained to me that the Squadron was well below strength, consisting at the moment only of three troops—in total about a hundred sabres; reinforcements of men, horses, and equipment were daily expected. The Squadron's operational duties were, first, the protection of a sector of the Talavera-Toledo road; secondly and following from this, reconnaissance of the few miles of country between Santa Olalla and the Tagus, beyond which lay enemy territory. This road was vital to the Nationalist communications between their rear areas and the Madrid Front. There were Republican forces in the mountains to the north as well as in the country beyond the Tagus to the south; a combined attack from both directions, by cutting off this link at a vital period of the Madrid battle, might inflict disaster on the Nationalists. The road was very thinly held—a small garrison in Talavera, ourselves and a company of Falange militia in Santa Olalla, and a company of soldiers in Torrijos, about sixteen miles to the east. The Squadron was supposed to organize pickets by night and, by day, patrols between these posts to deal with enemy raiding parties and give warning of enemy movements; it was also to act as a mobile reserve in case of attack.

'It is very hard work for so few men,' said Llancia sadly, 'especially when they are not even half trained. But what can we do? All the troops are needed for Madrid; we must hold this long front as best we can.'

Like all of us at this time, he was convinced that a great assault was about to be launched on Madrid; then, he had been assured, our squadron would have its rôle in the battle as part of a mobile column.

I was given a horse, a powerful black beast with a beautiful mouth; also an old Mauser carbine and a sabre, the later of very poor quality steel, with a metal scabbard whose glitter would attract attention from some distance. There was no 'bucket' for the carbine, which had to be carried slung across the back, causing considerable discomfort when riding at any pace other than a walk. The only automatic weapon the Squadron possessed was one old Hotchkiss light machine-gun; I believe, but I am not sure, that there were two people in the Squadron who knew how to use it.

Llancia lent me a Spanish manual of training and indicated to me the movements, mounted and dismounted, which we should use.

During this time I worked hard at my Spanish, studying my Hugo, reading newspapers and carrying on conversations as best I could; but I found it helped me little when I tried to understand the patois of my Andalusian companions. This did not matter so much on parade or patrol, for I soon learned to follow the others, but it made it difficult to enter the life of the Squadron—or would have done had they not been so friendly and determined to make me feel at home.

For the first week I did not go out on patrol, but otherwise took my part in all duties. At six o'clock we were awakened by the beautiful Spanish bugle call of *diana* or reveille. We lined up outside the barracks for breakfast—a piece of bread and a mug of sweet, black coffee. 'Stables' followed. The rest of the morning was spent in drill or training, followed by watering and feeding the horses. *Rancho*, usually some form of stew, was at half past twelve, with a break until half past two. The afternoon was occupied in much the same way as the morning, with water and feed for the horses at half past four. After this there was a lecture, followed by prayers and, at six-thirty, the evening *rancho*. At ten o'clock the bugles sounded *silencio*.

On Sundays there were no parades except one, at noon, for Mass, which was celebrated by the chaplain of the Falange company, there being no chaplain in the Squadron.; although a Protestant, I naturally attended. At first I wondered why there was no priest in the village, but I soon found out.

It was usual for one troop to be on patrol while the other two were on training. I was in Llancia's troop; when he was busy with administration we were commanded by Sergeant San Marano, a dark, clean-shaven stocky Reservist, an excellent N.C.O. who took great care of his men.

I had night guard duty about twice a week. This entailed standing sentry in front of the barracks for two hours between *silencio* and *diana*. It would not have been arduous but for the intense cold and the fact that the sentry had to stand motionless throughout his period of duty.

Obviously, I was not very good at this drill; even so I was not much worse than the rest, who were the despair of our officers for their inability to learn the simplest movements, although they were competent enough horsemen. Officers and sergeants carried *fustas*, pliant riding crops, which they laid across the shoulders of any defaulter, mercifully excluding me. This punishment was usually taken in good part by the victim, accompanied by howls of joy from his companions.

But there was a grimmer side to the discipline, which reminded me how far I was from the O.T.C. The day after my arrival two troopers reported for duty incapably drunk; apparently they were old offenders. The following evening Llancia formed the whole Squadron in a hollow square in the main barrack-room. Calling out the two defaulters in front of us he shouted, 'There has been enough drunkenness in this Squadron. I will have no more of it, as you are going to see.' Thereupon he drove his fist into the face of one of them, knocking out most of his front teeth and sending him spinning across the room to crash through two ranks of men and collapse on the floor. Turning on the other he beat him across the face with a riding crop until the man dropped half senseless to the ground. He returned to his first victim, yanked him to his feet and laid open his face with the crop, disregarding his screams until he fell inert beside his companion. Then he turned to us: 'You have seen, I will not tolerate a single drunkard in this Squadron.' The two culprits were hauled, sobbing, to their feet to have half a bottle of castor oil forced down their throats. They were on duty next day, but I never saw either of them drunk again.

The Falange company stationed in the village were Canary Islanders. They were a gay and feckless lot who spent all their money in the taverns and most of their time singing and playing mouth organs, at which they were remarkably skilful. They seemed to regard the war as a joke and anything military as utterly ridiculous. We became very friendly with them, joining at their parties in the evenings and carousing happily together. Although they were horrified that we let ourselves be worked so hard, there was none of the animosity that too often strained relations between Requeté and Falange.

With the villagers we were on excellent terms. They would often invite us into their homes—the few that remained—for a meal or a glass of wine. From them I learned what had happened to the village priest. In August *milicianos* had come to Santa Olalla from Madrid—strangers to the place. After shooting a number of prominent villagers they crucified the priest in front of the rest. The villagers, who were fond of him, would have saved him if they could; but they were powerless before this armed rabble. 'At Alcabón, five kilometers from here,' they told me, 'the *milicianos* burnt the priest alive.' For all I have been able to find out it seems that a very large number, if not the majority, of such atrocities were committed by armed bands who came into the countryside from large towns, rather than by local peasants.

By the end of November I was allowed to accompany my troop on patrols. This was the most satisfying part of our work. We would ride out in the clear, keen air of a December dawn, when the first sunlight was flushing the snowy tops of the Gredos with fingers of rose. Usually we patrolled southward over the brown fields and through the olive groves towards the Tagus. As the morning ripened, the tawny, undulating landscape with its silver olive trees and sunlit hillocks unfolded in brilliant clarity, a pattern of bright light and blue shadow rolling away to the river and the mountains beyond. There lay enemy territory; the enemy would occasionally cross over to raid or ambush, and so we had to move with care.

Sometimes we would split into sections, each under a corporal, to carry out our various tasks of reconnaissance. After being in the saddle all day, with the occasional halt to rest the horses or to eat, we would reform as a troop towards evening and trot back to Santa Olalla in the dusk.

At about three o'clock one morning, about the middle of December, we were awakened by shouts and the sound of distant gunfire. There was a message that the enemy was attacking Talavera. We turned out and made ready to move off. No orders came until, just before dawn, we heard that a Republican force of unknown strength had crossed the river and attacked a guard post between Santa Olalla and Talavera; at the same time artillery had shelled the town. After a brief fight the enemy had retreated and were believed to be making their way back across the river. We were to intercept if possible.

We moved off about seven, one troop to the north-west in case the enemy made for the mountains, the remaining two, including mine, towards the Tagus. We split into groups of three to reconnoitre the country, but took care to keep in touch with Llancia and Squadron headquarters. After we had ridden for two hours without seeing anything Sergeant San Merano halted us while he sent out scouts. We were in a field of water melons, on which we breakfasted—not sharing Mr. Hemingway's views on the only proper use for the Castilian melon.

Suddenly we received orders to mount. We closed in to join the troop in the cover of some olives on a small hill. I noticed my companions pointing and talking excitedly; following their gaze I saw, some distance away to the right, a mass of dark specks moving across a wide gully. What could this be but our enemy? We drew our sabres, formed line and cantered down the hill and up the opposite slope. As we came over the crest San Merano gave the order, 'Charge!' Spurring our horses, we swept downhill in a cheering line, leaning forward on our horses' necks, our sabres pointed. In a moment of mad exhilaration I fancied myself one of Subatai's Tartars or Tamerlane's bahadurs. Whoever, I exulted, said the days of cavalry were past? Preoccupied with these thoughts and with my efforts to keep station I never thought of looking at our target; nor, it seemed, did anyone else. For the next thing I knew we were in the middle of a bleating, panic-stricken, heard of goats, in the charge of three terrified herdsmen. A sharp crack on the elbow from the butt of my carbine shattered my dreams; so ended my first and only cavalry charge.

One morning I was standing in front of a doorway with Llancia and Medina when we heard the sound of an aircraft approaching. As we looked up we saw at the end of the street a bi-plane circling about fifty feet up. We had time to glimpse the red marking on its tail before it banked and dived towards us. As we leapt for the shelter of the doorway bullets began to spatter the street and the walls of houses nearby. The aircraft circled again, fired several more bursts at the barracks, then made off in direction of the river. There were no casualties, but Llancia said gravely, 'You will have to watch out for those birds when on patrol.'

About this time a new Ensign came to us, the Polish Count Orlowski. He was small, dark and beautifully turned out. To my joy, he spoke perfect English as well as Spanish, pronouncing both languages in a careful, precise manner, as though each word were a trip-wire that might set off an explosion. Having served in the Polish cavalry, he was not only a superb horseman but also had a fair knowledge of horsed cavalry tactics; he was horrified by our slovenliness, incompetence, and ignorance. I was now a sergeant, owing my promotion more to Llancia's kindness than my own merit, though he may have been impressed by my O.T.C. certificates. Colonel Alkon was good enough to confirm my appointment on the only occasion he favoured us with a visit.

Much as I enjoyed my life in the Squadron, and fond I was of the officers and men, I was getting impatient at the delay in bringing us into action and at our obvious unfitness for operations. None of the expected reinforcements had arrived—not a man, not a horse, not one round of ammunition. It would clearly be a matter of months before we could hope to operate effectively. My impatience was shared by all ranks throughout the Squadron. Captain Barrón, who was supposed to command us, had not yet put in an appearance.

From time to time I was given twenty-four hours' leave to go to Toledo, where I would collect my letters and money from the Bank. On one of these visits, a few days before Christmas, I dined with a delegation of six British Conservative Members of Parliament which was visiting the Madrid front. There was a Spanish Press Officer in charge of the party, one of the most remarkable characters I have ever known.

Don Gonzalo de Aguilera, Conde de Alba de Yeltes, Grandee of Spain, was a hard-bitten ex-cavalryman of what I believe is known as 'The Old School'. That is to say, he was a personal friend of King Alfonso XIII, a keen polo player and a fine sportsman; he spoke English, French and German perfectly (he told me that he had a Scottish mother); although widely traveled he was no absentee landlord, but spent the greater part of his time looking after his estates near Salamanca; he was widely read, very knowledgeable about literature, history and science, with a brilliant if eccentric intellect and a command of vituperation that earned him the nickname during the Civil War of *El Capitán Veneno* (Captain Poison).

Loyal friend, fearless critic and stimulating companion that he was, I sometimes wonder if his qualities really fitted him for the job he was given of interpreting the Nationalist cause to important strangers. For example, he told a distinguished English visitor that on the day the Civil War broke out he lined up the labourers on his estate, selected six of them and shot them in front of the others—'*Pour encourager les autres*, you understand.'

He had some original ideas on the fundamental causes of the Civil War. The principal cause, if I remember rightly, was the introduction of modern drainage: prior to this, the riff-raff had been killed off by various useful diseases; now they survived and, of course, were above themselves. Another entertaining theory was that the Nationalists ought to have shot all the boot-blacks. (The boot-black is as integral a part of the Spanish scene as the man who sells newspapers.) 'My dear fellow,' he explained to me, 'it only stands to reason! A chap who squats down on his knees to clean your boots at a café or in the street is bound to be a Communist, so why not shoot him right away and be done with it? No need for a trial—his guilt is self-evident in his profession.' For the Requeté ideal he had an amused contempt: 'They call themselves Traditionalists, and what is this tradition that they're always talking about? The Salic Law, imported from France by the Bourbon kings, which has no place whatever in Spanish law or custom.' For the Church, in fact the Christian faith, he appeared to have no time at all; yet he was no Nazi—indeed he hated all 'isms' and was scornful of all authority, except that of the hereditary nobility of Spain.

He sympathized with my impatience to see more active service. 'I'll fix that for you,' he said. 'I'm taking these fellows—he indicated the M.P.s—'to see the Front to-morrow. I'll have a word there with my friend, Colonel Rada. He's Inspector-General of the Requetés, and also commands the Central Sector.'

When I saw him the following evening he said 'It's all arranged. You're going to be attached to Rada's Staff. Your Movement Order will be sent to your Squadron in a few days. I don't know what Rada will do with you—probably give you a motor-bike and let you carry dispatches. Anyway, it ought to be more interesting than what you're doing now.'

About this time I was disturbed to receive a letter from my mother, saying that my father was ill in bed. Although there was no indication that anything was seriously wrong, I worried because he had already taken the greatest pride in his physical fitness and it was very unlike him to take to his bed.

I spent Christmas with the Squadron. On Boxing Day my Movement Order arrived from Rada's Headquarters.

---

[1] While I was in the ranks I was, of course, given my keep. Later, as a Requeté ensign, I drew a ration allowance which covered my mess bill, and pay equivalent to rather less than £1 per week.

CHAPTER FOUR

I reached Toledo too late in the evening to continue my journey to Getafe, where Rada had his headquarters. Having booked a room at the hotel, I went to one of the cafés on the Plaza de Zocodover, where I found the journalists, Steer, Holme, and Massock, with whom I spent the evening. Both Steer and Holme subsequently quarreled with the Nationalist authorities and were expelled, to return to Spain on the Republican side; they covered the fighting on the northern front during the Nationalist offensive against Bilbao in the summer of 1937. Both played an important part in working up feeling in England against the Nationalists over the bombing of Guernica, of which I shall have something to say later.

I know nothing of the reasons for Holme's expulsion, but Steer, whom I had known before as a man of initiative and courage, could fairly be described as a natural rebel. The incident which precipitated his expulsion is worth recording, as illustrating the fury of an Englishman confronted with Spanish plumbing.

It seems that the Nationalists authorities eventually decided to grant the journalists' pleas for a visit to the Madrid front. They laid on a specially conducted tour, starting from Toledo. There were not only English and American journalists, but French, Italian, German and some South American as well. There were some senior Staff Officers from the Army, to explain the situation as it should be presented. A senior official of the Ministry of Press and Propaganda was in charge. A fleet of cars was assembled, ready to leave from the hotel at 8.30 in the morning. Soon after nine o'clock the party was ready to start, but there was no sign of Steer. After waiting a while in a fury of impatience, they were about to start without him when he appeared on the steps of the hotel with a set, exasperated expression on his face. In clear tones he addressed the assembled party:

'You pull—and pull—and pull—and nothing happens. You pull again . . . and the shit slowly rises. That's Spain for you,' he roared, 'in a nutshell!'

*   *   *

I arrived at Getafe in a lorry in the middle of an artillery bombardment; it was not a heavy bombardment, but scattered shells were falling around the village. A leaden grey sky was fading into the night; it was bitterly cold. I dismounted, retrieved my suitcase and started to walk up the deserted main street. The North wind whistled sadly over the roofs of houses, most of them empty; here and there a few candles flickered through open doorways. An atmosphere of squalor and gloom, rather than of danger, pervaded the place. I found Rada's headquarters off a side street, in a house that might once have been a rich man's villa. An orderly showed me into a room where several officers were sitting, some of them were Requetés, other in Army uniform. I was greeted in English by a spare, clean-shaven Requeté lieutenant, who gave his name as Espa; he told me he was the doctor:

'The Colonel is busy in his office now; we'll see him at dinner.'

Espa took me across the road to his own house, where we sat in virtual darkness, lit only by one candle, for more than an hour, before going to a tiny, dirty tavern for a glass of vermouth. An occasional shell still exploded nearby, but before long the bombardment had ceased.

'We nearly always have this in the evening,' he explained. 'The Reds have an excellent observation post at the top of the Telefónica building in Madrid. Those guns are Russian "12.40s"; they're good guns, which they handle very well. At the moment this sector is quiet, although of course there's always something happening down the road at Carabanchel Bajo. Our positions there are in houses, right next-door to the enemy.'

Colonel Rada was a cheerful, tubby little man, who spoke with a strong Andalusian accent. This made him almost unintelligible to me, but fortunately Espa was there to translate. After the usual compliments the Colonel said, 'I'm afraid it will be rather dull for you here. If you want to see some action I can send you to Major López Ibáñez, who is in command at Carabanchel Bajo. Report to me at eleven o'clock to-morrow morning if you want to go there.'

But next morning I found the Colonel had gone to a conference with General Orgaz and would not be back until the evening. After lunch I went for a walk in the direction of Madrid, along a path beside some fields. One of our batteries began firing somewhere behind me, I could not see where the shells were falling, but I heard them sighing as they passed on their way above. Enemy artillery replied, their shells whining close overhead to land in or behind Getafe. Other batteries joined in; soon the air was humming with projectiles. Undisturbed by the commotion a peasant continued to work in the middle of the field beside me. To him all that mattered was his field; if other men were fools enough to waste their time in fighting, that was their affair.

Reporting the day after, I found the Colonel with a gaunt, lanky lieutenant in army uniform who fortunately spoke some English. 'Lieutenant Urmeneta,' said Rada, introducing him, 'will conduct you to Major López Ibáñez at Carabanchel.

Good luck to you.'

I thanked him. 'Go with God,' he said.

* * *

The lorry stopped with a jerk, causing me to bang my head against the windscreen. Urmeneta, sitting beside me in the driver's cabin, smiled, showing an irregular line of yellow teeth with gold stoppings. We jumped down and stood for a moment stretching ourselves in the drizzling rain. A hundred yards ahead of us the road came to an end in a high barricade of sandbags, behind which huddled a sentry. It was a depressing scene—bare, crumbling red-brick buildings, the street torn with shell-holes and littered with rubble, no sound but the occasional sharp impact of a bullet against a wall and the faint rumble of gun-fire to the north.

On the right of the barricade was a small hut built of wood and sand-bags; inside, the smell of gun-oil blended with the reek of cheap tobacco, wet clothes and unwashed men. Three soldiers were lying sprawled about a machine-gun—a pre-1914 Hotchkiss whose barrel pointed through an aperture in a parapet of wooden beams and sand-bags. Looking through this opening I saw a patch of grass-covered open ground, three or four hundred metres wide, and beyond it more houses and another barricade—all that was visible of our enemy.

'It seems quiet enough, doesn't it?' said Urmeneta, 'but don't show your head or you'll have it shot off. People get careless—' we all ducked instinctively as there came a sharp whirr followed immediately by an explosion and the sound of spattering fragments. 'That's a mortar bomb,' he explained. 'We get them all the time. You can't hear them coming till it's too late. Let's go and have some lunch.'

We picked our way through the ruins of houses and along trenches to the dug-out where Urmeneta had his Platoon Headquarters. Several times we passed a strong-point, holding a machine-gun or light Hotchkiss, with a sentry on duty; other men lay around eating, smoking, or sleeping. These posts were strengthened by sand-bags shored with stout wooden beams, and roofed against mortar bombs with iron bedsteads and odd pieces of furniture. Elsewhere, the defenses consisted sometimes of shallow trenches, in which we had to bend ourselves double, or rough barricades; but more often of the walls of houses, the windows being bricked up or blocked with sand-bags or bedding, leaving only a loop-hole for a rifle. For the barricades and parapets every kind of article and material was used—sand-bags, mattresses, bedsteads, furniture of every kind and even, in one place, an old violin.

While we ate, Urmeneta explained our position. By this time the assault on Madrid had given place to a siege, which was to last for more than two years. When the Nationalists were thrown back from the gates of Madrid by the International Brigades in November, they took up fortified positions in the University City, the Casa del Campo, and the suburbs of Carabanchel Bajo and Usera; for the next few months these places were the scenes of bloody fighting as one side or the other tried to improve its position or gain a little ground.

The 8th Battalion of the 27th Regiment of Argel, which Major López Ibáñez commanded, was holding a large part of Carabanchel Bajo. Urmeneta's sector wound in and out of houses and across streets in a confusing series of salient and entrants that I never managed to understand; in some places we were as much as six hundred metres from the enemy, in others no more than ten metres. From many points we could see Madrid, its domes, spires and houses gleaming wetly through the mist, with the high tower of the Telefónica forming a clear and hateful landmark.

The men were conscripts—'Pipis', as they were called in Army slang—from the western province of Extremadura, where the Battalion had its depot; they were admirable soldiers, cheerful and willing, calm in danger, undismayed by the unremitting strain of street fighting. They were fortunate in their officers, especially in Urmeneta, whom they looked upon as a father; although he was the same age as they—only a year or two older than myself—he had a gravity and sense of responsibility beyond his years. A Basque from Pamplona, the capital of Navarre, he had joined the Requetés at the beginning of the war. He had been posted to this battalion after completing an officers' *cursillo* at one of the infantry schools. He was studying to be a lawyer in civilian life.

In the afternoon we went to see Major López Ibáñez. At one point our way lay through a coppice which Urmeneta warned me was a dangerous spot, being exposed to enemy fire. Crouching behind a wall he whispered, 'This is where we run! Keep well down and don't stop running till we've reached that wall on the other side.' We had not gone more than a few yards among the trees when the bullets started to fly around us, hissing through the branches and slapping against the trees. Knowing we had to go back the same way, I was not comforted when Urmeneta told me that the enemy were using a new dum-dum bullet made in Mexico. The Major was a short, thick-set, dark officer who bristled with self-confidence and gruff good humour.

'Where would you like to go?' he bayed. 'We have every kind of position here. You can go to a very quiet one, a very dangerous one, or'—he indicated Urmeneta—'you can stay with this officer.' In very politeness I could do no less than choose to remain with Urmeneta; in any case this is what I preferred.

On the afternoon of New Year's Eve a runner appeared to summon Urmeneta to Company Headquarters. When he returned he looked pre-occupied:

'We move tonight to a very bad position, right in the middle of the enemy—are you still sure you want to come?'

'Of course.'

* * *

It was nearly midnight when, having handed over to our relief, we formed up the street and moved off quietly on foot. I remember that journey well: the silent blackness of the bitter night, the stars twinkling frostily overhead, the whispered orders passed down the column, the muffled clink of arms, the clatter as someone kicked a fallen tile, the muttered curses and occasional quick flash of Urmeneta's torch. How differently would my friends in England be welcoming the New Year!

I had no idea where we were going, and in the darkness it was impossible to keep any sense of direction; it was all I could do to follow the man in front of me. There was a faint grey light in the sky when Urmeneta halted us and went forward to see the Company commander. Returning half an hour later, he said to me: 'You stay here with Platoon Headquarters while I settle the men into our new positions.' I heard them shuffling off into the gloom.

It was daylight when he came back.

'Let's go. Keep close to me. When you see me duck keep well down, and run like hell when I tell you. There are some places that are dangerous to cross in daylight. Above all, when we reach the position don't speak above a whisper. The enemy are very near.'

I kept close behind him, followed by his batman and the two platoon runners. Twice we were fired upon—I never knew from which direction, for I did not stop to look—but we reached the first house of our new position without a casualty. This was a small, single-storey building with a patio opening off a street. It was held by one of the two sections of our platoon.[1] We stopped here for a rest while Urmeneta spoke with the sergeant in command.

Between this and the other house in our position ran a broad, straight street, both ends of which were held by the enemy. This was crossed by a narrow tunnel built on the surface, consisting of a double line of loop-holed sandbags and roofed with planks and sandbags. It was defended by two light machine-guns, one pointing each way; it was just high enough for a man to crawl through on hands and knees, just wide enough for him to edge himself with difficulty past the defenders.

Crawling through the tunnel we came to the main position, held by the remaining section. This was a two-storey building, built round a patio like the first. A gallery, approached by an open staircase from the patio, encircled the upper story, the windows of which were barricaded and loop-holed. In two adjacent rooms, opening off the patio, Urmeneta established his office and sleeping quarters; the latter, where we had our meals, was a bare room about thirteen feet square, lit by a single smelly carbide lamp; it was furnished by a deal table and a few chairs, the rest of the space being taken up by old mattresses, on which six of us slept—Urmeneta, his sergeant, his two runners, his batman, and myself. A half-platoon of Regulares occupied two rooms of a ruined house next to ours; they had nothing to do with the defense of the position, but were there for sniping, reconnaissance and an occasional *coup-de-main* raid. They were happy, giggly little men—some of them fairer in complexion than myself, and one of them red-haired. They soon became very friendly and would bring us cups of sweet mint tea.

Our only line of communications with Company Headquarters and the rear was the tunnel of sandbags. Through this had to come all our food, water, ammunition and supplies; through this we must evacuate our wounded. It could only be done at night, which meant that a wounded man might die before he could receive proper attention, for we had no doctor. Water was so scarce that there was no question of washing, or even cleaning our teeth. In a few days we were all infested with lice. Our food, which consisted chiefly of mule steak and dried codfish, was cooked at Company Headquarters.

The rough sketch, which I drew at the time, gives some idea of our situation[2]. The enemy occupied houses enclosing us on three sides at a distance of between ten and thirty meters. Having pin-pointed the position long ago, they continually dropped mortar bombs and hand-grenades on us by day and night. That was the danger of talking above a whisper: The enemy could hear exactly where we were and would land a shower of bombs all round us. Worse, they seemed to know exactly where our latrine was situated—an exposed and shattered room at one corner of the patio; their attentions did much to expedite the process of nature.

I think there is something in the Spanish character that is stimulated by danger and discomfort; for throughout the ensuing fortnight everyone maintained an astonishing cheerfulness. We learned to take pleasure in the smallest comforts—the arrival of an unexpected bottle of brandy or box of cigarettes would put us in a happy mood for the whole day.

We suffered a daily drain of casualties. Although mortar bombs and hand-grenades could not penetrate the ceilings of the rooms, which were strengthened with beams and sandbags, they could have a devastating effect on the patio. Too often an explosion outside would be followed by the sound of scuffling and childlike whimpering; we would hurry outside to pick up a torn, bleeding figure, which we would rush into the office and lay on a mattress; there he would lie in pain until nightfall—if he did not die first. Even the dead had to be sent out through the tunnel, for there was nowhere we could bury them.

There were serious losses from sniping; I think the enemy had machine-guns trained on some of the more vulnerable places. Our men were keen snipers too, and in their excitement would sometimes expose themselves to enemy fire, with fatal results. Urmeneta did not at first discourage this activity, believing it would be good for morale; until one morning when they carried in the senior corporal with a ragged red hole in his forehead and a little white dribble of brain oozing from the back of his head. He had been a pleasant-faced, blonde youth, an excellent soldier, efficient and cheerful, cool in danger, loved by everyone. He seemed to be trying to say something, although he must have been unconscious; all we could hear was a continuous, low-pitched, snuffling moan. Urmeneta bent over him to recite the prayer for absolution, holding his own gold crucifix to the dying man's lips. As he straightened up, one of the soldiers said, 'Mateo was too confident; he would never keep under cover.'

It may be wondered why we tried to hold such a pernicious position, seeing that it cost us so much more than it was worth. I do not know the answer, but throughout this war the most dangerous and useless positions were defended by both sides with absurd tenacity and at great cost. I suppose it was reasons of prestige that prevented either side from voluntarily giving ground.

The fighting in November and December convinced both sides of the folly of attacking fortified houses by day; but we were subjected to frequent night attacks. The first came on the night of January 2nd. About 8.30 Urmeneta and his sergeant were sitting at the table about supper, giving me a Spanish lesson in whispers; all was quiet outside. Suddenly there came a burst of fire from one of our machine-guns upstairs, followed by a series of sharp detonations above and around us. In a moment the whole house was shaking with the blast of mortars and grenades, the night became a chattering cacophony of rifle and machine-gun fire. I snatched my rifle and followed Urmeneta and the sergeant through the door. In the few hideous moments of danger as we raced across the patio and up the stairway of the gallery I saw the darkness lit everywhere with flashes. As I took my post at the loop-hole I became aware of another sound, like hail—bullets striking the walls all round us. At first I could discern no target in the darkness, and confined myself to firing at enemy rifle flashes; but now our men were lobbing grenades, and by the flash of an explosion I could see a shadowy figure on the ground below or on the neighboring roof-top or balcony—a brief glimpse barely sufficient for a snap shot. I blazed away until it occurred to me that I must be wasting a good deal of ammunition, and so must my companions. The same thought seemed to occur to Urmeneta; for, coming up behind me, he shouted in my ear: 'Don't shoot unless you've got a good target—we must conserve our ammunition. That goes for grenades too.' I had lobbed a few grenades, more for practice and to give myself the impression that I was doing something than for their effect. But for every grenade we threw the enemy threw a dozen at us. Fortunately the standard hand-grenade used by both sides was the percussion 'Lafite'. This was a metal cylinder, a little larger than a 'Brasso' tin, filled with high-explosive; once the weighted safety-tape had been unwound, as it would be in the course of flight, the grenade would explode on the slightest impact. But as the case was very thin there was little danger from fragmentation, and the blast effect was limited to a few feet. On this and other occasions during the Civil War I was thankful that the Mills grenade was not in use.

For two hours the battle—or at least the firing—continued; then it died as quickly as it had begun. We tended our casualties, which were four wounded, only one seriously, posted guards and went to bed.

I doubt if the enemy suffered more casualties that night than we did. Had they pressed home their attack and succeeded in forcing an entry, I do not see how any of us could have survived; for they out-numbered us many times. We had these alarms almost every other night. Sometimes, as on this occasion, they were genuine attacks; more often I believe they were started by a jittery sentry or machine-gunner loosing off at a shadow; his companions would join in, and the enemy, thinking we were attacking, would reply. A great deal of ammunition would be wasted over nothing. Men whose nerves were overstrained by constant danger and lack of sleep tend to see shadows.

About this time there was a rumour throughout the army that the enemy were about to use gas; we were all issued with German gas-masks in cylindrical metal containers. The scare soon evaporated, and it was not long before the masks were discarded and their containers used as water-carriers.

One morning, about the middle of the second week in January, an N.C.O. came to the door of our office, asking to speak to Urmeneta. They whispered together; Urmeneta told us to keep quiet, then went down on his hands and knees, his ear to the floor. He stayed there about a minute, then motioned to the sergeant to do the same. When he had finished he scribbled a message for a runner to take to the Company Commander. He looked very worried.

What's wrong, Miguel?'

'I'm afraid the enemy are mining underneath. I heard their picks just now.'

'But are they right underneath this house?'

'No, I don't think so, not yet; I fear they soon will be.'

A new warfare was beginning around Madrid. The Republicans were employing miners from Asturias and Pozoblanco to drive mines underneath Nationalist positions in Carabanchel and the University City, in which they proved themselves extremely skilful. By this means they inflicted severe losses on Nationalists at very little cost to themselves, even forcing them to abandoned some positions. The Nationalists enlisted the most experienced engineers from Italy and Germany in attempts to put a stop to the mining; but they were unable to do more than limit its effect. In their turn the Nationalists began to use flame-throwers, especially in the Usera suburb, to blast the Republicans from their fortifications. I am told by witnesses that their effect at close quarters was devastating.

Happily I did not stay long enough to experience either forms of warfare. On the afternoon of January 13th we received orders to prepare to move out. Soon after dusk we were relieved by an infantry platoon from another regiment. We formed up outside Company Headquarters; at 7 p.m. the whole Battalion began to move in column up the road to Getafe. We arrived three hours later at the barracks where we were to sleep. Although supper was ready for us we were too tired to be bothered with it, and went straight to bed.

We slept the whole of the next morning. In the afternoon I was ordered to report to Colonel Rada. He received me very warmly and told me to put up the silver *fleur-de-lis* of a Requeté alférez, or second lieutenant.

A fortnight later the entire position we had last occupied at Carabanchel was blown up by a mine; a whole company perished in the ruins.

* * *

On January 16th I received from an aunt the following telegram: '*Your father sinking fast come at once.*'

I was all the more shocked by this because the last news I had heard was that my father was much better; nor had I any idea what was the matter with him.

Urmeneta and Major López Ibáñez were full of sympathy; permission for me to leave must, however, come from Colonel Rada. Urmeneta went with me to see him. He was very kind, but seemed doubtful whether even he had authority to give me leave outside the country. However, when I gave him my word to return to his command at the earliest moment, he issued me with a return *salvoconducto* as far as the frontier. Within two hours of receiving the telegram I was sitting in the back of an open lorry bound for Toledo.

As I huddled myself into my overcoat against the bitter wind, I tried to detach my mind from contemplation of the tragic circumstances that must have inspired that telegram, and how to concentrate on my immediate problem—how to get home with the least delay. But I could not concentrate. I thought of the last time I had seen my father, at Newhaven; of our day in London buying my kit for Spain; and, with remorse, of the frequent disagreements, even quarrels, that had previously clouded our relations. I thought of how lonely my mother was going to be, with my brother at sea in the Navy and myself in Spain—for I must keep my word to return to Colonel Rada. I could not doubt for a moment that my father was dying; such a telegram would have never been sent if there were any reasonable hope of recovery. My great fear was that he would die before I could see him.

I had no idea how I was going to get to the French frontier, but decided I was to make for Ávila, where I hoped to find a train. Another difficulty was that I had no civilian clothes, so that I should have to cross France and arrive in England in my Requeté uniform; perhaps my teddy-bear coat and scarf would conceal it satisfactorily.

In Toledo I stopped long enough to draw the rest of my month's allowance from the Bank—about £10 in pesetas—and to have a *café-cognac* to fortify myself against the numbing cold. In Talavera, after various inquiries, I found three men who were leaving for Ávila in a very old, small car; I had difficulty in persuading them to take me, for they were doubtful if the car would get them to Ávila over the snow-bound Gredos. They had grounds for their fears, because we broke down twice on the Puerto Del Pico. Arriving in Ávila about nine p.m. I found there was a train at 11.30 as far as Medina del Campo; there I must change and catch the Salamanca-San Sebastian 'express'. This would at least give me time for a meal, my first since breakfast.

In the Hotel Inglés I found Harold Cardozo, Pembroke Stevens and other journalists. They were naturally eager for a first-hand account of the fighting around Madrid; I willingly answered their questions, stipulating only that my name should not appear in print, because the British Government was beginning to enforce the policy of 'non-intervention' in the Spanish Civil War, and I was anxious to avoid any trouble in getting back into Spain.

I reached San Sebastian the following afternoon, after a cold and uncomfortable journey. There I was lucky enough to meet a friend who gave me pounds and francs for my pesetas, and drove me as far as Irun. I had some anxious moments passing through the French frontier control at Hendaye; I was afraid I should be made to take off my overcoat, thus revealing my Requeté uniform. But I caught the night train to Paris without difficulty, and was home late next afternoon—twenty-four hours after my father's funeral.

*　　*　　*

I stayed a fortnight in England. It was neither easy nor pleasant to explain to my mother why I must return to Spain so soon. It may be that I was wrong to go; let those judge me who have been in a like situation. My mother made no complaint and did all she could to hide her distress. She would be quite alone; for my brother, who had been given only twenty-four hours' leave to attend the funeral, had rejoined his ship before I arrived.

Two days before my departure the local Police Superintendent rung up. Somehow he had heard of my activities in Spain and of my intention to return. He did not propose to try and stop me, but only warned me that I might find myself liable to prosecution under the provisions of the Foreign Enlistment Act of 1880, or some such date. I said I doubted whether the Act applied to Civil Wars, and anyway I would chance it. He was kind enough to wish me luck.

*　　*　　*

The major on duty in the *Comandancia Militar* in Ávila was clearly in a very bad temper. He was not at all impressed by Colonel Rada's *salvoconducto*. A fussy, bald, bespectacled old man evidently dug out from a peaceful retirement, he regarded me with unconcealed suspicion. It was obvious what was going through his mind: what did this damned Englishman think he was doing, asking him for transport to Getafe? Whoever heard of an Englishman in the Requetés? Everybody knew the English were all on the Red side, in the International Brigades. Obviously the fellow was a spy! He might have fooled the Requetés but he wasn't going to fool the Army—least of all an old Regular soldier with forty years' service.

These thoughts he presently expressed to me, forcibly and fast, through ill-fitting false teeth that obscured the details but left the general meaning only too clear. He ended by saying that if I appeared before him again he would put me under close arrest. 'Do me the favour of removing yourself!' were his concluding words.

This was really too bad. I had expected some difficulty in getting back into Spain, but this was the first time I had met with anything but courtesy and helpfulness in the country. I had crossed France wearing the same clothes as before, with an overcoat and scarf over my uniform. In Biarritz the Conde de los Andes warned me that, owing to the 'non-intervention' regulations, I should require a visa from the British Vice-Consul in Bayonne in order to get through the French frontier control. The British Vice-Consul turned out to be a bad-tempered old Swede with a white, pointed, beard. He seemed very suspicious and was only partially satisfied by Collin Brooks's letter; but he gave me the visa. I crossed the frontier without difficulty in one of Andes's cars, which took me as far as Salamanca. This was now Franco's General Headquarters. I arrived there late on Sunday night, the 7th of February.

Next day the Nationalist troops entered Málaga. This offensive was the first occasion on which Italian troops were in action. They played an important part in the fighting, but did not endear themselves to the Spaniards, who had also fought hard, by their claims to have captured the town unaided. Particular indignation was caused by some Italian officers who had the words: *Vincitore di Málaga* printed on their visiting cards. Nevertheless, it was a spectacular victory, for Málaga was one of the principal Republican strongholds as well as the scene of some of the worst excesses of mob violence. Before the final assault the Nationalists cut the roads east of the city and, with their command of the sea, were able to prevent the escape of a large number of leading Republicans. Among those captured and subsequently executed was the infamous García Atadell, leader of the terrible *Brigada de Amanecer* (Dawn Brigade), so called because its members used to drag suspects from their homes in the small hours and shoot them. Some distinguished foreigners were captured at the same time, but later released; these included Mr. Arthur Koestler and his host, Sir Peter Chalmers Mitchell. The latter, a keen Republican supporter, was a little naïve in his efforts to palliate the actions of the extremists in Málaga. He admitted to a friend of mine that some thousands of people had been executed there by *milicianos*: 'But,' he added, 'it was all straight shooting.'

On Monday afternoon I was on a bus to Ávila, hoping to find transport there to take me to Colonel Rada. After my rebuff at the *Comandancia Militar* I decided to try my luck at General Mola's Headquarters. Within twenty minutes I had my *salvoconducto* stamped, and a place reserved for me in the official postal car leaving the next morning.

We crossed the Gredos in glorious spring weather, very different from the blizzard of my last crossing three weeks earlier. In Talavera I lunched with Pablo Merry del Val, a senior official of the Ministry of Press and Propaganda and the younger son of the famous Ambassador. He had been educated in England and still retained the austere manner and appearance of a Sixth Form prefect confronted by a delinquent from the Lower Fourth; he became a very good friend of mine, and I am indebted to him for a great deal of kindness, but I always had the feeling that at any moment he might tell me to bend over and take six of the best.

On the road to Toledo I passed my old cavalry squadron, now in Torrijos; stopping a moment to talk with the men, I learned that Llancia, Elena, Medina and Orlowski had all left for other units. I reached Getafe at 6.30, to be told that Colonel Rada had moved to Pinto, about seven kilometres to the south-east, off the main road to Toledo. I found a lift to Pinto, but Colonel Rada had moved to La Marañosa, twelve kilometres further east, above the Jarama valley. I decided to stay the night in Pinto, where an infantry officer kindly lent me a mattress in his room.

Three days earlier, on 6th February, the battle of the Jarama had begun. This Nationalist offensive, directed by General Varela, had as its objective cutting off the Madrid-Valencia road, and, in particular, the capture of the town of Arganda on that road. This was the last direct supply line remaining to the defenders of Madrid from their bases in the Mancha and on the Mediterranean. Colonel Rada, who was commanding one of the formations under Varela, had launched his attack on Pinto the first day.

The country over which the battle was fought was an undulating plain, covered with scrub, sloping gradually eastwards to the Jarama valley; the most important tactical features were the heights of La Marañosa, six hundred feet above the Manzanares, and the so-called Espolón de Vaciamadrid, a ridge overlooking the confluence of the Manzanares and Jarama rivers. Farmland and olive groves covered the valley of the Jarama on both sides of the river. On the eastern side of the valley were hills thickly covered with olives.[3]

By the time I reached Pinto, on February 9th, the Nationalists had overrun the country to the west of the Jarama and occupied the heights of La Marañosa and the Espolón de Vaciamadrid; from the latter they were able to shell the Valencia road. On February 11th, they forced the crossing of the Jarama and occupied the hills beyond to a distance of about four kilometres from the river. There they were held by the determined resistance of the International Brigades, including the British, who suffered very severe losses. Heavy fighting followed. The Republicans counter-attacked all along the line, but failed to regain any ground. By February 24th, the battle was over. The Nationalists failed in their main objective, which was the capture of Arganda, but they were able to dominate the Valencia road with their artillery fire and deny its use to the enemy. Thereafter, the only ground communication between Madrid and Valencia was along the Aragón road through Alcalá de Henares and across the country to Cuenca.

The morning of the 10th February was bright, clear and spring-like. As I sat in the back of an open lorry, jolting along a very bad road towards La Marañosa, and looking at the fresh quiet countryside I found it hard to believe that a battle was being fought only a mile or two away. But I was soon reminded of the enemy's proximity by the sight of a battery of anti-tank guns deployed for action by the side of the road, their German crews crouched alertly behind them.

La Marañosa could scarcely be called a village; it consisted of about a dozen houses, on either side of the track from Pinto, and a disused ordnance factory. Immediately to the north the ground rose to the heights where our positions were situated. Colonel Rada's Headquarters was a small house with a garden and a low wall, standing on the left of the road. There I found the Colonel with Espa and others I knew. They seemed surprised to see me back. Rada said he would send me to the Requeté *Tercio del Alcázar*, which was due to arrive in La Marañosa the next day; he could not return me to the 8th Battalion of Argel because they were no longer under his command.

While we were talking there was a small air-raid; Rada took us out into the garden to watch; half a dozen enemy *'ratas'*—Russian fighters—were machine-gunning the area, concentrating on the positions above us, and to the eastward. They dropped three small bombs which landed harmlessly in open country.

As we were sitting down to dinner that evening an enemy battery opened fire, obviously trying to hit Rada's headquarters. The shells fell close around the house, damaging one or two of the other buildings and causing several casualties. There was a feeling of expectancy and tension in the air which made me realize that something important was to happen to-morrow. After dark a *bandera* of the Foreign Legion formed up outside—dark, hard-bitten, grim-looking soldiers with a tremendous pride in their bearing, they were singing the two great Legion songs, *El Himno del Legionario* and *El Novio de la Muerte*, thrilling tunes that moved us all as we heard them chanted with such spirit by these men who were about to die. Indeed, many of them were dead within twenty-four hours; at dawn they went into action, nearly six hundred strong, to force the crossing of the Jarama; by the evening there were barely two hundred left.

Next morning the *Tercio del Alcázar* moved into La Marañosa. I reported to the Commanding Officer in his headquarters opposite Colonel Rada's. Major Emilio Alamán was tall and stout, with a loud guttural voice. He was a fine soldier; skillful, experienced and courageous. He had distinguished himself in the defence of the Alcázar of Toledo, in which he had been wounded. By nature a jovial and good-hearted person, he was clearly still suffering from the strain he had undergone during the siege; this made him liable to sudden and unreasonable outbursts of temper, terrifying in their violence.

He spoke no English and was clearly not very pleased to have a strange Englishman thrust upon him; but he received me well enough. He said that I had better stay with him at Battalion Headquarters for the present. I was allowed a batman and a corner of a room in an adjoining house to sleep in. This room I shared with five others, including a French alférez, a jolly, tubby, middle-aged man with a voluble manner and a passion for his food; he used to spend a lot of time in the kitchen, before and after every meal, giving hell to the cooks. An additional sleeping companion was a tiny mongrel, who hung around the kitchen by day and came to sleep on one or other of our beds at night. We were all fond of him, and would have been fonder but for his habit of making a mess on the bed of his choice. Our chief discomfort was lack of water, for there was no local supply and all our water had to come from Pinto in lorries; there was barely enough to drink, none for washing. The wine, though not scarce, was atrocious.

The first two days were uneventful but for intermittent shelling from across the river; this ceased on the third day. Air-raids continued, usually in the early hours of the morning. They seldom came by day, for two reasons: firstly because we were well protected by anti-aircraft; secondly because the Nationalists were beginning to win command of the air from the Republicans. Credit for this was due primarily to the initiative of one man, the fighter pilot García Morato. García Morato, who commanded a formation of Fiat CR 42 bi-planes, trained his pilots to pitch a perfection far ahead of the enemy. When he brought them into action over the Jarama they chased the Republicans out of the sky.

I usually slept during the night raids, which of course were not comparable with those of the last war. But on one occasion I was awakened in the middle of a raid by infuriated shouts from the Frenchman: '*Merde! C'est le chien qui chie!*' The little dog had chosen his bed that night.

A day or two after my arrival we were joined by a young German officer, Lieutenant Von Gaza. He was something of a mystery, because he claimed to be a lieutenant of machine-guns in the Reichwehr, and was wearing German army uniform; yet it seemed extraordinary that he should be sent by himself. He spoke

English but no Spanish; he was polite but formal in his manner, speaking in a precise, clipped voice and seldom smiling. He told me that he came from East Prussia and that he was an orphan, his parents having been murdered by the Russians in Riga after the First World War. We had one or two Germans in this unit, but Von Gaza held himself aloof from them, causing them grave offence. He soon transferred from us to the Foreign Legion, where he served under Captain Cancela, who subsequently became my own Company Commander and who told me something of his story. He was indeed a Regular Army officer, and came from a Junker family; but, having committed some serious offence which had brought upon him the displeasure of the German military authorities, he was given the choice of a court-martial or service in Spain—but with the proviso that he must not serve with his own countrymen. He was killed by a chance shell two months later, while playing cards in a bungalow with three other officers of his bandera. Cancela told me that he was the best officer he ever had.

There was a German press photographer called Franz Roth, who had taken up his quarters in La Marañosa, with whom I became very friendly; he worked for Associated Press, had travelled widely, and was in Addis Ababa at the time of Mussolini's invasion. He and I used to climb one of the hills overlooking the Jarama to watch the fighting on the other side. Through our binoculars we could see the battle raging among the olives, white puffs of bursting shrapnel in the air, the dark smoke of high explosive between the trees, and the incessant sound of machine-gun fire reaching us faintly from across the valley.

One day Roth asked me to accompany him down to the Jarama. He had heard a report that a company of Frenchmen from the International Brigades had been destroyed by a tabor of Regulares while trying to cross a bridge over the Jarama and that the Moors had castrated their victims. I agreed to go because I felt that this sort of report should be checked, in view of the wild atrocity stories that were circulating about the Moors; anyway I wanted to see the Jarama. We set off on foot in the early afternoon and after about a mile descended into the *vega*, or cultivated plain, of the Jarama. Beside a ruined farmhouse we came upon a German anti-tank gun, with its crew, commanded by an officer. We made to approach and Roth called to the officer in German; but they shook their heads and would not let us come near. The bright sun shone golden on the fields and the olives; it shone also on the huddled corpses of the Frenchmen, heaped around the bridge where we had expected to find them. Most of them had been stripped of their boots and outer garments by the Moors and lay there in their underclothes in every attitude, grotesque and stinking, shriveled by two days' hot sun. With ghoulish intensity Roth probed among the bodies, urging me to do the same. We found no trace of mutilation, but after ten minutes of this grisly business I was violently sick and told Roth I could not go on. My legs would hardly carry me back to La Marañosa, where I drank nearly half a bottle of Roth's brandy before I began to recover. If this is the sort of thing I have to do to prove myself a man, I thought, I think I'll stay a mouse. Roth was quite unmoved.

On the morning of February 15th Major Alamán asked Von Gaza and me if we would like to be posted to one of the positions on the heights of La Marañosa. We were delighted, for we had nothing to do at Battalion Headquarters and felt we were always on the Major's toes. We each took a rifle and pack and set off along a path leading up the hill past Colonel Rada's Headquarters. It took us about twenty minutes to reach our new position. This was on the right of our line, on a ridge overlooking the plain of the Manzanares. Below us, about three-quarters of a mile distant, was a broad belt of olives stretching away to our left. A track led from it straight in front of us for about half a mile to a deserted village. Beyond the village ran the Manzanares. The country between the Manzanares and ourselves was supposedly a no man's land. Von Gaza and I were astonished that no patrols were sent to reconnoiter it at night; we offered to go ourselves, but were told it was unnecessary.

The defences consisted of rough earthworks, with shallow trenches and parapets of earth and stones, bolstered with a few sandbags. There was a Hotchkiss machine-gun and a light machine-gun of the Lewis pattern. About a hundred yards back from the position was a small empty house in a little grove of trees; this was Platoon Headquarters, where we slept.

At dawn on the morning of the 17th we awoke to the sound of heavy firing away on our left. We ran to our trenches and took up firing positions. At first we could see nothing, for the valley below was still hidden in the river mist. But as the haze rolled back in the rising sun, we saw groups of little dark figures moving towards us along the track from the village and across the fields. We held our fire, letting them reach the olive trees undisturbed. Surely, I thought, they can't mean to attack across those open fields in front, with no artillery preparation. It's sheer suicide although they do outnumber us many times. But in a moment they emerged from cover and began to advance at a trot towards us. We waited until they were well in the open, then, at a sharp word from the Platoon Commander, our machine-guns opened up; we joined in with our rifles. The little trotting figures halted and toppled down in heaps. A machine-gun in the olives started firing at us, its bullets flying high overhead; some of the enemy in the open tried to cover the advance of their comrades with light automatic weapons, but in those fields, devoid of cover, they stood no chance against our fire. Soon they were running back for shelter, leaving their dead and wounded strewn among the stubble; many more fell as they ran. It's sheer bloody murder, I said to myself. What criminal staff officers they must have, to send them into battle this way! Possibly, well-trained, experienced troops might have been able to find some dead ground for cover, though I doubt it; certainly no experienced commander should have asked them to do it. It may bet that they counted on surprise, but if so they had planned it very badly. From the sounds of firing I judged that the attack was being pressed on both our flanks. I was a little disturbed that we seemed to have no artillery. But the enemy had; for soon there was a whistle as a shell passed overhead. It was followed by several more, each one landing a little closer. It was fortunate that we could hear them coming, for our earthworks were flimsily built and our trenches much too shallow, so that we had to crouch down each time a shell came over. It was clear that they were shooting at the house, and so the Platoon Commander ordered its evacuation: none too soon, for a succession of shells hit it immediately afterwards, reducing it to a ruin. Then they concentrated on the position itself and their shells began to fall uncomfortably close, one or two of them causing casualties.

Now the enemy were advancing again, threading their way among the bodies that had fallen in their first attempt. Again we opened fire and again they were thrown back, leaving more of their number on the ground. Yet a third time they advanced, fewer of them now, and flagging in their pace.

'Hold your fire!' shouted our Platoon Commander. 'Let them get a bit closer this time.' We kept under cover.

They came on in bounds, one group giving covering fire while another advanced. When the nearest was within four hundred yards, and all were well out in the open, we had the order: 'Fire!'

It was murder. The poor creatures fell in heaps. The survivors turned and ran for cover, dropping their weapons in their haste. When the last few survivors had vanished into the olives, the whole plain in front of us was littered with bodies. Von Gaza told me he saw two officers shot by their own men while trying to stop the rout. Our own casualties numbered some half-a-dozen.

For a while there was a lull and no movement in front of us. Suddenly we heard the sound of heavy engines, and from our right front appeared six Russian tanks, each carrying a 37 millimetre gun in its turret. One after the other they crossed in front of the olives, then turned towards us and began to approach in line. This looked awkward for us, and would have been if any infantry had followed them; but the latter had no fight left in them. If the tanks had preceded the earlier attacks the result might have been very different; even so, we were expecting rough handling. At that moment our artillery, silent before, came into action. It found the range quickly and soon we saw black puffs of smoke bursting all round the tanks. They wavered, then came to a halt. A moment later one of them was enveloped in black smoke as a shell struck it squarely; it began to burn. Then another was hit at the base of the turret. The remaining four turned, spread out and made off.

About midday, when the fighting had died down on our front, a runner arrived with news that the two companies on our left had suffered heavily and were in need of reinforcements; our Platoon Commander was required to send any men he could spare to report to Battalion Headquarters. Von Gaza and I were among those who went. At Battalion Headquarters we found a young man, Felipe Pallejá, a Catalán who spoke good English. He told us that the positions in the centre and on the left had been under heavy fire from artillery and mortars all morning; Major Alamán was up there now and Pallejá would take us to him.

The enemy were evidently respecting the hour of the siesta for everything was quiet when we arrived. The Major was in very good heart, although he expected the attacks to be renewed in the afternoon and next day. Most of our heavy machine-guns were concentrated on the centre position; Von Gaza was sent there, where his special knowledge would be most useful. For the moment I was to stay with Alamán.

During the afternoon we were subjected to intermittent shelling, but no new attack developed. It seemed that the enemy were re-grouping for a further assault on the morrow. They had established themselves in the olives. I accompanied the Major on visits to our two positions. These followed the crest of the heights, the centre facing north across the valley of the Manzanares and the belt of olives, the left curving back and facing more to the north-west, towards Madrid. The Major expected the main attack to be launched against the latter, in an attempt to turn our left flank and cut the road to Pinto. It was arranged that Pallejá and I should move up there in the evening.

The defences had not been as severely damaged as I had expected; the enemy artillery could not have been of very heavy caliber. Most of the casualties had been from mortars. In places where the parapet had been demolished men were repairing the damage with earth and sandbags. It struck me that the trenches were very badly constructed, being much too shallow to give proper protection, and dug almost in a straight line instead of with traverses. Throughout the Civil War it was my experience that Spanish troops could not be induced to dig proper trenches; this applied even to the Foreign Legion. They seemed to think it indicated cowardice to dig themselves in securely.

We returned to Battalion Headquarters to snatch a meal. There I found the French lieutenant; he had found time during the lull to slip away from his post to give some more hell to the cooks about the soup they had sent up.

At dusk Pallejá and I went up to our new station. We found a dug-out to sleep in, which we had to share with eight others; it was a bit cramped, but it would do for the little sleep we were expecting. We went to report to the Company Commander, whose name, if I remember rightly, was Santo Domingo. We found him in his dug-out with another captain, called Frejo, and Father Vicente, the Company Chaplain, a stern-faced, lean Navarrese with the face of a fanatic gleaming behind his glasses. Captain Santo Domingo had a great reputation as a soldier in this *tercio*, and was beloved by his men, whom he led by the sheer force of his own example. He was a man of about forty-five with a strong, gentle face, full of character. Father Vicente, in great spirits, dominated the gathering. He was the most fearless and the most bloodthirsty man I ever met in Spain; he would, I think, have made a better soldier than priest.

'Holá, Don Pedro!' he shouted at me. 'So you've come to kill some Reds! Congratulations! Be sure you kill plenty!' The purple tassel of his beret swung in the candle-light. Santo Domingo frowned:

'Father Vicente , you always talk of killing. Such sentiments do not come well from a priest. The Reds may be our enemies, but remember they are Spaniards, and Spain will have need of men after the war.'

'Of good men, yes. But not of evil.'

'Of good men,' repeated Santo Domingo, 'and of evil men converted.'

I was fascinated, as the argument became heated, to see the roles of priest and soldier reversed; but I noticed that Father Vicente was alone among the party in his condemnation of all Reds as traitors who must be killed. He needn't worry, I thought, we'll have to kill all we can to-morrow, if only to save our own skins.

Captain Frejo spoke: 'It will be a hard battle to-morrow; they must outnumber us by at least ten to one. We have no other defences to fall back on, and if we break the whole Jarama front will fold up.'

'God will not desert us,' pronounced Father Vincente.

None of us felt like sleep; it was long after midnight before Pallejá and I returned to our dug-out, to throw ourselves full dressed on the ground. The imminent prospect of a violent, if glorious death, tends wonderfully to concentrate the mind on past misdeeds and future hopes of salvation. I will admit that I said a few prayers that night and even made some resolutions; but I wish I could honestly record that the pattern of my life changed radically after my deliverance. I was not the only one who found it difficult to sleep. I must have dozed, for the next thing I knew was that someone had lit a candle, and my companions were stirring themselves. I put on my belt, pouches, and steel helmet, took my rifle and crawled out into the open. I stood up on the hillside, taking deep breaths of the clear, cold air, which revived me wonderfully after the dusty atmosphere of the dug-out.

It was beginning to get light. I could make out dimly the shape of our own trenches and the position on our right, lined with tense, waiting figures. As the light grew, I stood looking down into a mist-draped valley where the enemy lay hidden in the gloom. Not a sound came from it. Now I could see the tops of the olives beginning to appear through the grey blanket. From the right a single shot broke the stillness.

The next moment the whole valley exploded into countless flashes and the thunderous noise of firing; the air around me was humming with bullets. I ran the few yards to the trench and flung myself against the parapet, with my rifle to my shoulder, as our own line burst out in reply.

All around us the earth was thrown up again by shells and mortar bombs, the air torn by bullets. Once again the enemy machine-guns were firing high, but their artillery already had our range, while mortar bombs were landing on the parapets and in the trenches. As the mist parted we saw that under its cover the enemy had been moving towards us. The plain in front of the olives was full of them, and more could be seen coming up from the river. As Major Alamán had forecast, they were working round on our left flank.

My throat was dry, my face hot and my hands shaking as I feverishly loaded and fired my rifle. With a great effort I pulled myself together and began to fire more slowly, checking my sights, resting my elbows on the parapet and taking careful, aimed shots. This had a steadying effect on me and I began to feel much better. I began, too, to feel a kind of pity for my enemies, exposed in the open to this murderous fire, so that, as I aligned my sights on one of them and pressed the trigger with a slow, steady pressure, as I had been taught, I found myself praying that my bullet might put him out of action, but not maim him grievously for life.

Once again the enemy's planning had let him down. His troops were, indeed, nearer to their objective than on the previous day; so also were they further from cover. Their only chance seemed to be a rapid advance, regardless of casualties. About three or four hundred yards in front of our trenches was a line of low hillocks extending to our left; these, if they could reach them, would afford them some protection, enabling them to concentrate for a final assault. At first they made no progress against our fire. Many fell; some lay down where they were and fired back at us, others turned and ran in all directions, looking for cover, not realizing that this was the most certain way of being killed.

The morning drew on with occasional brief lulls in the fighting, which gave us time to evacuate the dead and badly wounded, dress lesser wounds, repair defences where possible, replenish our ammunition and take a drink from our water bottles. But the mortars in the olives gave us no rest.

The bombardment intensified as a new wave of attackers surged forward, in much greater strength than the first. They had learnt by now to use what little cover there was, and to combine fire and movement more skillfully than before. In spite of their losses, numbers of them reached the shelter of the hillocks, where with rifles and light machine-guns they opened fire on us to cover the advance of their comrades.

The bombardment was reaching a climax. Our ears were throbbing with explosions, our eyes almost blinded with dust; not so blinded, however, that we could not see that the enemy was getting closer, finding his way surely round to our left flank. Bullets from his light machine-guns were slapping against the parapets and whistling by our heads. Sometimes a Requeté, carried away by excitement, would clamber up on the parapet, half out of the trench, to get a better shot; in a moment he would slump back, torn with bullets, or fall forward over the parapet to roll a few yards down the slope in front. Whenever the latter happened—and I personally saw it happen several times—Father Vicente would leap from the trench and run down the hill to where the body lay, the purple tassel of his scarlet beret flying in the wind; there he would kneel, oblivious to the bullets churning the earth around them, while he prayed over the dead or dying man.

Major Alamán was moving along the line between us and the position on our right, limping on his heavy stick, now quite imperturbable in the heat of battle, his harsh guttural voice croaking encouragement to us all. Looking over my shoulder I saw Frejo and Santo Domingo on top of the parados, each standing behind his men, each wearing his red beret and wrapped in a *capote*, unmoved by the bullets flying around him, calmly directing the fire and encouraging the defence. This was the true Requeté tradition. Even when Frejo collapsed with a shattered shoulder and was carried away unconscious with pain, the inspiration remained with us.

My ammunition pouches were empty, the barrel of my rifle was too hot to touch. Near me lay a dead Requeté; I stooped over him to replenish my pouches from his, and to take his rifle. As I straightened up to return to my firing position there was an explosion almost on top of me, which threw me to the ground, where I lay for a moment with my ears singing. Realizing that I was not hurt I got up, adjusting my steel helmet. A bit of it seemed to be pressing against my forehead, and so I took it off; I found a large dent in front, where a piece of metal had hit it. Hitherto I had been inclined to laugh at tin hats.

It was nearly noon. There seemed no prospect of reinforcements for us; our ammunition was running low and the enemy, now within three hundred yards of us, was preparing for the final assault. We were so heavily outnumbered that there could be only one outcome if he reached our trenches. The firing died away and a lull descended, while the enemy collected his forces for the attack and we made ready to meet them.

Then we heard a new sound from the left flank beyond the enemy—the sound of tank engines. In a few moments a column of our own light tanks swept into view—about sixteen of them, each with two machine-guns. They came on fast, fanning out into line abreast, then opening fire together on the enemy's unprotected flank and rear. The battle was decided. The Republicans had no chance. Caught between our fire and the guns of our tanks, they were shot down in swathes as they ran for the shelter of the olives. Few of them reached it; those that did continued their flight to the Manzanares and beyond. Their mortars were silent; even their artillery ceased fire.

I was conscious of Father Vicente beside me; his spiritual duties finished, he was bent on seeing that we did not allow the fleeing enemy to escape unpunished. He kept on pointing out targets to me, urging me shrilly to shoot them down, and effectively putting me off my aim. It seemed to me that he could barely restrain himself from snatching my rifle and loosing off. Possibly recollecting that I was a heretic, and therefore little better than a Red, he soon left me to concentrate on my neighbours. Whenever some wretched militiaman bolted from cover to run madly for safely, I would hear the good Father's voice raised in a frenzy of excitement:

'Don't let him get away—Ah! *don't* let him get away! Shoot, man, shoot! A bit to the left! Ah! *that's* got him,' as the miserable fellow fell and lay twitching.

It had been a very near thing. If our tanks had not arrived, or they had arrived even a little later, we should almost certainly have been overrun. I do not know where they came from; they were German tanks, though the crews were Spanish. As we had been told to expect no reinforcements we were as surprised to see them as the enemy must have been. I have reason to believe that these tanks consisted nearly the whole of General Varela's mobile reserve; if so, he used them brilliantly, to strike at exactly the crucial moment to turn impending defeat into total victory.

Thus ended the two-days' battle of La Marañosa. Although we were shelled heavily that afternoon and frequently during the next few days, we were not attacked again. This had been part of the Republican General Miaja's counter-offensive, which he now switched to other points on the Jarama front. The formation that had carried the brunt of the attack against us was a Spanish brigade with the inspiring title of 'The Grey Wolves of La Pasionaria', named after the notorious Communist Deputy, Dolores Ibarruri. Certainly their fiasco was due to no lack of courage—indeed they showed remarkable bravery in such hopeless circumstances.

Our own losses were considerable. At the beginning of the battle our fighting strength was about three hundred; of these we lost more than a hundred in killed and seriously wounded; I think we were lucky to get off so lightly. Major Alamán, who had contributed notably to it, expressed himself as well satisfied with our performance, and both Colonel Rada and General Varela sent us personal messages of commendation.

By the 24th February the Republican counter-offensive was exhausted. Conducted as it was, it is not surprising that it achieved no success. The battle of the Jarama might have been a decisive victory for the Nationalists if they had had more troops; but at the time of General Varela's original offensive, at the beginning of February, a large part of the Nationalist effort was directed against Málaga.

At the beginning of March I received a letter from my mother, asking me if I could get leave to come to England for a few weeks to deal with some legal business arising out of my father's death. At the same time I heard from my brother, who was in the cruiser *Neptune* at Gibraltar, offering me a passage home in his ship if I could get there by the middle of the month. Colonel Rada gave me leave to go, but advised me to have it confirmed in Salamanca if I wished to return to Spain afterwards. I left for Salamanca the next day.

---

[1] A Spanish infantry platoon is divided into two sections, or half-platoons, of 20-25 men, each commanded by a sergeant. It is confusing that the Spanish word for platoon is *Sección*, and the term for a section, or half-platoon, is *Pelotón*. A *Pelotón* contains three *Escuadras*, each commanded by a corporal, or senior private.

[2] Please see the Publisher's note at the front of the book.

CHAPTER FIVE

It was something of a shock to find a constable in the uniform of the Metropolitan Police answering me in fluent Spanish; yet this is what happened on the North Front at Gibraltar when I asked my way to the Rock Hotel.

Thanks to Pablo Merry del Val, whom I met in Salamanca, I had no difficulty in getting permission to return to England. In the Gran Hotel I was introduced to a tall, distinguished-looking Spaniard, the Marqués de Manzanedo, who was then serving in the Nationalist Diplomatic Service. A great anglophile, he was extremely kind to me and gave me a lift to Seville two days later. There I took a bus to Algeciras. I crossed the frontier at La Linea in the same disguise I used to cross the French frontier, and with the same success. But in the bar of the Rock Hotel, where I could not very well keep on my overcoat and scarf, I felt considerably embarrassed. There my brother joined me with the news that his ship was sailing in two days' time and that he had the Captain's permission for me to sail in her.

'I'm afraid there's no cabin for you, and I'm damned if I'm going to give up mine, so you'll have to sleep in a hammock. As a matter of fact, I think you'll find it very comfortable.'

I can never forget the kindness and hospitality I had from Captain Benson and the officers of the H.M.S. *Neptune* during the voyage. She was a very happy ship. My brother, Neil, who was in the Fleet Air Arm, piloted the seaplane that she carried; five years older than myself, he had achieved distinction in the Service as a naval historian and writer on naval subjects. Among his fellow-officers he was known as 'Three-plank' because, they told me, when he walked the deck each of his feet covered three planks; they took one look at me and christened me 'Two-plank'.

Neil was right about the hammock. Once I had learnt how to climb into it—it was slung at about shoulder height—I slept in it very well; moreover, because it swung with the motion of the ship, there was no sensation of rolling. But there was one drawback; it was slung immediately over a hatch, usually open, which led down to the boiler-room. This did not worry me when I went to bed loaded with ward-room whisky, but it gave me a fright, on waking with a thick head, to look over the side into a gaping black pit.

It was my brother's last voyage in *Neptune*, she was paying off in England before going out to South Africa. It was a sad blow to hear, in 1942, that she had struck a mine while chasing three Italian cruisers in the Mediterranean, and capsized with the loss of every man on board.

* * *

The bearded Swede in the British Vice-Consulate at Bayonne flew into a temper when I presented myself again with Collin Brooks's letter; he abused me as he stamped my passport and almost spat at me as I left his office. There is no doubt, I said to myself, that he isn't in the least deceived. If I have to cross this frontier again I must find another way.

It was now the middle of April. After the failure of their offensive against Guadalajara the Nationalists finally abandoned their efforts to take Madrid. Instead, they began a full-scale offensive against Bilbao. Despite their superiority in aircraft and artillery they were faced by an enemy fully as brave and determined as themselves, well entrenched in positions that they had been preparing all winter; by some of the most difficult terrain in the Peninsula, and by weather that often made operations impossible. It seemed, therefore, that Bilbao would be an unconscionably long time falling.

It would have taken longer still if the Basque Republicans had not wasted their best troops at the end of November, 1936, in a disastrous offensive concentrated on the town of Villareal, the gateway to Vitoria. Some fifteen thousand men, mostly *Gudaris*, or Basque militiamen, were thrown into the attack against a garrison of about six hundred men—Regular Army and Requetés. These beat back all attacks until relieved on December 5th by a column from Vitoria, under Colonel Camilo Alonso Vega. The Republicans renewed their assault on 18th December with disastrous results to themselves; they were forced to abandon their offensive, having suffered appalling casualties. Unfortunately they had not even bothered to organize casualty clearing stations or hospitals, or to provide themselves with medical supplies, such as anti-gangrene serum. In a single night more than four hundred of their wounded died of gas-gangrene.[1]

I saw Orlowski on my way through Paris. He had gone to the *Tercio del Alcázar* after leaving the cavalry squadron in January; he had been slightly wounded in action with them at a place called Cabezafuerte, not far from La Marañosa, but had left just before my arrival, finding the Major's temper too much for him. Through friends of his I had an introduction to the O'Malley-Keyes family, who lived in an enchanting house on a hill at Anglet, near Biarritz; with them I stayed while waiting for my *salvoconducto*, which would allow me to enter Spain. What would have been a period of tedious waiting thus became a delightful interlude.

I arrived in Spain on April 21st in the middle of a political crisis. The only public announcements of it were, first, an official statement that Señor Hedilla, the leader of the Falange, was under arrest; secondly a decree amalgamating the Requetés and the Falange and abolishing all other political parties. The new organization was to be known as *Falange Española, Tradicionalista y de las Juntas de Ofensiva Nacional-Sindicalista*—and, added the Spaniards with their irrepressible love of ridicule, *de los Grandes Expresos Européos*. Parties with more divergent political views than the Requetés and the Falange could scarcely be imagined. Writing of 'this magnificent Harlequin', Señor de Madariaga says it was 'as if the President of the United States organized the Republican-Democratic-Socialist-Communist-League-of-the-Daughters-of-the-American-Revolution, in the hopes of unifying American politics'. Either the Falange or the Requetés would have to dominate; the skill at intrigue of the former, and the political ineptitude of the latter made the outcome certain; the Requetés ceased to exert any serious influence on Spanish politics.

The day after the announcement of Hedilla's arrest the Falangist newspaper, *Arriba*, appeared with thick black borders. Officially the news was hailed as a statesmanlike move to achieve national unity; but public uneasiness persisted, nor was it allayed when General Faupel, the German Ambassador, was sent packing. Clearly there had been a conspiracy. The full details are still imperfectly known abroad, but in brief what happened was this: the Germans were anxious, for their own reasons, to see the war ended quickly. For some months they had been dissatisfied with General Franco, whose strategy they regarded as archaic and likely to lead to an indefinite prolongation of hostilities. But General Franco is a gallego (Galician), with all the obstinacy and subtlety of that race; it was his war, and he was going to run it as he thought fit. The Germans therefore decided to replace him with a creature of their own; Señor Hedilla, as the leader of the most pro-German party, was their ideal tool. He was persuaded by General Faupel to stage a *coup d'état*, which very nearly succeeded. But General Franco reacted vigorously, suppressed the conspiracy, sent Hedilla to prison for ten years and demanded the recall of Faupel. To complete his ascendency he appointed himself head of the new, and only, party. He continued to run the war in his own way, and it was not until March, 1938, that he launched an offensive along the lines advocated by the Germans.

Having made up my mind to be transferred to a unit on the Bilbao front, I went to Salamanca to arrange a posting. From there I was sent to Ávila to see General Monasterio, the ex-cavalry leader, who was now in command of all militia forces. It was an alarming interview. The General, a man of austere appearance, whose face seemed more suited to the wig and scarlet robes of a High Court Judge than the uniform of a soldier, was surrounded by half-a-dozen officers, none of them below the rank of Colonel. They fired a bewildering succession of questions at me in Spanish, to which I could only reply in a high-pitched croak, for I was suffering from laryngitis. Sweating and trembling I left the room, with orders to await my posting in Salamanca.

Architecturally Salamanca is one of the most beautiful cities in Europe. I spent long hours admiring the perfection of the colonnades in the Plaza Mayor and visiting the University, the two cathedrals, and the Casa de las Conchas. Less beautiful among the sights of Salamanca at this time but, it seemed, scarcely less firmly established, was the figure of General O'Duffy, who commanded the Irish Brigade. I met him through his A.D.C., Captain Meade, a charming man, half Irish and half Spanish, with all the tact and patience that his job required. The General was sitting at a table in a corner of the lounge in the Gran Hotel, a bottle of whisky in front of him; with him were Meade, another officer of his staff, and the Rector of the Irish College at Salamanca. Meade, whom I had met before, came over to my table and asked me to join them; as we crossed the room he whispered to me, 'Please be careful what you say to the General. I'm afraid I must tell you that he loathes all Englishmen.'

A former Chief of Police of the Irish Free State, General O'Duffy launched into Irish politics in the 1930's, forming his own United Party, or 'Blueshirts'. Seeing in the Spanish Civil War a chance to increase his prestige in Ireland, he raised a 'Brigade' of his countrymen to fight for the Nationalists. The 'Brigade' was in fact equal in strength to a battalion, but O'Duffy was granted the honorary rank of General in the Spanish Army. Few generals can have had so little responsibility in proportion to their rank, or so little sense of it. Whatever the ostensible purpose of the Irish Brigade, O'Duffy never lost sight of its real object, which was to strengthen his own political position. He therefore gave the most responsible appointments to his own political supporters, regardless of their military experience; one of the most important he gave to an ex-liftman from Jury's Hotel in Dublin, a man who knew nothing of soldiering and was prepared to learn nothing. In favour of such men as this he declined the service of experienced ex-officers who did not happen to belong to his party. Like some other Irishmen and some Americans—happily a minority—whose minds cherish the memory of past enmity he had a pathological hatred of the English, which he never tried to conceal. To his men he was known as 'General O'Scruffy' or 'Old John Bollocks'.

His secretary and shadow was 'Captain' Tom Gunning, a brilliant journalist who had formerly made a name for himself in Fleet Street. The story Gunning put around was that his Irish Republican sympathies made it impossible for him to set foot in Fleet Street again. Closer inquiry revealed more compelling reasons. A skilful intriguer, he contrived, so long as he remained O'Duffy's secretary, to keep the Irish Brigade divided against itself.

The administration of that unhappy unit was described to me by Lieutenants FitzPatrick and Nangle, who, to their fury, were transferred from the 5th Bandera of the Foreign Legion to serve under O'Duffy, and by Lieutenant Lawler, who came out from Ireland with him. The men were crammed like cattle into the stinking holds of an ancient, unseaworthy ship, with bad and inadequate food and barely enough water to drink. Disembarking at a port in Galicia, they entrained for Cáceres, which was to be their depot. Their route ran through Salamanca, where they arrived at about ten in the morning, having had no breakfast; they were received on the station by a delegation of the Nationalist authorities, who gave them a *vin d'honneur*, attended by senior Army officers. Lawler said to me: 'I knew it was going to be sheer bloody murder with the boys drinking all that wine on empty stomachs. I tried to see if we couldn't get them some food, but it was no sue. Sure enough, when the time came to get back into the train the boys were so drunk it was all we could do to push them into it. And even that wasn't the end of our troubles! When we'd got them all in, and the train ready to start, the band struck up the Spanish National Anthem, and all the officers and generals came to attention and stood at the salute. And all the time the band was playing, there was one of our lads—drunk as a coot he was—leaning out of the carriage window being sick all the way down the neck of an old general. And the old boy—I was watching him—stood there like a rock at the salute through it all. But I could see he wasn't liking it.'

Misfortune followed them even to the front; their first casualties were at the hands of their allies. One of their companies, marching in column to take up positions on the Jarama, was fired on by a unit of Falange, who unaccountably mistook them for a unit of the International Brigade. The first shots did no harm, but the Company Commander, who had been chosen for his political loyalties rather than his military experience, allowed a minor battle to develop.

It was only fair to add that when the Irish eventually went into action, in the Valdemoro-Ciempozuelos sector, the Spaniards were filled with admiration for the bearing and courage of the troops. Indeed, the quality of the men was superb. They were truly inspired with the ideal of fighting for their faith. With good leadership they could have been the worthy successors of the famous Corps that fought for France in the 18th century:

> On the mountain and field from Berlin to Belgrade
> Lie the soldiers and chiefs of the Irish Brigade.

But they had no chance with the leadership O'Duffy gave them. Quarrels with the Spanish authorities became more frequent and more bitter. In the summer of 1937 the Irish Brigade went home.

*   *   *

Impatient at the delay over my posting, I obtained permission from General Monasterio to move to Vitoria. There I hoped to expedite matters, since it was the headquarters of Generals Mola and Solchaga. The former was in charge of all operations on the northern front, the latter commanded the *Brigadas de Navarra*, comprising the Requeté units on that front. Most of the foreign correspondents were concentrated in the town, including Harold Cardozo, who was sharing a flat with a Frenchman called Botteau, the correspondent of the Havas agency; these two asked me to stay with them while I was waiting. I did not see much of them during the daytime because they were usually at the front; the Nationalists had at last relaxed some of their restrictions on the movements of journalists, who were now able to make frequent visits to the front in the company of Captain Aguilera and his colleagues.

The Republicans were countering the Nationalist offensive against Bilbao with a propaganda offensive of their own; at this time it was concentrated on the famous Guernica incident. It was very cleverly handled, and a great deal of money was spent on it abroad—Botteau was told by his head office that the Republicans spent about six hundred thousand pounds in Paris on propaganda about Guernica alone. The story circulated—and widely believed—was that Guernica, an open town, was destroyed by incendiary bombs dropped by Nationalist aircraft; Cardozo was indignant at the success it was having in England. He was in Guernica immediately after its occupation by the Nationalists, and so was able to make a pretty thorough examination. It was clear to him, he said, that the Republicans themselves had set fire to the town before leaving, just as they had burnt Irun, Eibar, and Amorebieta in the course of their retreat through the Basque Provinces; he himself had witnessed the burning of Amorebieta. Certainly Guernica was bombed by the Nationalists, but it was not an open town at the time it was bombed; it was packed with Republican troops, and was, in fact, a Divisional Headquarters. After watching the burning of Amorebieta, he had entered into it the next day, and talked to some of the few inhabitants that were left. Before abandoning the town the *milicianos* had come to their houses and taken all their food and clothing, even what they were wearing, so that they were dressed in pieces of sacking; then they had set fire to the town. 'We know,' those poor people had told Cardozo, 'who burned Amorebieta. So we can guess who burned Guernica.'

It seems to me that nothing illustrates better the superiority of Republican propaganda over Nationalist than the Republican story about Guernica was given immediate and world-wide publicity, and is still generally believed; whereas the Nationalist case scarcely received a hearing.

About the middle of May I fell ill with an attack of jaundice, brought on by influenza, which left me very weak and depressed. I owe a great deal to Cardozo and Botteau for their kindness to me during the three weeks I was ill. I was fortunate in having friends in Vitoria who came to cheer me up; among them were the Duquesa de Lécera, whom I had met my first day in Spain, and an English girl, Gabrielle Herbert, who had been running her own hospital in the Huesca sector of the Aragón front; Huesca was invested on three sides by the enemy, and Miss Herbert's hospital was under direct fire from enemy artillery for several months.

I approached Captain Aguilera about my posting and, as usual, found him sympathetic and helpful. Through him I obtained entry to the headquarters of Generals Mola and Solchaga. Here I met with courtesy, compliments and promises—General Mola was particularly affable—but nothing materialized. I was beginning to despair of ever getting to the front, when I met an Englishman called Edward Earle; a leading Bilbao industrialist, he had financed a *tercio* of Requetés, named the *Tercio de Nuestra Señora de Begoña* after the Virgin who is the Protectress of Bilbao. He promised that I should be taken on its establishment; within a week he had arranged this personally with the commanding officer. Now all I needed was a *salvoconducto* from headquarters in Vitoria to allow me to join them at the front. On June 9th I applied for it, only to be told that I must first produce a certificate signed by Colonel Rada, my last commanding officer, granting me permission to serve on the Bilbao front. This, I felt, was something they might have told me three weeks earlier, when I first applied to them. However there was no help for it but to find Colonel Rada. Nobody seemed to know where he was, but I was advised to go to Salamanca and ask. After two days' inquiry in Salamanca I heard that he was in Ávila; there, to my surprise, I found him, and obtained my certificate without difficulty.

My two days in Salamanca are memorable for one incident: I was lunching at a restaurant with the charming name of 'The Friar's Widow', when a lanky lieutenant of the Foreign Legion came in and sat at my table:

'Excuse me,' he said, 'but you have been pointed out to me as the English Requeté. My name is Noel FitzPatrick and I am English, too—or rather, Irish,' he added hastily. It turned out that we had a number of friends in common in England. He was a most entertaining companion with a highly developed sense of the ridiculous, especially where it concerned himself; I was to see a great deal of him during the next few months and he became and has remained, one of my closest friends. Over lunch he told me something of his pat history, and a great deal about General O'Duffy and the Irish Brigade. He was now in his early thirties.

After leaving Sandhurst he had been posted to a famous line regiment, which he later left, he said, 'with the enthusiastic cooperation of my commanding officer'. He transferred to another regiment; but, deciding not to pursue a career in the regular Army, he was put on the Supplementary Reserve, attached to the Irish Guards. 'At the time the war broke out,' he told me, 'I had a motor business of my own in London. But then I discovered that my secretary, whom I rather fancied, was sleeping with my manager, and I reckoned they were both having a good laugh at me. So I packed it up and came out here. That was in August.' On arrival in Spain he was attached to Major Castejón of the 5th Bandera of the Legion, where he met an old friend and brother-officer, Bill Nangle. They were both mentioned in dispatches during the advance on Toledo, and were among the first dozen to enter the Alcázar when it was relieved. He remained with the 5th Bandera until November 1936, when he and Nangle were transferred to the Irish Brigade. Now he was in Salamanca, trying to arrange a posting back to the 5th Bandera, where Nangle had already preceded him.

*   *   *

On June 3rd, to the grievous loss of the Nationalist cause, General Mola was killed in an air crash. He was a man of great personal integrity and powerful influence, not only with the Requetés but throughout the country; had he survived it is possible that he would have been a check to the ascendancy of the Falange and to the growth of totalitarian rule.

On the 11th June, after an intense bombardment by artillery and aircraft, the Nationalists launched the last phase of their offensive. This was against the defences of the famous 'Iron Belt', the main line of fortifications defending Bilbao. The advanced positions were stormed on the first day, the main defences breached on the second. When I set out from Vitoria on June 19th it was clear that the fall of Bilbao was imminent. Nobody knew exactly where my new unit, which formed part of the Colonel Sánchez González's 5th Navarre Brigade, was operating. Earle thought they were in the region of Las Arenas, a seaside resort about eight miles from Bilbao on the right bank of the estuary of the Nervión. I found Las Arenas clear of the enemy, but there was no sign of my new *tercio*. It was a day of brilliant sunshine, hot inland but cool here with the sea breeze blowing. From up the river came the sound of battle as the *Brigadas de Navarra* stormed the last Republican defences on the heights overlooking Bilbao. The estuary was crowded with boats, from dinghies to small streamers, trying to make their way to safety; they had little chance, for they were within range of Nationalist artillery and machine-guns; most of them were forced to turn back. One steamer alone tried to struggle on. Through my glasses I saw spouts of water leaping up all around her as a Nationalist battery found the range: then one flash after another on board as the shells struck. Smoke and steam poured from her; she heeled over and sank in a vortex of foam.

It was early evening before I found the *Tercio de Nuestra Señora de Begoña*. They were resting in the woods on the heights of Archanda, which they had stormed that afternoon. This ridge was the last enemy line of defence, and now there was nothing between us and Bilbao, which lay beneath. With me, however, it was a matter of 'Go hang yourself, brave Crillon!' for they had fought a bloody battle all day, struggling up the almost vertical hillside through the trees under a murderous fire of mortars and machine-guns from the defences on the top—defences, moreover, manned by fanatical Asturian miners, who did not run away or surrender, but stayed and fought it out to the last man. This *tercio*, already well under strength, had started the assault with a hundred and seventy men; there were barely forty left when I joined them. Among the forty, however, I found my old friend, Father Vicente, from the *Tercio del Alcázar*, who had joined this unit at the beginning of the offensive. To-day he had led one wing of the assault, mounted on a white horse and still wearing his scarlet beret with the purple tassel—a perfect target. As so often happens with such people, he was only slightly wounded, in the hand, while the Requetés behind him fell like corn at harvest-time and his fine horse was killed under him. He was at the top of his form, full of sympathy with me having missed the battle. He took me to the Commanding Officer, Major Ricardo Uhagón. 'We shall march down to Bilbao at dawn to-morrow, so I suggest you find somewhere to sleep.' He told his batman to get me a blanket. When he brought it I walked up the hill, past a deserted pill-box, to a small meadow at the top, where some Requetés were standing, sitting, or lying around in the gathering dusk. They gave me a hunk of bread and some sardines from a tin. I was very thirsty; but so was everyone else, and there was no water, nor wine either. A grinning Requeté offered me a canteen full of brandy; like a fool I drank some and became much thirstier. When I handed it back he tilted it to his lips and appeared to swallow most of its contents in three or four gulps.

'Why do you drink it like that?' I asked him. 'It all goes down at once and you get no pleasure from it.'

'Of course I do,' he laughed, 'Now it's all inside me and the pleasure comes from there.' This was the way that nearly all Spanish soldiers used to deal with a bottle of brandy when they got hold of one.

I was terribly cold that night, even with the blanket; after months of sleeping in a bed, and after my illness, the hard ground pressed painfully against my hips and shoulders. I lay awake for hours, feeling ashamed of my softness and very lonely among these strangers.

It was still dark when we were roused and I stood up to stretch my cold and aching body. My Requeté friend gave me some more of his brandy, and this time I was really glad of it. By daybreak we were formed up on the road, awaiting the order to move. The sky was clear and the day promised to be hot.

At six o'clock we had the order to march and moved off in column down the almost vertical, winding road towards Bilbao. I was marching with Major Uhagón at the head. There was no sign of Father Vicente. Our *tercio* led the line of march and we thought we should be the first troops to enter the city; but half way down we heard that the enemy had evacuated it yesterday, and advanced elements of our forces, principally tanks, had entered the previous evening. On the way we passed groups of civilians, looking thin and strained, who watched us apathetically.

Lying in a deep valley, hemmed in by almost perpendicular heights, Bilbao on a fine day has a steamy, relaxing atmosphere. By the time we had reached the river, or *Ría* as the Nervión is locally called, I was already feeling tired. Here we turned left and marched into the Plaza de Arenal; this is a wide square with a small public garden beside it, on the bank of the *Ría*. The bridges had been blown, and sappers were working to construct pontoon causeways. Nearby, field kitchens were working, where we were given a mug of black coffee and a piece of bread. It was Sunday, the 20th of June. After breakfast we formed up in the Arenal for Mass. There must have been well over five thousand troops assembled in the square, facing the church at the eastern end; the *Tercio de Nuestra Señora de Begoña* was in front. The Mass was attended by senior officers of all three services, including the Generalissimo himself. Who should preach the sermon but Father Vicente, his bandaged hand in a sling, his enraptured, ascetic face raised to heaven, his loud, strident voice thrilling with emotion as he poured out his words of faith and triumph in stately measured periods, thundering the repeated refrain of his text:

Contra Dios no se puede luchar! [2]

* * *

Although it wore a sad, neglected appearance Bilbao seemed to have suffered remarkably little damage during the long siege. She is a town accustomed to sieges, having suffered many during the Carlist wars of the last century. The streets were full of broken glass and debris; some of the windows were smashed, others sandbagged and loop-holed for defence, but generally the houses and shops were intact; there seemed to have been remarkably little looting, at least during the evacuation, although there had been more during the early days of the war. Factories and industries were undamaged, though without power. Most serious was the shortage of drinking water, for the enemy had cut off the city's supply and it was a month before it could be restored. The condition of the civilian population was tragic. The first day we were constantly besieged by pathetic, emaciated figures—men and women of every age and class, with wasted flesh, sallow skins, and eyes bright with famine, begged piteously for a little bread. The Nationalists tackled the problem at once, rushing in supplies of meat, potatoes, rice and bread, and opening restaurants where any civilian could get a free meal. The city came back to life very quickly; by the middle of the week power and light were restored and trams were running; even the shops were open, although there was very little in them. There were a few cases of typhoid but no epidemic.

We stayed a fortnight in Bilbao, recruiting officers and men from sympathizers who had remained underground among the civilian population during the Republican régime; we had more applications than the shortage of equipment and instructors allowed us to enlist. I was given a platoon with, fortunately for me, two very efficient sergeants.

* * *

In England the summer of 1937 was one of the gayest pre-war years; to me in Spain it was a period of extreme frustration. Having worked so hard to get into a fighting unit on a fighting front, I had arrived too late for the battle. Now I was to spend my time in training and garrison duties on a front that had become stabilized. Moreover I began to receive letters from well-meaning friends and relations at home, urging me to 'think of my future'—in other words, come home and find myself some more permanent and lucrative employment than that provided by the war in Spain. Of course they were right. But having continued so long in the war I could not bring myself to leave it before the end; nor did the promise of financial security appeal to me.

Early in July we moved to Las Arenas, where we were headquartered in luxurious villas belonging to *émigré* Basque Nationalists. This was a relief from the heat, humidity and dirt of Bilbao. We were now about four hundred strong and all our working time was spent in training the recruits.

As an Englishman, my prestige in Las Arenas was very high. This was due to the selfless courage of an English governess, a Miss Boland, who had lost her life while trying to save her employer's family from execution during the Republican régime. They were Basques called Zuburría, who lived in Las Arenas. Miss Boland had been the children's governess and had remained with them after they were grown up. There were four sons, the youngest still a schoolboy, the eldest married just one year. The day before the Nationalists entered Las Arenas, *milicianos* came to arrest the four boys and the wife of the eldest. Knowing that they were going to be shot, Miss Boland went too; in her efforts to save them she was herself executed, the first of them all.

Our training completed, we left towards the end of July for a small village on the border of the provinces of Vizcaya and Santander, near the sea. The village, El Castaño (the Chestnut-tree), was in the mountains a few miles north of Valmaseda. The positions marking the front lay across the top of two peaks connected by a ridge, about half a mile above the hose where we had our Battalion Headquarters. Now we formed part of the 2nd Navarre Brigade under the command of Colonel Muñoz Grande, a magnificent soldier—and incidentally a man of great charm—who later became well-known as the General Officer Commanding the Spanish Blue Division operating against the Russians in 1942. Before leaving Las Arenas we received a large draft of officers who had just finished *cursillos* at infantry schools; this brought our officer strength above establishment. As fully trained officers, the newcomers were obviously entitled to commands in preference to volunteers like myself, and so I reverted to the status of supernumerary officer at Battalion Headquarters.

We stayed idle at El Castaño for nearly a month; we were in reserve, the positions above being held by an Army battalion. Although unsatisfactory to me, it was a pleasant enough existence; having few duties, I spent much of my time bathing in a small cove a mile or two away, or walking in the hills of that lovely country, in company with other officers of the *tercio*. Sometimes I went to Bilbao to have a talk and a drink with Tom Pears, the British Consul, and Charles Purgold, a British resident of San Sebastian, who had come to Bilbao to broadcast to England on the Nationalist radio. Our sector of the front was very quiet, interrupted only by occasional exchanges of artillery fire. Between ourselves and the sea were grouped the Italo-Spanish 'Mixed Brigades' of the *Flechas Negras* and *Felechas Azules*. There was no love lost between the Italians and us. The *'Vincitoria di Malága'* were very much above themselves; not that they had any reason to be, for they had suffered some sharp reverses, because of their own impetuous stupidity, during their advance along the coast during Bilbao. From these they had had to be rescued by neighbouring Spanish units. Spanish soldiers, though they fight stoutly under their own officers, are seldom amenable to foreign command.

During this month we were daily expecting to resume our advance, this time against Santander. The reason it was delayed until the middle of August was the Republican offensive against Brunete on the Madrid front. The Republicans knew that the Nationalists had concentrated a large part of their fighting strength on the campaign in the north; it was only to be expected that they would try to relieve the pressure there, and at the same time exploit the Nationalist weakness before Madrid, by taking the offensive themselves. They had a very able Chief of Staff in General Vincente Rojo, a Regular Army officer, who was the contemporary and—before the war—a friend of my former commanding officer, Major Alamán. He had been caught in Madrid with his family by the outbreak of the Civil War and, to save his family, consented to serve the Republic. This did not excuse him in the eyes of the Nationalists, who would have shot him if he had not escaped from Spain at the end of the war. He was responsible for the planning of the Brunete operations; they were well planned but not well carried out.

On July 6th the Republicans attacked with fifty thousand men in the region of Brunete, north-west of Madrid, and with a further twenty-five thousand in the sector of Villaverde, south-west of the capital. their objective was Navalcarnero, the main centre of communications for the whole Nationalist front. Had they succeeded they would have inflicted a major disaster on the Nationalists. The battle raged savagely in intense heat until July 26th, and resulted in the total rout and virtual destruction of the Republican forces; it has been estimated that their casualties were in the neighbourhood of thirty thousand. However, the offensive did oblige the Nationalists to withdraw large numbers of troops from the north, and so delayed their attack on Santander.

On August 14 the Santander offensive began; but from the south, and not, as we expected, from the east, where we were stationed. For the moment our orders were simply to stay where we were while the main attack, launched by three Spanish Navarre Brigades and two Italian regular divisions, broke through the enemy defences round the town of Reinosa. For the first two days the Republicans fought stubbornly in terrain particularly suitable for defence; but on the 16th the Navarrese took Reinosa, while the Italians, attacking boldly in the face of determined opposition, stormed the Escudo Pass. These two victories forced the gateway through the Cantabrian Cordillera, and the Nationalists continued their advance against rapidly disintegrating opposition.

On August 22nd the 6th Navarre Brigade on our left occupied the positions in front of them without firing a shot or finding an enemy. At 10.30 the next morning we received the order to advance. We climbed steeply for two and a quarter hours under the blazing sun; then started to advance along a spur leading towards the enemy trenches. We were at the tail of the column, but we should have been in no greater danger had we been at the head; the enemy had fled the night before and there was no sign of them. I noticed that their trenches were skilfully sited and deep. During the afternoon we continued our advance westward along the top of a ridge; on either side of us was a deep valley, with a corresponding ridge beyond it, along which I could see parallel columns of troops advancing. Progress was slow, and when we halted for the night we seemed to have covered only a few miles. Where we rested were some dug-outs, abandoned by the enemy, with dry straw inside. Thinking I should be warmer there, I very stupidly lay down to sleep in one of them; but I found sleep impossible, owing to the attentions of a million fleas.

The advance continued soon after dawn. Our *tercio* was detached to act as a flank guard to the column, which meant that we had to go down into the valley on our left and reconnoitre the villages there—picturesque little mountain hamlets with enchanting, evocative names, like *Nuestra Señora de las Nieves* (Our Lady of the Sorrows). There were no traces of the enemy, but we had plenty of hard work climbing in and out of the ravines that intersected the valley. In the early evening we arrived at a cluster of white, red-roofed houses, surrounded by cornfields and orchards, called The Bridge of Guriezo; here was a crossroads and a bridge over the River Aguera that had not been destroyed. We had orders to halt for the night. Major Uhagón detailed one company for outpost duties; another was sent to patrol the village, on the look-out for enemy stragglers who might be in hiding, and for booby-traps. A series of small explosions soon showed that this last precaution was fully justified; the enemy had laid a few traps in the form of hand-grenades, which were easily discovered and caused no casualties. We need not have worried about enemy stragglers, for the villagers were heartily sick of the Republicans and themselves handed over two *milicianos* who were in hiding. When Uhagón, by nature a kind and gentle person, heard what these men had done in the village, he had them shot out of hand.

The following morning the remainder of the 2nd Navarre Brigade arrived and halted around the village. Nobody seemed to know what the next move would be; but just after lunch news arrived that Santander was on the point of surrender, and our troops were to enter the city the following morning. The previous day the 1st Navarre Brigade had captured the town of Torrelavega, west of Santander, cutting the only escape route to Asturias; a large part of the Republican Army was trapped. Uhagón sent for me and suggested that I should take a fortnite's leave: 'We shall have nothing to do for a while,' he said, 'and so I am sending off any officers I can spare. Start as soon as you like.'

It turned out that the news of the surrender of Santander was a little premature; I have already told how Rupert Bellville and Ricardo González discovered this to their cost.

When we reached Bilbao that evening I found an American friend, Reynolds Packard, the United Press correspondent, and Dick Sheepshanks of Reuters. They were about to leave by car for Santander, which they hoped to enter with the first of our troops; they suggested I should come with them. We started just before one and drove all night, having to make a long detour to the south. About 6 a.m. we were held up for two hours by an Italian picket, but by nine o'clock we had reached a hill looking across the marshes to Santander. A column of Italians was formed up on the road, headed by a squadron of their miniature two-man tanks.

After half-an-hour's wait we saw two men approaching wearily along the road from the city; they turned out to be the Garrison Commander and the Chief of Police of Santander, coming to parley with the Nationalist commanders, General Dávila and General Bergonzoli, who stood apart in a field beside the road. Both delegates looked very white, but whereas the policeman remained quite steady and dignified throughout the brief discussion, the soldier seemed on the point of collapse. The interview was brought to a close when one of them expressed the hope that the Nationalists would spare the women and children; at which gratuitous insult General Dávila ordered them to withdraw.

Squadrons of Nationalist aircraft flew low over the city in close formation, while a mountain battery was assembled and trained on the town in case of resistance. Nothing happened for another hour; then the column beside us formed up to begin their march. The tanks went first, clattering down the steep hill in single file at a dangerous speed, followed by a column of motorcyclists, each carrying a light machine-gun mounted on the handle-bars. Then came the two Italian Divisions, *Littorio* and *XXIII de Marzo*, followed by a nondescript and scruffy Italian militia unit, the *Fiamme Nere*. Spanish troops were entering the town by another route.

We left our car to walk with the leading Italian infantry. It was a hot, glaring day and we were choked by the dust thrown up by the tanks and motor-cyclists. Parties of *Guardia Civil* accompanied our column, some on foot, others on motor-cycles. On our way we met groups of men hurrying away from the town; most of them were wearing blue overalls, clearly militiamen making a last pathetic attempt to escape. They were rounded up by the *Guardia Civil* and made to fall in at the rear of the column under escort; later they were all herded into the bullring to be screened. I was walking with a Spanish friend, a Requeté temporarily attached to the Press Office; we had out-distanced the infantry and were some way ahead of the column when we saw a camouflaged car coming towards us from the town with four militiamen inside. We held it up with our pistols and ordered the occupants to produce their papers; when they failed to do so, we made them get out, disarmed them and handed them over to some police who appeared at that moment. They were too demoralized to resist. My friend, who had his own car, suggested that I should take possession of this one, a fine new Citroën coupé. Thinking it would be useful to my *tercio*, which was very short of cars, I drove it a little way off the road, locked it and rejoined the column. As we neared the centre of the town we found the road lined deep with civilians, who waved to us, pelted us with flowers and cheered as though they had gone mad. I noticed women and girls wearing their best clothes, pathetically shoddy though they were, their faces transported with joy, yet showing the signs of months of fear and famine that no make-up could conceal. Republican rule in Santander had been particularly savage; hundreds of Nationalist supporters were thrown to their death from the top of the cliffs near the lighthouse on Cabo Mayor.

I left the triumphal procession to wander through the town on my own. Almost the first thing that struck me was that the side streets were crowded with dejected militiamen, some of them still carrying arms, but all paralyzed by the suddenness and extent of their disaster. They ignored me, showing neither hatred nor fear at the sight of my uniform. The civilians, on the other hand, were far from indifferent when they saw my red beret; men would come up to me and shake me by the hand, women would embrace me, kissing me on both cheeks—much more often old women than young, I reflected wistfully. Noticing my height and fair colouring they would ask me if I were German. When I replied that I was English their enthusiasm was overwhelming. Some of the Nationalist soldiers were natives of Santander; there were moving scenes as they found members of their families, or anxiously questioned friends for news of them. I saw no signs of damage in the town, in contrast to the broken glass and debris that had littered the streets of Bilbao.

By half past three I had seen enough, and so decided to return to Bilbao. My new Citroën was full of oil and petrol, obviously in preparation for a long journey. On the outskirts of town I stopped to ask an Italian sentry if he knew whether the coast road was clear of the enemy, of whom a large number must have been trapped between Santander and our troops advancing from the east. He assured me it was clear. For the first twenty-five miles the road was deserted; I saw neither human beings nor animals. The car went beautifully. Leaving the promontory with Santoña and its lighthouses on my left, I drove on without incident until I approached the little fishing port of Laredo. The outskirts and the narrow streets of the town were thronged with men in blue overalls and black berets, carrying rifles slung from their shoulders, pistols and grenades at their belts. It was only when the press in the street forced me to slow down to a walking pace that I realized who these were; I had driven right into the middle of the Republican Army, or a portion of it which had been cut off by our rapid advance to Santander. It was impossible to turn the car; my only hope was to drive on as unconcernedly as I could and hope that I would be taken for the advanced guard of the victorious Nationalists, come to accept their surrender. Of course it would be too bad for me if they had no mind to surrender; wearing my scarlet beret with the silver *fleur-de-lis* and carrying a large 9 millimetre automatic, I was only too obviously an enemy.

Ironically I was reminded of the words of a charming little song from this town, which our Requetés used to sing:

Yo no te quiero, chica
Yo no te quiero, no!
Porque los mis amores
Son de Laredo, son!

Now I knew something of what the former occupants of my Citroën must have felt when we stopped them outside Santander. However, I forced my feature into what I hoped would seem a confident grin and drove on, sounding my horn to clear the way. The *milicianos* stared at me curiously but no one tried to stop me until I was beginning to get clear of the town. Then a couple of men with white arm-bands signaled to me to stop, though without pointing their rifles at me; as I passed them I called out, in what I trusted was an authoritative voice, '*Tercio de Nuestra Señora de Begoña!*' and drove on. In the driving mirror I saw their faces gaping in blank astonishment. I tried this formula on two subsequent occasions with the same success; but I confess I felt relieved when at last I met the advanced units of our 'Mixed Brigades' near Castro Urdiales. It was with some astonishment that I heard the B.B.C. News announce the following day that ten thousand Basque Republican troops had taken up defensive positions on the road between Santander and Castro Urdiales.

I decided to spend my leave in San Sebastian, where I was certain of finding friends at this time of year; but I would go first to Vitoria to collect my mail from England and some pieces of luggage I had left there. Next morning I set out proudly in my new car and reached Vitoria without incident. there disaster overtook me, through my own inexperience and stupidity. I was foolish enough to think that I could get oil and petrol from the Army Service Corps with the excuse that the car was to be used by my tercio. As I had no papers to support my statement, and as the car had a Santander number-plate, it was promptly impounded; moreover I had no identity card, and in the heat of Vitoria and my chagrin at losing my new car I flew into a rage, was very rude to the officer at the depot and was lucky to escape arrest.

I was not disappointed in my expectation of finding friends in San Sebastian. Arriving at the Hotel Continental, I was welcomed almost as a son by the manageress, a generous-hearted French-woman who, at the risk of her own life, had protected many Nationalist sympathizers during the period of Republican rule in San Sebastian. Next, walking into Chicote's Bar for an early drink to help me forget the loss of my car, I found Noel FitzPatrick with another friend of mine, Michael Larrinaga, the son of a well-known Liverpool shipowner; having retained his Spanish nationality, Larrinaga had come to Spain early in the war to enlist in the Artillery. They were sipping two of Perico Chicote's Specials with the air of rapt concentration which is due any masterpiece. Before the Civil War Chicote's in Madrid was already famous; now he had opened in San Sebastian. If there is a world hierarchy of barmen—and I suggest hierarchy as the most suitable word—Perico Chicote must be one of its principal Cardinals; famous in two continents, as much for the warmth of his heart as for the skill of his hand, he radiated through his bar in San Sebastian an atmosphere of *simpatía*, in which past troubles and dangers, future worries and fears alike were forgotten.

In Chicote's the men liked to let their hair down and relax; sweethearts and wives, therefore, though not forbidden, were discouraged. They went to the Bar Basque, where the men usually joined them after their drinks at Chicote's.

I had learnt one thing about the Requetés; for all their courage and endurance, their patriotism and self-sacrificing idealism, they lacked the strict discipline and technical training that are so necessary in modern warfare. This war had altered radically since the early days, and the old qualities of willingness and valour were no longer enough. Only in the Foreign Legion, I was convinced, could I hope to learn first-class soldiering. They were the troops on whom General Franco depended for the most difficult operations. Somehow, I decided, I must join the Foreign Legion; but having worked my way from the ranks to be an officer in the Requetés, I was reluctant to enlist as a private in the Legion and start again. After a great deal of thought I decided to go to Salamanca and see if I could get a posting to the Legion in my present rank.

On my way I stayed a night in Burgos, where I ran into Pablo Merry del Val; with him was Sir Arnold Wilson, Member of Parliament for Hitchin, whom I had met when I was the Secretary of the Conservative Association at Cambridge. One of the most controversial figures of his time, Sir Arnold Wilson had a distinguished and sensational career, mostly in the Middle East; he was an outstanding authority on Persia and Iraq. A man of abnormally forceful personality, absolute integrity and decided political views, he could tolerate no opposition, however sincere; he therefore made numerous and powerful enemies. He was gifted with truly phenomenal mental and physical powers: for instance, he could memorize a book after reading through it once, and his idea of a pleasant summer holiday was to sign on for three months as a stoker in a cargo boat in the Persian Gulf. When the war broke out with Germany he became, at the age of fifty-five, a Pilot Officer and rear gunner in the R.A.F., having passed every physical test that could be devised to stop him. 'I will not,' he said, 'shelter behind a rampart of young bodies.' He was killed the same year, when his aircraft was shot down in flames over Holland. His character was a remarkable mixture of ruthlessness and kindness; personally I experienced the greatest kindness from him, and will always value the memory of his friendship.

Over dinner I told them of my wish to join the Foreign Legion. 'You're in luck,' said Merry del Val. 'General Millán Astray is here in the hotel. I'll have a word with him afterwards and see what can be done.' General Millán Astray, the famous 'Father of the Legion' and its co-founder with Franco, was the most famous, even fabulous, figure in Nationalist Spain, because of his legendary courage and the number of times he had been seriously wounded. A flamboyant personality, with one arm and one eye and a severe limp, he attracted immediate attention in any gathering. In matters concerning the Legion his power was absolute.

Merry del Val spoke to him for a few minutes, then called me over. The General shot questions at me like a machine-gun, concentrating his one eye upon me in a fierce unblinking glare. Apparently my answers satisfied him, for he concluded by saying, 'I will speak personally to the Generalissimo and recommend that you be admitted to the Legion as Alférez. Go to your *tercio* of Requetés and get your discharge. Then wait in Salamanca for your orders from the Legion. Good luck to you!'

---

[1] Lojendio, *Operaciones Militares de la Guerra de España*. (Montaner y Simón, Barcelona 1940), pages 265 and 266.

[2] Against God no man can fight.

CHAPTER SIX

I found Major Uhagón and his *tercio* at Riaño, north-east of León and just south of the famous Picos de Europa, on the borders of Asturias. The war in the north was virtually over and Uhagón thought it unlikely that they would see any action before it finished. I was tempted to linger longer with the Requetés in the delightful village beside a swift and swirling trout stream, where the yellowing birches under the clear September sky made a warm contrast against the grey and sombre grandeur of the eight thousand foot peaks which towered above the valley. But my orders from Millán Astray were to go as soon as possible to Salamanca; and so I said an affectionate farewell to Uhagón and my other friends.

There was a cosmopolitan atmosphere in Salamanca. The long centre table in the Gran Hotel dining-room was reserved for the German military observers, most of them senior officers; a general presided. They were an earnest party, who seemed to take little pleasure in their food or drink, and who kept very much to themselves. At a smaller table nearby sat the newspaper correspondents, among them Randolph Churchill, Pembroke Stevens, Reynolds Packard and his wife and Philby of *The Times*; Churchill's clear, vigorous voice could be heard deploring with well-turned phrase and varied vocabulary the inefficiency of the service, the quality of the food and, above all, the proximity of the Germans, at whom he would direct venomous glances throughout the meal. 'Surely,' he exclaimed loudly, 'there must be one Jew in Germany with enough guts to shoot that bastard Hitler!'

O'Duffy's brigade had gone home; but a few stragglers remained, including my friend, Peter Lawler, a hard-bitten little Irish-Australian who had served with the A.I.F. in the First World War. During the troubles in Ireland he had been an intimate and trusted lieutenant of Michael Collins; in his own part of the country he was still known as 'The Commandant'. At this time he was waiting in Salamanca to collect six months of back pay due to him from the Spaniards, who were responsible for paying the Irish Brigade. When he received it, a month or so later, he returned to Ireland, very bitter against O'Duffy.

Standing one day in the hall of the hotel I was accosted by a Falstaffian figure with a high, bald forehead and a small blonde moustache, who introduced himself in a direct, almost abrupt manner as Archie Lyall, an author and free-lance journalist. He had just come from Santander, where he had been reporting the trials of war criminals by the Nationalists. As a qualified barrister he considered that they had been very fairly conducted and that the sentences on those found guilty had been just. Previously, he had written a multi-lingual vocabulary entitled *Lyall's 25 Languages of Europe*, some travel books on the Balkans, Portuguese West Africa, and Soviet Russia, and a gay little satire, which I had read called, *It Isn't Done: Or the Future of Tabu Among the British Islanders*.[1] He had also founded and administered a donkey hospital in Fez, supported by contributions from rich and charitable old ladies in the United States of America. When I met him he was about thirty-five years of age. An entry under his name in *Who's Who* described his hobbies as 'Reading, travelling and collecting matchbox labels.'

I found him an ideal companion during this time of waiting; for not only was he a witty conversationalist, but he had a remarkable faculty for nosing out the best places in town for food, drink and entertainment; the second of these was important because bars were supposed to close at midnight, after which the only place where we could get a drink was in the *Barrio Chino*, or brothel quarter. Here Lyall found a night club where we could drink and listen to the *guitarrista* and a singer, who gave a brilliant and moving interpretation of García Lorca's lament for Sánchez Mejías.

Sometimes Lawler would come with us; but such occasions had explosive possibilities because of Lyall's tendency to tease Lawler and the latter's quick temper. When Lawler would start to inveigh against O'Duffy and the ruin he had brought so fine a fighting force, Lyall would interrupt with some such observation as: 'But surely you can't expect the Irish to be any use in Spain? There aren't any hedges here for them to shoot behind.' As half an Irishman myself, I would repudiate the slander, but Lawler would storm out, shouting: 'Ye great buckin' whore!'

About this time Pablo Merry del Val suggested that I should accompany him and Sir Arnold Wilson on a quick tour of Castille and the Basque Provinces. My orders to join the Legion might not arrive for another month, but Merry del Val arranged that I should be notified immediately if they came while we were away. With us came Wing-Commander Archie James, Conservative Member for Wellingborough, who was in Salamanca for a brief visit. Sir Arnold Wilson was collecting material for an article he was writing for *The XIXth Century and After*, of which he was then a director.

Arriving in Toledo we went to examine the ruins of the Alcázar. We were looking across the Tagus beyond the Alcántara bridge when a battery of field guns opened fire behind us; we heard the shells bursting across the river. Soon afterwards there came the sound of intense machine-gun fire. 'This takes me back,' said James. We later heard that a *bandera* of the Legion, supported by two *tabores* of Moors, had attacked and cleared the enemy out of the positions from which they had been able to shell and snipe at Toledo. Although I did not know it at the time, the bandera was the 14th, which I was to join.

The same evening I was sitting in a café opposite the Alcázar, waiting for the others, when a large party of officers of the Legion came in; by their yellow flashes I knew they were from the 5th Bandera, in which Bill Nangle was serving. FitzPatrick had told me to make myself known; I was anxious to meet Nangle and so I approached the party and asked for him. When he came in a few minutes later, he joined me at my table.

I had heard a great deal about him and his strange career from FitzPatrick. After leaving Sandhurst he joined the Indian Army; but although he was an efficient soldier he found the life monotonous; moreover he was unable to show a proper respect for senior officers. At the end of his tour of duty in command of Fort Alexandra in tribal territory on the Frontier, which is alleged to be the highest fort in the world, he was required to write a report for the Staff at Simla. This he did, couched in the correct official phraseology, but spoiled the effect by adding as a postscript the irrelevant question: 'How much string does it take to go round St. Paul's?' By the time it reached the Staff, Nangle had gone to England on six months' leave. He had sent in his papers but, without waiting for them to be accepted, enlisted in the French Foreign Legion. He was enjoying his new life when the Prince of Wales, with whom his family had some influence, intervened with the French authorities; to his disgust Nangle found himself discharged. Now he had been just over a year in the 4th Bandera, where I discovered from his brother-officers, he was greatly respected and liked. He suffered from recurrent attacks of *cafard,* which had first come upon him during his service in the Sahara and which made him an awkward, sometimes dangerous companion. Family reasons obliged him to return to England in December of 1937, so that it was nearly six years before I saw him again.

When we had completed our tour of the north I returned to Salamanca. On the 26th October I received orders posting me to the First Tercio of the Legion, with the rank of alferez.[2] I was to sign on and draw my uniform at Talavera, then report to the headquarters of General Yagüe, General Commanding the Legion, at Illescas, on the road between Toledo and Madrid.

* * *

Harold Cardozo once told me that there were two ways of breaking into

London journalism: the first, and hard, way was to serve an apprenticeship on the staff of a provincial newspaper; the second was to solicit influence. The trouble about the latter was that the editor and staff were inclined to look on you as a badly house-trained puppy; you were an object of resentment and any mess around the office was automatically attributed to you.

The same was true, though I did not then appreciate it, of the Spanish Foreign Legion. This was the *corps d' élite* of the Spanish Army; during the war it attracted the most efficient officers of the Regular Army and the most adventurous of the reservists and volunteers. Selection was strictly by merit. Apart from one or two, who had risen from the ranks, non-Spanish officers serving with banderas were virtually unknown. FitzPatrick and Nangle were two exceptions; now I was a third. Naïve as I was, my reception came as a surprise; rather than gratitude for having come so far from home to fight in their cause I encountered at first only distrust and resentment from my fellow-officers; I was made to feel a gate-crasher. It was two months before they accepted me as one of themselves.

At the depot in Talavera I found a sour-faced captain, who made me sign a document committing me for the duration of the war, and issued me my uniform. Very proud of myself in my new green forage-cap with its red-and-gold tassel, I reported to Major Merino, General Yagüe's adjutant, at Illescas. Merino, a broad-shouldered man with a domed forehead, a sympathetic manner, and a quiet, commanding personality, told me that I had been posted to the 14th Bandera, which was now at Getafe. I arrived there on the night of October 31st, very tired after two days of travelling and virtually no sleep. The Bandera was quartered in the infantry barracks. I reported to the commanding officer, Major Alfonso de Mora Requejo, whom I found on the point of going to bed; he told me to report again at nine o'clock the following morning. I found a billet at a private house in the town. After impressing on my landlady that I must be called not later than eight next morning, I went straight to bed.

I awoke to find an agitated legionary standing over me. '*Mi Alférez*,' he began, 'the *Comandante* sends me to ask why you have not reported at nine o'clock as he told you. He requests that you come at once.' I looked at my watch; to my horror I found it was half past nine. Angrily I asked my landlady why she had not called me.

'Oh well,' she said serenely, 'we knew you were tired, and you were sleeping so soundly that we didn't like to wake you.'

'This is a fine start,' I thought as I threw on my clothes and followed the legionary out of the house.

Major de Mora, now in his early thirties, was a small, lightly-built man with finely chiseled features, a strong jaw, prominent nose and clear grey eyes, above which dark, curly hair receded from a high forehead. A lieutenant in the 4th Bandera when the war started, he had won the Medalla Militar—a rare distinction for a junior officer—at the storming of Badajoz in August 1936. His company led the assault on Puerta de la Trinidad—a gateway to the same walls that had caused Wellington's troops such terrible casualties—in the face of an intense concentration of rifle and machine-gun fire; of the whole company one officer and fifteen men remained to enter the city. Standing on the ramparts and waving the Nationalist flag to encourage his men, Mora was struck by a bullet that exploded the magazine of the pistol he carried on his hip. Two years later he was being treated daily by the Medical Officer for the still open wound; yet I, who saw him almost every day, knew nothing of his disability until told of it by another officer at the end of the war. A strict disciplinarian despite his quiet manner, he was a superb commander and a brilliant tactician. In battle, even when things looked blackest, I never saw him ruffled nor lose for one moment control of the situation; his mere presence in action filled us with confidence. At this interview, however, I felt no confidence at all. Dismissing contemptuously my apologies and excuses Mora gazed at me coldly.

'We require discipline in this unit,' he observed. 'I have assigned you to the 56th Company, which is the machine-gun company. Do you know anything about machine-guns?'

'No sir, but I can learn.'

'You'd better. Report now to Captain Almajach.' He ordered a legionary to conduct me to my new Company Commander.

Captain Gutiérrez Almajach was one of the best company commanders in the Legion. Of medium height and well-built, he wore a perpetual half-smile on his thin lips, which gave a first impression of humour, even of joviality; but his eyes behind the thick glasses were hard, and the half-smile more often than not turned into a sneer. Infinitely painstaking, ruthlessly efficient, undismayed in danger, he was at the same time the most bloody-minded man I have ever known. The legionaries feared him for his cruelty but respected him for his competence and courage. He chased me rigorously and unremittingly, as a result of which I learned much more than I would have done from some milder commander.

By the look he gave me when I reported to him I thought that he was going to summon the sanitary squad; then he asked my nationality, and I was certain of it:

'I shit on Englishmen,' he said simply.

The 14th Bandera was a newly-formed unit, composed partly of veterans from older banderas, partly of officers and other ranks fresh to the Legion. The four company commanders were all veterans. The leading company, the 53rd (in the Legion the companies are numbered consecutively throughout the Corps), was commanded by Captain Eduardo Cancela, a slender, handsome gallego with a rich, rakish laugh, a warm heart and a gay and gallant manner, which he fully maintained in battle; he it was who told me of Von Gaza's death near La Marañosa. He was the one officer who from the first accepted me as a friend and comrade. I shall have more to say of him later. The 53rd was the happiest company in the Bandera, nor was it by any means the least efficient.

A small dark officer, Captain Rodríguez, commanded the 54th Company. He had a likeable, ugly face and a pleasant, quiet personality. For some reason I never saw much of him or his company.

The 55th Company, when I arrived, was under the command of Captain José Luengo, a strange, erratic creature with sandy hair and pale blue eyes who always gave me the impression of being detached from his surroundings. He was an officer of many years' seniority in the Legion; but his career in Morocco and Spain had been punctuated by a series of distressing incidents, which eventually convinced his superiors that he would never be amenable to discipline. His eccentricities were a byword in the Corps; among them I remember the story of an occasion during manœuvres in Morocco when his commanding general, having expected to find him at the head of his platoon, and having commented unfavorably on his absence without leave, saw him the next day fighting a bull in the Ring at Málaga. Fearless in battle, he was unfortunately too much inclined to bring the atmosphere of the battlefield into the bar; after a few drinks in a café he would draw his pistol and, slowly and with great dignity, shoot out the lights one by one. He was universally loved in the Bandera, and even Mora had a soft spot for him; but eventually he went too far and was dismissed from the Service by a court-martial.

These three were rifle companies; the machine-gun company, as I have already said, was commanded by Captain Almajach. The officers of each rifle company had their own separate mess; those of the machine-gun company messed with Bandera Headquarters, that is to say with the *Comandante*, the Chaplain and the two Medical Officers. When I joined there was no Second-in-Command and no Adjutant.

The Chaplain, whose name I never knew because he was always addressed as *Páter*, was a Regular Army padre. He was a podgy, serious-minded man in his late thirties. A very devout, conscientious and kind-hearted person, he had to endure a good deal of teasing on account of his home town, Cuenca, which is a regular butt for Spanish comedians, in much the same way as Wigan used to be on the English music-hall. His chief and almost only relaxation was *julepe*, a card game at which most of the officers in the Bandera used to gamble— sometimes for much too high stakes; I was warned against learning this game by the amount of quarrels and bad blood that I saw it engender. Although he deplored my religion—he shook his head, deeply shocked, when I told him that clergymen of the Church of England were allowed to marry—he was unfailingly courteous to me, showing me many small kindnesses and always taking my side in arguments with other officers over Britain and the policy of the British government. He was greatly relieved when I assured him that I was not a Freemason; he had been convinced that all Protestants were Masons—a belief shared by most of the other officers. It was a waste of time trying to explain to Spaniards that English Freemasonry was a different thing from the Continental variety, which they abhorred because of its connection with the Popular Front governments in France and Spain. My friend FitzPatrick told me that what eventually finished his career in the Legion was his admission, in the course of an argument, that he was a Mason.

The senior of the two medical officers, Lieutenant Larrea, was also of the Regular Army and very like many of his opposite numbers in the R.A.M.C. A big man with a loud voice and bluff, hearty manner, he irritated me at first by his frequent attacks on England and the English, a country and people of which he knew nothing, and by his use of me as a target for his witty sallies or outbursts of bad temper. Later, when I found my way around, he became a good friend; indeed, it was impossible to dislike him, for he was fundamentally a conscientious and good-hearted man. When he was not baiting me he was baiting the Padre, his chief weapon being a flow of language that would have horrified many people not in Holy Orders. He was, I thought, unduly severe on the troops. On one occasion he shocked me by sending a man to the Punishment Squad for a fortnight because he asked to be sent to hospital for gonorrhea: 'Damned scrimshanker!' he exclaimed. 'Whoever heard of sending a man to hospital for a dose of clap?' His assistant, Alférez Ruíz, was a friendly little officer with a small moustache. He was cheerful, hard-working and very much liked.

The senior of my two fellow-officers in the machine-gun company was Lieutenant Noriega, a small, wiry, grey-haired man of many years' service, who had risen from the ranks. In general, legionaries do not like their ranker officers, but Noriega was an exception, for he treated them with a perfect blend of severity and kindness; they knew that he would never call upon them to do anything that he was not able and willing to do himself. Quick to discern and despise inefficiency or cowardice, they found neither in Noriega. He had a taciturn manner, a dry sense of humour and a remarkable knowledge of the world. Before joining the Legion he had been a seaman and had served aboard Pierrepoint Morgan's yacht. Subsequently, he had smuggled arms to one or other of the belligerents in the Gran Chaco war—I think to the Paraguayans.

Another officer, Alférez Colomer, a Catalan from Gerona, was about the same age as myself. He was a noisy, rancorous little man, for ever bickering with his brother-officers and bullying his men. He had been badly wounded in an earlier battle, which had perhaps affected his temper; but he always seemed to me to have a chip on his shoulder. His contentious nature was, literally, the death of him: one day, after I had left the Bandera, he became very drunk after a battle, and challenged another officer to a stupid competition to see which of them could pick up more of the unexploded hand-grenades lying in front of their trenches. Colomer picked up one too many; it blew his head off.

Among the Regular Officers in the Bandera were several who had been cadets at the Military Academy at Zaragoza when Franco was Commandant. Respected as an efficient soldier, he was equally feared as a martinet; many were the traps he laid for the unwary or undisciplined cadet. For instance, when he noticed one of them approaching down the street he would sometimes turn to look in shop window, apparently absorbed by what he saw; if the cadet was foolish enough to pass him without saluting, thinking himself unobserved, he would not have gone many paces before he would hear that dreaded, soft, high voice calling him back; betrayed by his reflection in the plate-glass window, he might be on the mat next morning.

He was just as severe on matters not strictly military but reflecting indirectly on the health and efficiency of the cadet. A model of rectitude in his own private life, he was also well aware of the temptations to which young men so easily succumb in a city. He therefore made it an order that every cadet, when walking out in the evening, must carry in his pocket at least one contraceptive. He would frequently stop cadets in the street and demand that they show him this armour; heavy was the penalty for him that failed to produce it.

As in all the banderas, with the exception of the extra one—the Jeanne d'Arc, composed entirely of French volunteers—the men in the 14th were ninety per cent Spaniards. The remainder were mostly Portuguese—good soldiers, although even the Spaniards found it hard to understand their speech. There were a few Germans—poor soldiers and despised by the rest—a White Russian and a

Turk. The Turk was even harder to understand than the Portuguese, but as he hardly ever spoke it did not matter. I soon found that my command of Spanish was not nearly so good as I had thought, nor as good as it needed to be, especially when it came to the flow of abuse which a legionary expected as the proper accompaniment to any order given him. I had to put this right when I found that, without it, my orders simply were not obeyed.

The legionaries, like their officers, were all volunteers. Some were attracted by the prospects of adventure and danger which this *fuerza de choque*[3] provided, others by the better pay and food, others by the *esprit de corps* and the extra latitude allowed to legionaries when off duty; the majority were impelled to join by a combination of them all. A few had signed on for five years, others for three, but most of them for the duration of the war.

Pay for officers and other ranks alike was about double that of the Regular Army; food was incomparably better. The usual midday and evening meals consisted of soup, followed by fish or *pasta,* a main dish of meat, and pudding or cheese, with wine and coffee; moreover the food was extremely well cooked. At the depots of Ceuta and Melilla it was served to the men on china plates by waiters in white coats. The officers had the same rations as the men, supplemented by a few luxuries bought out of their pay.

Spanish troops, when well led and properly disciplined, show superb qualities of courage and endurance. It was the pride of the Legion that it developed those qualities to their full. From the moment he joined it was impressed on the recruit that he belonged to a corps apart—the finest fighting force, he was taught to believe, in the world; it was up to him to prove himself worthy of the privilege. Battle was the purpose of his life; death in action was his greatest honour; cowardice the ultimate disgrace. The motto of the Legion was '*Viva la muerte!*' It is easy for more phlegmatic nations to deride this 'cult of death'; but it is essentially in keeping with the Spanish character, and it produced the best soldiers of the Civil War—men virtually impervious to cold and hunger, danger and fatigue. As an Englishman I can only say that the thrill of serving with and commanding such troops was one of the greatest experiences of my life.

The turn-out and bearing of the legionary, whether with his bandera or on leave, was expected to be, and was, far superior to that of other units. The greatest freedom was allowed to him when off duty; he was taught to take pride in his individuality; his full official designation was '*Caballero Legionario*'— Gentleman Legionary. In contrast, discipline on duty and the field was extremely strict, even savage by English standards. Orders were executed at the double and usually reinforced by threats or imprecations; the slightest hesitation, laxity or inefficiency was punished on the spot by a series of blows across the face and shoulders from the *fusta*—a pliant switch made from a bull's pizzle, which was carried by all officers and sergeants. More serious or persistent defaulters were sent to the *Pelotón de Castigo*, or Punishment Squad, where they toiled at the most exhausting tasks from before dawn until well after dark under the command of a corporal, usually chosen for his ferocity; in this mobile glasshouse food was meagre, beatings frequent and severe. A dirty rifle was enough to earn a man a month in the *Pelotón*. Insubordination, whether or not in the face of the enemy, was punishable by death on the spot.

Men trained under such discipline were apt to emerge with blunted sensibility, a callous indifference to suffering, whether in themselves or in others, and an unfeeling disregard for the horrible and squalid aspects of war. One of my machine-gun sergeants told me with great satisfaction how his comrades had contrived to spend a comfortable night in the open in pouring rain after an attack in the Casa de Campo: the ground, he explained, was waterlogged but fortunately (sic) it was littered with corpses; these they collected, arranged them in rows, and laid down on them, covering themselves with their greatcoats. FitzPatrick, after the capture of Talavera by the 5th Bandera, found a legionary hammering at the face of a dead militiaman with the butt of his rifle; when FitzPatrick pointed out that the man was dead, the legionary answered serenely, 'I know sir, but look! He has some fine gold teeth.'

*   *   *

The 14th Bandera had been 'bloodied' in action about a fort-night before I joined, in the operation which Archie James and I witnessed from the Alcázar at Toledo. It had come out of the battle well and with improved morale. Now everyone was certain that we would soon be thrown into some great offensive that would see the end of the war.

I had four machine-guns in my platoon, divided into two sections, each under a sergeant. The guns were Maxims, manufactured—and used—during the First World War; they had recently been taken from the Republicans. They were unsatisfactory factory weapons, already worn-out with service and very liable to go out of action through breakage of the firing-pin. There were twelve machine-guns in the Company, and two 81 mm. mortars.

The Bandera remained in Getafe for a week after I joined. My time was spent in routine training, getting to know my men, and learning about the guns under the instruction of one or other of my sergeants. I could have wished that I had been sent to a rifle company, for I knew nothing of the tactical employment of machine-guns, and nothing of their mechanism. Almajach, who would tolerate no inefficiency in his Company, drove me relentlessly with abuse and exhortation to abandon my slovenly Requeté ideals of soldiering and to perfect my fluency in Spanish.

I was *Oficial de Guardia* (Orderly Officer) one night and *Oficial de Vigilancia* another; the latter was a duty only performed when the Bandera was in reserve or resting. The *Vigilancia* was a squad of legionaries with a sergeant and a subaltern, whose duty it was to patrol the streets, to see that there was no rioting or disorderly conduct, and to eject legionaries from bars and brothels by midnight. The service was provided by each company in rotation. Sometimes it meant an energetic evening, when there were brawls between legionaries and soldiers of other units; then the call of '*A mí La Legion!*' would ring down the streets, bringing every legionary within earshot to the rescue of his embattled comrade, and the *Vigilancia* must hasten to separate the combatants. But on peaceful nights the *Vigilancia* and his sergeant could sit in the comfortable parlour of some quiet brothel, sipping coffee and brandy with Madame and listening to her complaints about the rising cost of living, of the pranks of her girls and of the scandalous conduct of the troops—not the gentlemen of the Legion, of course—who frequented her establishment.

On November 7th the Bandera received orders to move. We were to march to Leganés, two kilometres away, there to entrain for Talavera. our final destination was unknown, but it was rumoured that we were going to the Guadalajara front, north-east of Madrid. Within two hours the Bandera was formed in column outside the barracks. The order was given to march, my men shouldered the dismantled guns and the cases of ammunition and we set off for Leganés.

---

[1] The last of these works was, I believe, the forerunner of the U and non-U controversy; the first enabled a friend of mine to complete the seduction of a Lithuanian chambermaid in the space of fifteen minutes.

[2] I have already explained (Chapter 2) that the Legion was usually referred to as 'El Tercio'. In fact, at this time its official name was La Légion, and it was divided into two Tercios, each containing ten *banderas*, including one of tanks. The depot of the 1st Tercio was at Melilla in Morocco, that of the 2nd at Dar Riffien, near Cueta.

[3] 'Shock Troops'—i.e. Foreign Legion and Moors in the Nationalist Army, International Brigades in the Republican.

CHAPTER SEVEN

Rumour for once was right; we were bound, eventually, for the Guadalajara front, although it took us a month to get there. After three days' wait in Talavera we were put into another train and journeyed for two days and nights, via Salamanca, Valladolid and Burgos, to a place called Calatayud in Aragón, about fifty miles south-west of Zaragoza. Officers travelled in first-class carriages, five to a compartment, sergeants in second-class carriages and the men, singing lustily all the way, in cattle-trucks, where they must have frozen at night. Calatayud is an ancient town, grouped round the ruins of a Moorish castle, which dominates it from the top of a bare escarpment and from the name (Kalat Ayub, or Ayub's Castle) is derived. The poet Martial was born there. Today it is better known among Spaniards through the words of a bawdy song, which the men were forbidden to sing while we were there because it gave great offence to the inhabitants. Even the first four lines, which are harmless enough, sufficed to upset a Calatayudian:

> Si vas a Calatayud
> Pregunta por La Dolores
> Que es una moza lozana
> Y amiga de hacer favores.[1]

After a mug of coffee we embarked in a long column of open lorries—the men huddled in the backs of the vehicles, exposed to the keen wind—and were driven south to the small town of Calamocha, sixty-five kilometres away on the Teruel road. Here we were billeted very comfortably, the officers in private houses; we settled down and relaxed while awaiting further orders. Training duties were very light and we had plenty of leisure. Calamocha is a picturesque little place, hundreds of years old; its most attractive features, I seem to remember, were a church, surrounded by a shallow moat where mules used to paddle, and a humped bridge of stones across a rushing stream.

The people of Calamocha, like all people we met in Aragón, received us with the warmest friendliness and hospitality. The *maños*, as the Aragonese are called colloquially, have the reputation of being hard-headed, plain-speaking, obstinate and even stubborn. They are frugal and straightforward—the North-Country word 'jannock' describes them well; they are also, in my experience at least, among the most generous-hearted people on earth. I spent the greater part of a year in and around Aragón, where I noticed that, although he country looked bare and uninviting, the people fared remarkably well for food and drink. They had a great hatred and contempt for the Republicans, which was reflected in their new attitude towards us.

About this time I had a new batman assigned to me, a legionary about my own age named Paulino Albarrán. A peasant from a village near Salamanca, he was sturdily built, with a podgy, fresh-complexioned face, slightly protruding eyes and the expression of a friendly, puzzled little pig, which earned him the nickname of *Tocinito* (*tocino* is bacon, or fat meat). He was one of the best-natured fellows I ever met, but he was a better soldier than servant—at least when he first came to me.

In the afternoons I usually went for walks outside the town. The bare contours and harsh colours of the countryside were softened and refined by the mellow sunlight and clear air of late autumn. The grape harvest was in, and the peasants were making the new wine. One day, walking down a narrow track, I came upon a white-washed farmhouse; in a vineyard beside it was a wine press, where an old man with a white, pointed beard was working, surrounded by his family. When he caught sight of me he called out in a hearty, raucous voice: 'Come here, young man!' As I approached he roared at me. 'You know me? I'm Satan! Oh yes, they call me Satan because of my beard. Also, perhaps, because of the good wine I make. We'll drink some together, you and I!' First he made me sample some of the new must, pouring me out a great beaker of bubbly, purple liquid. When I had drunk this and praised it, while his family stood by, the men with broad and friendly grins, and the girls giggling happily, he went indoors and fetched a dusty bottle. It was tangy and heavy and very strong. He made me drink half of it, sharing the other half between himself and his two sons. Then he fetched another bottle. This he split with me, muttering the while, 'Oh yes, I'm Satan, I am,' and wagging his white beard, now flecked with purple. At last I was able to take my leave and make my way, unsteadily and with several halts to rest, back to Calamocha. At the entrance to the plaza I met the Padre, talking to Sergeant Lorios. 'Holá!' he cried, 'where have you been?'

'Drinking with Satan,' I gasped, and left him standing in the middle of the road.

Curro Lorios, one of the well-known family from Algeciras, had been at school in England and was married to an English girl. Before coming to us he had been attached to the Irish brigade as a sergeant-interpreter, and some of the bitterness and cynicism induced by the experience remained with him to be transferred to the legion. He had a just grievance, in that he should have been an officer; but General Yagüe had refused his application for a commission on the grounds that, at thirty-five, he was too old to be a subaltern. Larios believed the real reason to be that Yagüe, having strong Falangist sympathies, was prejudiced against anyone with an influential name; certainly, there were subalterns in the Legion over thirty-five. Larios left us just before Christmas for the 13th Bandera.

After a fortnight we moved by lorry to Torrecilla del Robollar, a village in the bleak uplands east of the Teruel-Zaragoza road, about twelve miles from Calamocha and three miles from the front line. Our life here was no more exciting than in Calamocha, except that we had to be ready to go into action at an hour's notice. The only event to interrupt the monotony was the Feast of the Immaculate Conception on December 8th, the *Virgen de la Inmaculada* being the Patroness of the Spanish Infantry. After Mass we celebrated the *fiesta* with an enormous lunch, preceded by a party at Bandera Headquarters which all the officers attended; there was also a special lunch for the men. It would have been unfortunate for us had we been called upon to go into action that day—or the next. But calm reigned on all fronts—a calm that preceded one of the worst storms of the war.

Two days later the lorries came for us again. We started off at 5 a.m., down the twisting mountain road to Calamocha and right, along the main road to Calatayud; there we turned left along the main Madrid- Aragón road, and it became clear that we were at last bound for the Guadalajara front. About midday we stopped for lunch at Medinaceli; then we drove north through Almazán and west along the course of the Douro, a large village dominated by a square castle, which stood by itself on a mound. Here we disembarked and once again moved into billets.

There was no question of relaxation now; our second Guadalajara offensive was about to start and we had to be ready to leave at any moment. On December 13th Mora summoned all officers to a conference.

'The operations against Guadalajara and Madrid,' he told us, 'are about to begin. I expect the order to move at any time now. There are three Army Corps taking part: on the left the Army Corps of Castile under General Varela; in the centre the two Italian divisions and the two mixed divisions of *Flechas*, on the right the Marroquí Army Corps, which includes ourselves, under General Yagüe. Together with the 16th Bandera and elements of cavalry, artillery and tanks, we constitute the *Brigada Móvil* of the Army Corps. Our job, once the front is broken, will be to press on ahead of the other forces, capture important points behind enemy lines and hold them until relieved. The 16th Bandera and ourselves, operating in lorries, will form the Brigade's motorized infantry group, under Lieutenant-Colonel Peñaredonda, whom some of you know.'

There was a laugh in the back and a voice said, 'Oh yes, the deaf one.' Mora stared stonily at the speaker and continued:

'I will brief you in detail before we go into action. Meanwhile, here are one or two general points I want you to remember: there seems to be an idea among officers that their proper place in an advance is always at the head of their troops —Company Commanders in front of their companies and Platoon Commanders in front of their platoons; also that an officer has a duty to expose himself to enemy fire the whole time, in order to encourage his men. Both these ideas are nonsense, and I will have none of them in my Bandera. The only time when an officer's place is at the head of his men is in the final assault, as you all know. Otherwise, the Company Commander should be somewhere in the middle of his three platoons, where he can control them all; similarly, the Platoon Commander should be in between his front and his rear *Pelotones*. I want this rule observed. I assure you all that I will deal very seriously with any officer I see exposing himself needlessly, or allowing his men to do so. There will, I have no doubt, be plenty of suitable occasions for the display of courage; otherwise, an officer must keep his vanity and exhibitionism under restraint.'

He went on to deal with technical details: the employment of our machine-guns, the use of covering fire, the importance of keeping touch, the use of runners and the clear and concise drafting of messages in the field.

'One final point; you will see that the rights of the civilian population are scrupulously respected and that there is no looting. If there is any case of an attempt on the virtue of a woman, it will be punished on the spot by death.' He concluded: 'The orders I have just given you for these operations will be observed in any subsequent operations under my command.'

*   *   *

The situation of the provincial capital of Teruel, held by the Nationalists since the beginning of the Civil War, had always been precarious. Only in a civil war would a serious attempt have been made to hold it; for its military value was negligible. Forming a salient from the Nationalist lines and dominated on three sides by the Republicans, its only means of communication and supply consisted of a single road and railway running north-east through Calamocha to Zaragoza and Calatayud. The Republicans could overlook this road from their positions in the Sierra Palomera to the east of it, and were able to keep it under shell-fire. But Teruel was a town of nearly twenty thousand inhabitants, and so could not be abandoned to the enemy.

While General Franco was concentrating his troops for his offensive on Guadalajara, the Republicans were preparing theirs on Teruel. On December 15th they attacked with seventy thousand men. In twenty-four hours they had cut the road and railway to Calamocha and enveloped the city. The Nationalist defenders—a Brigade totaling about three thousand men, with one battery of artillery—retreated inside the perimeter. On December 21st there was fighting in the streets, and the Republican High Command announced the capture of the city —prematurely as it turned out.

The Nationalist were taken by surprise. General Franco immediately abandoned his projected attack on Madrid and moved troops to Teruel. He has been much criticized for this. If he had continued with his original plan he would probably have taken Madrid, an important gain to him and a very serious loss to the other side; whereas the capture of Teruel would bring little military advantage to the Republicans. On the other hand, the capture of Madrid by the Nationalists would not necessarily end the war. Possibly a more certain way, in the long run, was to destroy the Republican army around Teruel, opening the way for an advance to the Mediterranean coast. This, at any rate, seems to have been the Generalissimo's idea.

On December 22nd began the Nationalist counter-offensive to relieve Teruel. General Aranda's Army Corps (Galicia), which had been in reserve near Zaragoza, advanced from the north; General Varela's (Castile), withdrawn from the Guadalajara front, attacked from the south-west. Slowly they forced the Republicans back until, on the last day of the year, they were poised for the final thrust that would break through to the beleaguered garrison. Then it began to snow. The temperature dropped to minus twenty degrees centigrade. Further advance was impossible. Caught in the open by the blizzard at an altitude of over three thousand feet above sea-level, without shelter, without warm clothing and with no possibility of lighting fires, the Nationalists suffered more casualties during the next three or four days from the cold than from enemy action. General García Valiño, commanding the First Navarre Division,[2] told me later that he had three thousand five hundred cases of frost-bite. The Republicans, better protected from the weather, renewed their attacks against the city. On January 8th the garrison was overwhelmed; by the time the Nationalist were able to renew their advance Teruel was in Republican hands.

We in Berlanga de Duero knew nothing of these events but what we read in the scant official communiqués. The tension raised by Mora's conference and the prospect of imminent battle relaxed after a few days, when it became clear that the original plan had been abandoned. We were obliged to settle into a peaceful routine of parades, training and long route marches in snow-blizzards to toughen us. I was getting to know my men, whom I admired for their keenness and efficiency and liked for their wit and cheerfulness; I noticed that there was mutual respect and likening between them and my two sergeants. I was even beginning to understand something about the mechanism and tactics of the guns —though I doubt if Almajach would have agreed about this—when a new hazard was thrust on us, in the form of mules to carry the guns and ammunition. There were thirty-one of them in the company, of which I had eight—one for each gun and ammunition. This seemed to put paid to any idea of our operating as a motorized unit. At first the poor beasts were the objects of bitter complaints and curses. The legionaries detailed to look after them resented the work, nobody seemed to understand the loading of the guns and ammunition, and the mules themselves showed an obstinate, though not unreasonable reluctance to keep formation on parade and on the march; moreover, on the icy roads and streets they slithered all over the place. But as we became used to them we began to appreciate their qualities of strength, endurance and courage. With good treatment they became very tractable, and during the subsequent operations we found that they would carry heavy loads all day over the roughest mountain country, with scarcely any food and very little water; nor did they panic under fire.

Another hazard, but one we could never get used to, was the arrival in Berlanga of Lieutenant-Colonel Peñaredonda—'the deaf one'. He was a tall, well-built officer of about fifty, with a fleshy face and a discontented, almost menacing expression; he was a man of few words, and those were seldom pleasant. He had none of the qualities of the mules except obstinacy, as I was later to find out. For the moment he concentrated on keeping us busy all day, devising exercises and route marches for us and criticizing everything he saw. Naturally, the company commanders whom he criticized passed on the rocket to us, we passed it on to the sergeants and they excelled themselves in passing it on to the men—all in a temperature of twelve degrees below zero. The earlier happy atmosphere evaporated without any corresponding gain in efficiency.

Just before Christmas Captain Luengo left us, much to the relief of the café proprietors of Berlanga. His place was taken by Captain Alonso de Castañeda, a tall, fair man with a handsome face and a dashing manner. He was a regular Legion officer of the same seniority of Mora, intelligent, of independent mind, unorthodox views and a strongly argumentative nature. He loved to poke fun at the Church when the Padre was present; or to cast doubts on the universal depravity of the Republicans or on the sincerity of all Nationalist leaders, when Mora or Cancela were there to argue with him. He took my side in all disputes concerning British policy or behavior, but I felt he did it from contrariness rather than conviction. For all that, he had a sensitive mind, with an intelligent appreciation of literature and a sincere love of poetry. He was an extremely competent soldier.

My billet was a small house near the *Plaza Mayor*, kept by a middle-aged working man and his wife. They had two pretty daughters of about fifteen or sixteen, to the elder of whom Paulino spent his spare time paying spirited but, I fear, wholly unsuccessful addresses. They were all very kind to me, treating me as one of the family. I was lucky to get such a billet, because Berlanga was already full of troops when we arrived—the 16th Bandera, a *tercio* of Requetés and a company of German anti-tank gunners; the latter, I think, were in charge of some new equipment for testing, because they kept entirely to themselves and discouraged all friendly overtures from the Spaniards. Their quarters were in the *Palacio*, a three-hundred-year-old building in the main square. They caused me plenty of trouble one night, about a week before Christmas, when I was officer of the *Vigilancia*.

It was soon after midnight when a panting legionary reported at Bandera Headquarters that a fire had broken out in the Palacio. When I arrived I found the whole building ablaze, lighting up the sky, the square and the surrounding houses; even the castle on its bare mound seemed to be floodlit. The Germans had neglected to inform anybody until the fire was well under way, although they had removed all their ammunition and equipment to a place of safety; I did not see them at all that night, but heard later that they had been finding themselves new quarters. It was lucky for the inhabitants that they had troops in the town, for if they had been left to themselves I think all Berlanga would have been burnt. The Requetés and legionaries worked with a will, the former climbing up walls and clambering over roof-tops with axes and hoses, the latter forming a chain to pass buckets of water from the river and fountain to the two fire-engines. These appeared to date from about the same period as the Palacio, being simple little machines, hand-drawn and hand-operated, each with a crew of four puffing, laughing peasants. The rest of the male population stood grouping in doorways around the square, smoking cigarettes and pointing gaily to the fire. 'Look how it burns!' they cried to me. 'We haven't had a blaze like this for fifty years!' Pained looks greeted my brusque suggestion that they join in the work. The fire was too strong for us to hope to save the palace; all we could do was to try and stop it spreading. Luckily it was a calm night with no wind.

I was on my feet all night, detailing patrols to keep the streets clear of spectators, organizing a water-carrying service and directing operations with a hose from a roof-top. About half-past three I noticed that the legionaries had disappeared, leaving me with my small squad of *vigilantes* and a few Requetés to deal with the fire, which was still blazing fiercely. Putting my sergeant in charge, I ran to the building where two of our companies were quartered, roused them and set some to carry water and others to work the fire-engines, whose crews, tiring of their fun, had gone to bed. By six o'clock the Requetés had gone home, frozen and dead tired; and so I had to find the two other companies and turn them out. I should have had help from the *Vigilancia* of the 16th Bandera, but they were occupied in finding new quarters for two of their own companies, who had been burnt out of their old ones.

About seven o'clock the townspeople, having enjoyed a good night's rest, began to appear to see how things were going—but not to help. On my rounds I came upon two fire-engines standing idle and abandoned. With some difficulty I found the *Alguacil*, who corresponds roughly to the Town Clerk; he was enjoying a quiet cigarette in a doorway. 'You may be interested to know,' I snapped at him, for my temper was wearing thing by the time, 'that two of your engines are standing over there, abandoned.' He took a puff, removed his cigarette and asked brightly, 'Do you mean that they should work?' However it turned out the engines did not belong to Berlanga, but to firemen from Burgo de Osma, fifteen miles away, who had been summoned when the fire started and had just arrived. I found four of these men strolling along the street, and told them sharply to get their engines working. They nodded genially: 'Certainly, sir! That's just what we're going to do—as soon as we've had a little drink to warm us up.'

I was thankful when my tour of duty ended half an hour later, and I could hand over to another officer. At half past eight I snatched a cup of coffee, shaved quickly and went on parade until lunch time. Somebody finally extinguished the fire in the late afternoon.

Christmas came, bringing a more optimistic tone in the official communiqués but still no orders for us. We began to wonder whether we were to remain forgotten in Berlanga while the greatest and, as we thought, culminating battle of the war was raging barely a hundred miles away.

The New Year opened sadly for me. On January 31st a Press car containing four friends of mine—Dick Sheepshanks, Kim Philby, and two American correspondents, Eddie Neil and Bradish Johnson—was passing through the village of Caude, eight miles north-west of Teruel, during an enemy artillery bombardment, when a 12.40 cm. shell burst beside it. Sheepshanks and Johnson were killed outright. Neil died a few days later; Philby escaped with a wound in the head.

On January 2nd a new alférez, called Campos, came to my company. Being senior to me he took over my platoon and I was put in command of the two 81 mm. mortars. It was a blow to me because I liked and thought I understood my men. They seemed to think so too, for a party of them, under a corporal, came to see me and begged me to ask the Captain to retain me in command. I was fool enough to pass this on to Almajach, who said coldly: 'Of course they want you. They can get away with more under you than they could under a Spanish officer.'

Campos was a tall, flabby young man, a little stupid and morose. He told me that he had been one of the original members of the Falange in Granada, and that he had taken part in the firing squad that executed the poet García Lorca. I prefer to believe him a liar. The Nationalists, including the Falange, strongly denied any responsibility for Lorca's death, attributing to the vengeance of his private enemies, of which he had a large number; certainly he had many good friends on the Nationalist side who would have saved him if they could. His murder was a crime that robbed the world of one of its greatest living lyric poets; the mystery of it has never been satisfactorily explained. I say this with all respect to Mr. Gerald Brenan, who claims to have fixed the responsibility of the *Guardia Civil*.[3] No two versions of the tragedy coincide. Campos's account was not circumstantial enough to convince me even at the time; he was careful not to mention it front of Alonso de Castañeda. The reason he alleged for the execution —that Lorca was a Communist, who was to have led a column against Granada —is too absurd to be worth consideration. In his lines on the death of his friend, Sánchez Mejías, it seems, lies Lorca's own epitaph:

> *Díle a la luna que venga,*
> *Que no quiero ver la sangre*
> *De Ignacio sobre la arena.*[4]

A day or two after the appearance of Campos a Subteniente arrived to join the 56th Company. This rank corresponds roughly though not precisely, to that of Warrant Officer Class I in the British Army; the rank, suppressed in the Regular Army, persisted in the Legion. This particular creature was a cocky, officious little man with a shiny red face and pert expression, a squeaky, angry voice and the appearance and manners of a monkey. He started to throw his weight about from the first moment, abusing the N.C.Os. and laying into the men with his *fusta* on the slightest pretext. It was impossible for us to control him, for Almajach approved of him, or at least his methods. With the officers his manner varied between impertinence to us ensigns and a sickening obsequiousness towards the Captain. Day and night the hours were made hideous by his squawks of complaint or abuse.

At last we received orders to move, and on January 10th we left Berlanga in a long column of lorries. To our disappointment our destination proved to be, not Teruel, but another part of the static Guadalajara front—the ruined and virtually deserted village of Almadrones. Situated just off the main Madrid-Zaragoza road, about 65 miles north-east of Madrid, it had suffered severely from bombardment during the Guadalajara battle of the previous March. Few of the houses were undamaged, and the only inhabitants were a handful of miserable, underfed peasants who wandered disconsolately through the dirty streets. We lingered here a week, then set off on foot with our mules and all our equipment and a twenty-mile march eastwards. It was a hard march, across difficult country, but the weather was bright and cold and the men were in excellent spirits, singing lewd songs from the different regions of Spain when neither the Padre nor the Major were around, both of whom disapproved of the communal bawdry. In the evening we came to the mountain hamlet of Torrecuadrada, about two miles from the front line.

The inhabitants of this region were the poorest I ever saw in Spain, the country the most desolate. It is to the credit of the Falange relief organization, *Auxilio Social*, that as soon as the war was over it directed a great deal of its effort towards improving conditions here. Every morning and evening at meal times the children of the village would gather round our field kitchens, each carrying a little jar or bowl, which the cooks would fill with meat, fish, vegetables and bread. After two days the villagers asked us to stop giving their children meat and fish, which they had never tasted before and which upset their stomachs. Even bread was a luxury to which they were unaccustomed, their normal—indeed their unvarying—diet consisting of a mess of beans or *garbanzos* (chick-peas). The houses were hovels, the streets mean, filthy and dangerously pitted. But the people, though underfed and miserably clothed, were kind and warm-hearted and did all they could to make us welcome and comfortable.

After three days we left Torrecuadrada for the front, to effect what the communiqués called 'a rectification of the line'. This meant occupying and fortifying a range of hills overlooking the valley of Tajuña. The enemy, evidently fearing an attack in strength, had withdrawn beyond the river, and so we were able to occupy the ground without loss. Noriega had gone on leave, and I had taken over his platoon of machine-guns. The work of fortification was extremely arduous, for the ground was hard—in some places it was rock—so that our picks and shovels made little impression. At the end of five days the men's hands were covered with blisters and sores. Much of the work was in view of the enemy and had to be done at night. There was no shelter; we had to snatch what sleep we could lying in the open, each wrapped in his *capote* and blanket, in a temperature well below zero. Luckily the weather was fine. The men worked with a will, their high spirits seemingly unaffected by cold, fatigue or the pain of their hands. My platoon was attached to Captain Cancela and the 53rd Company, an arrangement that gave me great pleasure, for he and his officers were such a gay and friendly crowd that it was impossible not to be happy in their company.

The Tajuña, which separated our new positions from those of the enemy, was barely more than a stream at this point, running through a valley about four hundred yards wide. We had therefore to be careful how we moved during daylight, for the enemy had us well-covered with his machine-guns and would open fire at once on anyone they could see. We suffered half-a-dozen casualties in this way, among them one of my runners, who was shot through the head as he was going to his lunch. He was an efficient and cheerful soldier, which made me rejoice the more when our mortars blew the machine-gun post to pieces that afternoon. On the third night we were favoured with three deserters from across the river, who crept up to our wire in the darkness and shouted to us to let them through. They were Catalans, poor nervous wrecks of creatures, half-starved and wretchedly clad. Under the influence of food and cigarettes they chattered freely to us. According to their account, which their own appearance supported, the enemy opposite us was in a state of alarm bordering on panic, and stood to all night in expectation of an attack. They complained bitterly of well-fed Political Commissars who came from Madrid or Barcelona to give them lectures on The Fighting Spirit or The Meaning of Democracy. I often wondered, but never found out, what happened to deserters after they had been screened—whether they were allowed to live in peace or were conscripted into our army.

On the sixth day we were relieved by an infantry battalion, and returned to Torrecuadrada for a rest. Although glad of the relief, I was sorry to leave my friends of the 53rd for the ill-humor of Almajach, the bickering of Colomer or the unceasing bray of the Subteniente.

On February 1st we left the Guadalajara front for good. We drove east through the day, arriving in the early evening at the small village of Torrijos del Campo, a few miles south of Calamocha. At last, it seemed, we were to take our part in the battle of Teruel.

The following day we were issued with new uniforms, which turned out to be forerunners of the British Army battledress—a green *cazadora*, or blouse, of rough serge; trousers of the same colour and material, which could be pulled in above the ankles, and strapped boots reaching half-way up the calf. We retained our open-necked shirts and tasseled forage caps. Most welcome of all, we were issued with thick, wide-skirted, green greatcoats to replace our worn-out *capotes*. The same day was marred for me by a most unpleasant incident. It was my turn to supervise the Company's midday *rancho*; I was standing by the cauldron in a corner of the village square, the men lined up in a double queue in front of me, the Subteniente and the *Brigada*, or C.Q.M.S., looking on from a distance. Having tasted the food and given the order to carry on, I was watching the distribution when I heard the Subteniente break into a gabble of rage and, out of the corner of my eye, saw him advance on one of the men at the end of the line; at first I paid no attention, being used to his behaviour by now. A moment later I heard the sound of blows as he laid into the man, followed by an angry shout. When I reached the scene I found the Subteniente, flushed and quivering with temper, standing in front of a legionary whose face wore a look of defiance and whose cap was lying on the ground, where the Subteniente had knocked it.

'Now pick it up!' shouted the Subteniente.

'I will not,' growled the man.

'You're under arrest!' I snapped at him. 'You, and you,' I called to two of the other men, 'escort him to the *Vigilancia*. Subteniente, will you please make a report in writing on this incident.

When I told Almajach, he was indignant.

'Did you not have a pistol?' I had, as had the Subteniente for that matter. 'Well, why didn't you shoot the fellow then and there? That's how we deal with insubordination in the Legion! Now we'll have a court-martial on our hands.' I wondered if I should ever make a Legion officer.

---

[1] If you go to Calatayud
Ask for Delores
Who is a lusty wench
And fond of doing favours.

[2] The former Navarre Brigades had by now been expanded to Divisions.

[3] The Face of Spain.

[4] Tell the moon it's time to rise,
   I do not want to see his blood
   Where split upon the sand it lies.

                    (Translation—Roy Campbell.)

CHAPTER EIGHT

On the morning of February 5th a cheerful sun in a clear blue sky brightened the harsh landscape of the Sierra Palomera. Down in the plain that we had left behind, mist still floated in wisps, hiding the valley of the Jiloca and the main road north from Teruel which we had crossed the day before. I was standing on a mountainside, about two hundred yards below the crest of a stony ridge connecting two great shoulders of rock that sloped back towards the plain; the whole formed a wide, semi-circular amphitheatre about half-a-mile in circumference. Now its craggy sides were swarming with troops—green-coated legionaries, Requetés in scarlet berets, khaki-clad infantry and gunners. The whole arena teemed with men, horses, mules, guns and equipment. Colonel Sánchez González's 5th Navarre Division, with the 14th and 16th Banderas, was massed below the crest in preparation for a great attack.

The previous day we had left Torrijos on foot, and crossed the river Jiloca and the Teruel-Calatayud road at the village of Caminreal; then we had struck east and south-east into the hills. Lieutenant Noriega had returned from leave, and so I was back with my mortars. But the fine weather and the certainty that at last we were going into action had raised the spirits of all of us; even the Subteniente was almost amiable. After a march of fifteen miles we halted for the night in the open, near the hamlet of Rubielos. Despite the cold we slept well, waking refreshed and happy in the frosty dawn. By the Major's orders we dumped our blankets and greatcoats before moving up to our assembly point; they would only impede our movement in battle, and they could catch up with us in the evening with the Bandera pack train, which would bring the rations. As we moved in a narrow column up a winding track, I saw Lieutenant Peñaredonda with his A.D.C. standing watching us. Seated on a white horse nearby was a small wizened old man with glasses and a white moustache; on his left breast he wore the crossed sword and baton of a general. I heard someone exclaim:

'Look, there's Papa Vigón! We'll be all right if he's planned this."

General Juan Vigón was the Generalissimo's Chief of Staff, a brilliant soldier whose careful planning was largely responsible for the Nationalist victories. As he caught sight of me Peñaredonda shouted: '*Holá*, Mr Peter! Are you looking forward to today?'

'So we really are going into action, sir?'

'Certainly we are. There are five divisions in this.'

As we stood on the mountainside, waiting for the artillery and air bombardment to begin, I felt the tension in the mass of troops around me. A hush seemed to spread over the whole area; men talked little and in undertones; the clink of weapons or harness sounded unnaturally loud, and the bray of a mule from half-a-mile away seemed like a trumpet call. I heard a strident female voice nearby and saw a girl in Legion uniform talking to a sergeant in the 53rd Company; she was about thirty but looked older, with a leathery, weather-beaten face and short, black hair. These *legionarias* were a common sight in all banderas; they usually acted as camp-followers, cooking, washing and mending for the men and generally making themselves useful; but it was not often that they followed a bandera into action. This girl had been a long time with the Legion; she had a good knowledge of first aid and assisted the *practicante,* or medical orderly, of the 53rd. She was as tough and brave as any of the men.

At this moment a voice behind me said in English: 'Excuse me, but didn't we meet at Cambridge?' Wondering if I was dreaming I turned and saw a lieutenant of artillery of about my own age, with a pleasant, clean-shaven face. He introduced himself as Guy Spaey. He had, in fact, been a contemporary of mine at Cambridge, where he was at King's; we had a number of friends in common. Of mixed Belgian, Dutch and German extraction, he had arrived in Spain in October 1936, and immediately joined the Nationalist forces. At the moment of our meeting he was Gun Position Officer of a battery of 10.5 cm. mountain artillery, attached to Lieutenant-Colonel Peñaredonda's command.

By half past ten the last of the mist had cleared. We heard a droning in the sky and saw a formation of silver, twin-engine bombers, with an escort of bi-plane fighters, approaching from the west; they flew over us towards the enemy lines; a minute later we heard the thunder of their bombs. At the same moment our batteries opened fire all round us, from the mountains on either side and from the foothills and the plain behind; the air was alive with the hiss of shells passing overhead. The aircraft returned to circle over us and made a second run; again we heard the roll of bursting bombs.

For two hours the bombardment raged, the guns keeping up an unceasing barrage while waves of aircraft flew over us to unload on the enemy positions. Not a shell came back in reply, nor was there a sign of enemy activity in the air. When the firing began we all made ready to advance, expecting the order at any moment; but as it became clear that the bombardment would be a long one, we gradually relaxed and made ourselves comfortable. I thought it odd that we had no briefing from de Mora before going into action and that none of us had the least idea of our plan of battle; but I concluded that we should be briefed when the time came. As I meditated I watched another formation of our bombers approaching. They looked almost beautiful as they came on in perfect formation, steady and unhurried, the sun flashing on the metal of their wings and bodies— flashing too, I saw, on a tiny object that fell from the leading aircraft. It took me a second to realize what was happening—then, as I heard Almajach shouting, I roared at my platoon:

'Down on the ground where you are. Hold on to the mules' head-ropes! Keep your faces down!'

As they dropped I saw a bright orange flash; a great fountain of earth erupted from the slope a hundred yards below us. I threw myself on the ground, pressing my face between my arms against the rock. The next moment the whole mountain side seemed to be torn apart in a convulsion of flame. The ground shook as from an earthquake and the air was full of flying metal and boulders. The explosions hammered our ear-drums and tore at our clothes. There followed a horrible silence. I struggled to my feet, deaf and battered by the blast, blinded by dust which hung in a thick cloud over the whole area. Gradually the singing subsided in my ears and I began to hear the groans and whimpers of wounded men, the screams of injured and frightened animals and a swelling roar of fury and indignation from the troops. As the dust cleared I could see that most of the bombs had landed among us—a whole division massed without cover on that mountain side, where the rocky ground added to the force and destruction of the explosions. I called to my men: although shaken they had suffered no casualties, apart from cuts and bruises. I started to examine the mules when renewed shouting made me turn and look upwards. The bombers had circled and were coming back over us, still in perfect formation, with the same unhurried, steady pace. Oh my god I thought, they can't be going to do it again! Please, dear god, don't let them do it again! To my horror, as I fixed my glasses on them I saw the leader unload his bombs, followed by the rest. Men began to run wildly in all directions, up the flanks of the mountain, in a mad, useless and suicidal rush to escape. Again I shouted to my men:

'Stay where you are! Get on the ground and hold on to your mule-ropes!'

Those bombs seemed an age falling. I found myself praying feverishly that I should not be hit, or at least not maimed. Once more there came the splitting detonations in my ears, the scream of flying fragments and the grisly silence after; then the dust and the cries of the wounded. When I got to my feet my legs were trembling so that I could hardly stand, my voice shaking so much that I could scarcely call to my platoon. But they had been spared again; one man was cut in the forehead by a piece of rock and so shaken by the blast that he was sick all day; a bomb had burst a few feet from him. Two of my mules were dead. Another had run away but was soon recaptured. I was astonished at the docility of the mules during the bombardment and after; one had a bomb fragment through the shoulder, but carried his load through the next two days' operations with no sign of pain or fatigue. The Bandera had been very lucky, losing only two legionaries killed and three wounded badly enough to need evacuation. Elsewhere the carnage was heart-breaking—over five hundred casualties, including one hundred and fifty-six killed, in less than five minutes. Our sister Bandera, the 16th, had suffered severely, losing one of their best company commanders, whose foot was taken off at the ankle by a bomb splinter. The whole of the mountain was like some nightmare abattoir, with disemboweled horses, shreds of human flesh and clothing, severed limbs and broken pieces of equipment strewn around. In the midst of it I noticed the girl medical orderly of our 53rd Company moving calmly and efficiently among the wounded, typing tourniquets and bandages, giving morphia pills and exchanging an occasional joke in her hoarse chuckle.

That was the last we saw, or wanted to see, of our aircraft for that day. How the mistake occurred is uncertain. We had white identification panels spread on the crest in front of us, to indicate our forward positions; but it is possible that the troops behind us had also spread them, in which case the aircraft would have taken us for the enemy; or it may have been simply an error of navigation.

The operation was now beginning to be known as the Battle of the Alfambra, or of the Sierra Palomera. The object of the Nationalist was to clear the Republicans from their positions in the Sierra Palomera, which commanded the road and railway north from Teruel, and to advance the Nationalist line eastwards as far as the River Alfambra. The plan was simple. The positions along the Sierra Palomera were too strong to be taken by frontal assault; but behind the mountain massif, to the east, the country opened out into a wide, undulating plateau, interspersed with a few hills and ridges, which sloped gently towards the valley of the Alfambra. This area the Nationalists selected for their battleground. The operation, a pincer movement, was on a larger scale than Colonel Peñaredonda's figure of five divisions had indicated. Preceded by a morning's artillery and air bombardment, the attack was launched simultaneously from three directions: from the south-west, from the direction of Teruel, by General Aranda's Army Corps of Galicia with four divisions; from the north-east by General Yagüe's Marroqui Army Corps with three divisions, and from the north-west by the First Cavalry Division and the 5th Navarre Division, both under the command of General Monasterio. The bombardment destroyed the opposing defences, opening the way for a general advance; Monasterio's cavalry swept across the open country to the banks of the Alfambra, followed, more slowly, by the 5th Navarre Division, while the two Army Corps pressed inwards steadily from the north-east and south-west. On the second day the 5th Navarre Division joined up with General Aranda's troops, completing the envelopment of the enemy in the Sierra Palomera. On the third and last day the cavalry made contact with the two Army Corps advancing from the north and south, completing the occupation of the line of the Alfambra; at the same time the 5th Navarre Division cleared the enemy from the Sierra Palomera, attacking from the rear. During the three days the Nationalists inflicted some fifteen thousand casualties on the enemy and took a further seven thousand prisoners at very small cost to themselves. From that moment the recapture of Teruel was no longer in doubt.

We junior officers knew practically nothing of this plan on that morning of February 5th. Half-an-hour after our disastrous bombing the fire of our batteries slackened and we received the order to advance. We climbed slowly to the top of the ridge behind which we had been sheltering all morning, and moved in single file down a narrow, stony track on the further side; the three rifle companies in our van spread out in open order to cross the flat country in front of us. Away on our left the cavalry were racing ahead, widely extended across the plain. We advance slowly towards a line of low hills. At any moment I expected to hear the patter of bullets falling among us; but the most we encountered were a few 'overs' from far away, and we reached the hills without casualties. The enemy had abandoned their defences under the inferno of bombing and shellfire; and after our experience of the morning I could not blame them. The effect on me had not yet passed off, and it was a long time before it did or before I could watch our own aircraft fly overhead without a shiver of apprehension. To tell the truth, I had been badly frightened and so, I found, had most of us. During one of our many halts that afternoon I overhead Captain Cancela talking to Almajach:

'That girl,' he said, referring to the *practicanta* of his company, 'has certainly got guts. She is still with the Company, and for any woman to want to go on after what happened this morning—well, I can only tell you that I feel like lying down at once if I think I hear an aeroplane!'

Towards the evening we came to a bare, snow-covered ridge overlooking another broad plain, in which lay the villages of Argente and Visiedo. The Republicans had abandoned the ridge and retired to the villages in the plain. We prepared to camp for the night on the bare hillside. An order came that no fires to be lit under any circumstances, and so we opened the tins of sardines and tunny that we had taken with us as emergency rations, and started to eat them in our numbed fingers while we waited for the pack train to bring our greatcoats and blankets. At over four thousand feet above sea-level the temperature was well below freezing, the faint wind a caress of ice.

'What I wouldn't give now,' said Colomer to me, 'for a litre of that red wine which we used to call undrinkable when we were at Berlanga!'

Some of the men had canteens of brandy, *anis* or the rough, aniseed-flavoured spirit called aguardiente, from which they drank despite our orders and warnings that it would only make them feel the cold more. When it became clear that the pack train would never find us in the darkness we lay down in the snow as we were. It was a clear night, and as I lay on my back looking up into the sky the stars seemed to wink at me in mockery of my efforts to sleep. Several times I stood up and paced around, trying to get some warmth and circulation into my body; then I lay down again, hoping to fall asleep before the glow passed off. I must at last have succeeded, for I awoke, without even knowing that I had been asleep, to find a sky a pale rose above the Alfambra valley in front of us. As I stood up I saw that the front of my jacket and breeches were stiff and white with hoar-frost; it was thick in my nose, my eyebrows and my hair, reminding me comically of that old colonel in London who had taunted me, before I first came to Spain, with Napier's description of the Peninsular War and the 'icicles in their noses'. But I was not so amused soon afterwards when I saw a group of legionaries bent over a stiff figure on the ground; he had died in the night from the cold. With the daylight came the pack train and permission to light fires. Gratefully we snatched our mugs of scalding coffee, swallowing them with nips of *aguardiente*—surely the best pick-me-up after such a night. As we started to advance, the warmth of the day and the movement of our limbs put new life into us; in the bright, cheerful sunlight we forgot our misery of the night before. After occupying the village in Argente—or what was left of it—we continued our advance Eastward across the bare plain to Visiedo. There was no sign of the enemy; only the sound of firing from the direction of the Alfambra indicated where he had gone. When we reached Visiedo in the late afternoon we received orders to halt for the night. This village seemed to have suffered less than Argente; a few houses were still standing, some of them inhabited. Best of all, we came upon the abandoned supply depot of one of the Republican divisions; this we put under guard, but not before we had distributed crates of every sort of tinned food to the various companies.

In this village we encountered our only opposition that day: a furious old woman who, about an hour after our arrival, stormed into the room where Mora had established his headquarters, complaining that our men had stolen one of her chickens.

'Villains!' she screamed, shaking her fist at us all, 'Bandits! They thought I didn't see them—but I saw them all right! Liberators, you call yourselves? You're worse than the Reds!'

Mora let her finish—I think she would have scratched his eyes out if he had interrupted. Then he asked her what she thought her loss was worth, paid her the sum she demanded and told the officer of the *Vigilancia* to find the offenders; they did a month in the *Pelotón*. I imagine the Duke of Wellington, who had his troops flogged for similar offences,[1] would have approved of Mora.

Setting out early the next morning we retraced our steps, marching westwards all day until, in the evening we encamped for the night on a ridge of the Sierra Palomera. Here, to my joy, I found Spaey again. I had been worried that he might not have survived the bombing of two days before; but he rode into our camp, leading a spare horse, and asked me to ride back to his lines and dine with him. Neither Mora nor Almajach raised any objection, only insisting that I should be back with the Bandera by first light. I was astonished how well the artillery looked after themselves in such conditions; for not only did we dine extremely well, with the luxury of good cooking and good wine, but Spaey found me a small tent to sleep in. He ordered his servant to call me half-an-hour before dawn with a horse ready saddled to take me back to the Bandera. His battery had been detailed to cover the movements of the 14th and 16th Banderas; although he had not been required to go into action, Spaey had been able to form a fairly clear picture of the course of the battle, which he explained to me. Tomorrow, he said, we were going to clean up the Sierra Palomera from the rear of the enemy, but it was unlikely we should meet with much resistance. We both reckoned we were due for leave when it was over, and agreed to spend it together in Zaragoza.

Next morning, accompanied by Spaey's servant, I cantered the two miles back to the Bandera in the crisp air of another bright dawn. All that day we climbed among the ridges of the Sierra Palomera, rounding up the broken remnants of the Republican forces. They were in no state to offer resistance, and only wished to surrender as quickly as possible. They were all Spaniards. In the evening we arrived exhausted at a ruined monastery in the mountains, where we spent the night. Tired though we were, it was a sleepless night for most of us; the wind howled and whistled among the bare rocks, cutting clean through our greatcoats and blankets. We were thankful when the day brought another sun to warm us. During the morning we completed our sweep of the Sierra, then made our way by steep, winding tracks down to the plain and Teruel-Calatayud road. Late that night we limped into the village of Torremocha, where hot food and comfortable billets awaited us. During the whole operation the Bandera had suffered less than half-a-dozen casualties from the enemy; these had been among the rifle companies on the first and third days. But the cold had killed an equal number of us.

*   *   *

From the stony soil of the Sierra Palomera to the comfortable bed in the Gran Hotel at Zaragoza was the sort of sudden change that we came to accept as natural during the Civil War. Torremocha was little more than three hours by road from Zaragoza, where Spaey and I arrived on forty-eight hours' leave a day or two after our descent from the Sierra. At this period of the war it was a sure place for meeting old friends. When, after soaking for half-an-hour in a hot bath and changing my clothes, I walked downstairs into the great marble lounge of the hotel to meet Spaey, I heard my name shouted from a table across the room. Sitting there, with three whiskies and sodas in front of him was Captain Von Hartmann, a Finnish cavalry officer whom I had met in San Sebastian.

'Goddamit!' he cried in a nasal twang, 'I see you two bastards crossing the room half-an-hour ago, so I order these whiskies. It's Spanish whisky and it's terrible! See if you can drink one.' I couldn't; nor could Spaey when he joined us.

'Neither can I,' said von Hartmann, I'm a cavalryman and I know what that stuff's made of. I guess we better settle for brandy.'

At first sight von Hartmann, though short and handsome, looked like the typical Prussian officer of stage and screen, with close-cropped hair, scarred face and monocle. The resemblance was only in his appearance. He had an enthusiastic, volatile temperament, a warm, generous nature, wild courage, and a keen sense of humour. A nephew of the great Mannheim, he had gone to war at an early age, serving in the German Army on the Eastern Front in the 1914 war, first as a cavalry officer, later as an aviator; afterwards he had fought under his uncle in the first Finnish war of Independence. In the early months of the Spanish Civil War he commanded a squadron of mounted Falange on the Santander front; later he was appointed to the command of a cadets' academy near Salamanca. There he became involved in the Hedilla plot, for his part in which he was placed under house arrest and relieved of his command. When we met in Zargoza he had just been released and was about to take over an infantry battalion; I think this leniency was due to his universal popularity. He had more wounds even than General Millán Astray, some of them showing in the scars on his face.

Judged by the standards of the 400 or the Milroy, night life in Zargoza offered poor entertainment. The girls depended for their charm more on make-up and dim lighting than on youth or beauty; the liquor would have given a bootlegger a bad name. But to us it all seemed glamour and gay. It was sometimes exciting as well; for, under the influence of cabaret brandy and, I suppose, war-strain, officers would sometimes become boisterous, then bellicose; pistols would be drawn and bullets start to fly across the room. On more than one occasion a hand-grenade was thrown, with resulting injury and loss of life. Once an Italian tank officer, being refused admittance to a night-club that was full, hurried to his lines and returned half-an-hour later in his small tank, which he drove through the door and on to the dance floor. On the afternoon of February 15th Spaey and I left Zaragoza to rejoin our units. About nine o'clock in the evening we reached the village of Monreal del Campo, some fifteen miles north of Torremocha, where we found Spaey's battery; they told me that my Bandera had moved to Torrecilla de Rebollar, where we had been in December. It was too late for me to reach them that night, but the battery were moving in that direction at dawn and would give me a lift.

After a few hours' broken sleep on the floor of a chilly, unheated room Spaey and I climbed into a lorry in the freezing darkness of early morning. With the rest of the battery we drove north to Calamocha, there turning east up the winding road to Torrecilla in the first grey light. Torrecilla was deserted but a mile or two farther on I found the Bandera commissariat and learned that the Bandera was in action about a mile to the north-east. I could hear the sound of incessant machine-gun fire and the occasional explosions of shells and mortars. With a legionary to guide me I hastened on foot towards the battle.

We followed the road eastwards for a few hundred yards, then turned left to descend a rocky valley studded with shrubs and pine trees. The going was difficult and we made slow progress, but as we stumbled on, the sound of battle grew nearer and seemed to intensify; bullets hissed through the branches above us and a few shells landed on the sides of the ravine. After about twenty minutes, when we had reached the bottom of the valley, they firing slackened. I saw a figure approaching slowly, with his arm in a sling; he was a young Catalan officer, Alférez Mentasi, from the 53rd Company. He was very pale and obviously in great pain, but he smiled a greeting.

'Watch your step up there, Peter,' he gasped. 'It's pretty bad. We've had a lot of casualties. I've a bullet in my wrist and it hurts like hell.'

He stumbled on, and I began to climb the ridge ahead of me, traversing it towards the left. About a hundred yards below the crest I found de Mora, the two doctors, the Padre, and Noriega; with them was the Subteniente, taking surreptitious pulls at a bottle of brandy.

The previous day the Republicans had launched a surprise attack on this sector with two International Brigades—one Canadian and one Anglo-American —supported by two Spanish Brigades. After the Alfambra battle the Nationalist front ran roughly north from the line of the Alfambra, through the road and rail junction of Vivel del Rio and the village of Segura, towards Zaragoza. With their first onslaught the Republicans overran the forward positions of the Nationalists, capturing the village of Segura; their further advance was blocked by a second line of defence in front of Villanueva del Rebollar, four miles east of Torrecilla. The two 'mobile' banderas—the 14th and 16th, under Colonel Peñaredonda— were rushed to the scene, with orders to counter-attack and retake Segura and the lost positions; they were supported by a battalion of infantry and one or two batteries of field artillery. It was an ill-conceived operation. The Nationalist command, which was vested here in General Camilo Alonso Vega's 4th Navarre Division, seemed unaware of the strength of the enemy and of the distance that their own troops must cover between their assault positions and their objective; this was about a mile of difficult going, a large part of it brutally exposed to the defenders' fire. In the event, a force of under two thousand men, with inadequate artillery and no air support, was ordered to attack in daylight an enemy of several times its number—an enemy firmly entrenched on a high ridge, well supplied with automatic weapons and enjoying at least equal artillery support. Under the cover of darkness the plan might have succeeded; but Spanish troops were not trained in night operations.

Between the opposing lines ran two valleys separated by a low pine-covered ridge; scrub and low bushes grew in the valleys and on the lower slopes. At first light that morning de Mora, with his company commanders, had made a personal reconnaissance of the nearer valley—the one I had just crossed—to select a route for his advance. They came under fire immediately. Captain Almajach received a bullet in the foot, which shattered the bone and crippled him for life. Noriega took command of the company. Taking advantage of such cover as the undergrowth afforded, the Bandera advanced down the forward slope against a murderous volume of fire from some hundred heavy and light machine-guns. In spite of casualties it crossed the first valley and reached the low ridge of hills about six hundred yards from the enemy. Here de Mora halted and placed his machine-guns. When I arrived he was about to continue the attack.

I was put in command of a machine-gun platoon on top of the ridge, on the right flank; two of its four guns had already been destroyed by shell or mortar fire. I hurried off to supervise the distribution of ammunition and arrange for the provision and carriage of fresh supplies during the ensuing engagement; then I prepared to bring my two remaining guns into action, to cover the rifle companies' advance. Across the valley I could make out where the enemy positions were located, well concealed among the pines and dominating our own; my orders were simply to maintain as high and accurate a volume of fire upon them as possible. My left-hand gun was emplaced behind a low, broken-down brick wall which had once formed part of a pigsty; it gave cover rather than protection; the other gun was shielded, inadequately, by a rough, shallow earthwork constructed by the crew.

As soon as the rifle companies began to move down through the trees in front, the enemy opened fire all along his line, sweeping the forward slope and the crest of our ridge with a steady rain of bullets, mortar bombs and shells. As I ran from gun to gun, crouching low and taking what cover I could from the formation of the ground, I wondered how any one could survive in the open against such a devastating weight of fire. I flung myself to the ground beside each gun in turn, straining to mark through my field glasses the impact of its bursts on the enemy positions, and passing corrections in elevation and direction to the sergeant in command, shouting my orders to make myself heard above the stammer of the gun. I tried to hold the glasses steady, to give my orders without a tremor in my voice and to ignore the vicious spatter of the enemy's bullets. The legionaries needed no encouragement from me; quietly, efficiently and with occasional jokes they worked the two guns, maintaining a steady rate of fire as if they were on range practice.

It was difficult at that distance to be certain just where our shots were falling, but when I had satisfied myself as best I could that we were firing on target I stationed myself and my two runners in between the guns, where I could control them both. The enemy artillery and mortars were searching for us, their shells throwing up earth and stones around us. Shells from our own guns on the ridge behind whirred close overhead, some of them landing short, uncomfortably near. We had been in action for twenty minutes or half-an-hour when a mortar bomb landed on my right gun, dismounting it and scattering the crew. I hastened to the spot, to find the gunner dead and the sergeant severely wounded in the face and chest; there were no other casualties, but the gun was wrecked beyond repair. I withdrew the survivors of the section behind the shelter of the crest and returned to place myself beside my remaining gun. It seemed only a matter of time before it, too, must be destroyed.

Some fifteen minutes later a runner arrived from Bandera Headquarters with orders for me to cease fire and report to de Mora. On my way down the hill I met the Subteniente, red-faced and puffing, on his way to take command in my absence. I found the Major with his Company Commanders and the other machine-gun officers. It was a grim and gloomy gathering; even Cancela had lost his usual ebullient good humour. The rifle companies had suffered heavily and made little progress; even if they were to reach their objective it seemed impossible that they should capture it against such superior numbers. De Mora, who valued the lives of men he had trained and formed into this fine fighting unit, was unwilling to sacrifice them uselessly in such an ill-planned operation. On his own responsibility, therefore, he halted the advance, having accepted that the 16th Bandera, too, could make no headway; then he sent back a report to Colonel Peñaredonda and Division, requesting at least some air support or more artillery. It must have taken a great deal of moral courage for him to make this decision in the face of his orders. In the event it nearly cost him a court-martial; but it saved the 14th Bandera—and probably the 16th as well—from annihilation.

It began to snow. With numbed fingers we opened tins of sardines and tunny, spreading the frozen contents on lumps of hard bread; I have never been able to eat either of those fish since that time. The enemy had ceased fire; a dispiriting silence pervaded the dismal landscape of the Sierra under the murky yellow sky. In all my life I had seldom, if ever, felt so disheartened. The other officers shared my gloom, but the men, whether from ignorance of our situation or from natural good spirits, seemed in excellent humour. I noticed, with gratitude and almost a feeling of shame, one of the survivors from the crew of the gun I had seen destroyed, an energetic little man with a flair for buffoonery, he darted from post to post cracking jokes with his comrades in a high, squeaky voice that brought shouts of laughter and applause. His unquenchable gaiety, together with de Mora's quiet confidence, put new heart into me.

I was to need it. In the afternoon orders came to continue the attack. Indignant that neither Colonel Peñaredonda nor anyone from Division had thought it necessary to come forward and see the position for himself, we dispersed to our battle stations. I grieved for the men of the rifle companies, sent to futile execution by this heartless lunacy; I could not bring myself to look at de Mora. Strutting in front of my only machine-gun was the Subteniente, a bottle of brandy in one hand; he offered me a swig, which I refused, though unwillingly.

'Come, Mr. Peter!' he shouted, 'Let's see if those *cabrones* in the front can kill us!' Taking me by the arm he swaggered forward about twenty yards down the slope; there he stood and spread his arms, shouting insults towards the Republican lines amid a chorus of titters from the men. Of all the silly ways to get killed, I thought, and cursed myself for not checking the exhibitionism of this drunken mountebank. Yet I felt I must put a good face on it in front of the troops —though I wonder if they would not have respected me more had I bawled him out on the spot. To my relief the enemy chose to ignore us—if they even saw us —and after I minute I said: 'The battle is about to start again, Subteniente. I think you had better go back to Lieutenant Noriega.' He scuttled off down the hill like a bolted rabbit.

As my guns on the left opened fire I threw myself down beside my sergeant and gave the order to engage the enemy, checking our bursts through my glasses. The enemy replied vigorously, his bullets coming from the front and both flanks; they seemed to come at us like hail, with all this hiss and splatter of a heavy storm. Soon his mortars and his artillery joined in, repeating the pattern of the morning's battle. I tried to look as though this were the one thing in life I enjoyed, but with dry throat and thumping heart I doubt if I succeeded. I am inclined to turn red in the face when scared, and I couldn't help laughing when one of the ammunition numbers cried out: 'Look at the colour of the Alférez's face! It's giving away our position.'

It had stopped snowing, but the light was beginning to fade; it was becoming increasingly hard to make out the enemy parapets among the dark pine woods. The Republicans must have found the same difficulty, for I noticed that they were beginning to fire high. Suddenly, ,to my horror, our gun stopped firing; as the crew wrestled with it I heard the sergeant mutter fiercely, '*Percutor!*' with tears of vexation in his eyes. The firing-pin had broken, as too often happened with these old weapons. There was no way of repairing it, nor any means of replacement. I had no alternative but to withdraw gun and crew into cover behind the ridge. When I reported the mishap to Noriega all he said was, 'It doesn't matter, Peter. The Major is breaking off the action.' De Mora had just returned from the rifle companies in front, and from a conference with the commanding officer of the 16th Bandera on our left.

At nightfall we received orders to withdraw. A dejected and depleted Bandera dragged itself wearily back to the ridge it had left that same morning. There, after posting guards, we lay down to sleep in the snow, too weary to eat, too sad to even talk of the day's misfortune.

Thanks to de Mora our losses had been remarkably light in the circumstances —four officers and about a hundred men killed or severely wounded; the 16th

Bandera had suffered more heavily, losing a large percentage of officers. We expected to have to renew our attack during the next two or three days, during which I accompanied de Mora on several reconnaissances to try to discover a fresh and safer route for the advance. On the second afternoon de Mora called all officers to a conference, where he gave us our operation orders for an attack at dawn next day—supported this time, by air bombardment and a much heavier concentration of artillery. But that night the attack was cancelled. We were favoured by visits from various senior officers, including the Divisional Commander and General Yagüe himself. They were evidently impressed by de Mora's arguments, for the next orders we received were to dig in on the ridge and stabilize the front.

The ridge we now occupied was high and steep, its reverse slope thickly wooded. Along the top we strengthened the existing trenches, adding new strongpoints. We put two companies into the line, keeping the other in reserve; all our available machine-guns were needed for defence, but we switched round the crews to give everyone a rest. Those of us who were in reserve set about making ourselves as comfortable as possible, building dug-outs in the side of the hill, where we slept warm at night and entertained each other with lavish supplies of drink brought from Zaragoza. My batman, Paulino, built me a roomy dug-out with an ingeniously constructed fireplace and chimney. In the wall he levelled out a wide ledge of earth, spreading it lavishly with dried grass and covering it with a blanket to make it a comfortable bed; he hollowed out smaller recesses for seats all around and put a rough table of packing-cases in the middle of the floor. To me it seemed like a palace. With excellent food, few duties and plenty of rest our spirits soon rose, and I look back on those days as being among my happiest in the Legion.

Each day we saw large formations of enemy bombers, escorted by fighters, flying over us in the direction of Teruel; but they never bothered us. After the recapture of Teruel by the Nationalists, on February 22nd, the enemy abandoned the offensive on our sector, only troubling us occasionally with artillery bombardments by '75s' and heavier field guns; these caused very few casualties, but were alarming because our dug-outs were only thinly covered with earth. One morning a shell from a '75' struck a tree where four or five of my mules were tethered. I ran to the spot, expecting to find a shambles; instead I found all the mules unhurt, apparently not even frightened.

About this time I had another lesson in the workings of chance, in the form of a letter from my brother, once again at Gibraltar. He told me that his new observer, Charles Owen, had a brother who was also in the Legion; did I know him? His family were half Spanish and had lived in Vigo before the war. As it happened, there was a lieutenant in the 55th Company who came from Vigo, a sombre but friendly character called Arrieta; upon inquiry I had found that he knew the Owens well: Charles, the elder, had entered the Royal Navy about the same time as my brother; the younger, Cecil, had joined the Requetés at the beginning of the Civil War, had transferred to the Legion and was an officer in, Arrieta thought, the 14th Bandera. Now that FitzPatrick and Nangle had gone home, Cecil Owen and I must have been the only two British officers in the Corps; meanwhile our only brothers were in the same ship, flying together in the same aircraft. After receiving a citation for the Medalla Militar, Cecil Owen was killed in the Battle of the Ebro at the end of August, serving with the 16th Bandera.

During these days I saw much of Cancela and his officers in the 53rd Company; we would spend almost every evening together talking and drinking sherry, brandy or red wine in one or other of our dug-outs. They taught me to drink wine from the *bota*, the peasant's wine-skin which is held at arm's length to squirt a jet of wine down the throat. Only a little practice is needed to learn this method of drinking, and it is worth learning; a well-matured *bota* will vastly improve the roughest wine; slung from the shoulder it is easy and comfortable to carry. Thereafter I was never without one during my active service with the Legion; the trouble was that no sooner had I nursed my *bota* to maturity than someone would steal it and I would have to mature a fresh one.

Cancela's second-in-command was Lieutenant Torres, a dark, good-looking officer of about twenty-five, whose family operated a fruit-canning factory in Logroño, captain of the great wine-producing district of the Rioja. When I knew him he was a quiet-mannered, serious-minded young man, intending to go into the family business after the war; but he had been a wild youth in the stormy days of the *Frente Popular* government, earning his living in Madrid as a *pistolero* for his political party, the Requetés. All the political parties employed these professional gunmen, he said, to provide bodyguards for their leaders and to intimidate their enemies. On the outbreak of war Torres enlisted in the Requeté Militia, and was severely wounded in the lung. He was a conscientious and competent officer, much respected by the men. With the loss of Mentasti—the wounded officer I had met on my way to join the Bandera at Villanueva—the company had only one other officer, a young Andalusian, Antonio Marchán. A chemist's assistant from Seville, with all the Sevillano wit and *gracia*, he was inspired by a passionate enthusiasm for the spirit of the Legion and for Cancela as the personification of it. Gay, courageous and sincere, he was one of the sweetest-natured men I have ever met. He did not live long.

As a machine-gun officer I was neither very happy nor very efficient. Having resolved for some time to ask for a transfer to a rifle platoon, I now longed to join this cheerful and devoted company. One evening I summoned the courage to ask Cancela if he would take me in Mentasti's place. He readily agreed and promised to arrange it with de Mora as soon as we moved.

After a week of idleness I was ordered up to the line to take command of one of the machine-gun sections. My command post was a strongpoint on a hillock that dominated the position; it was comfortable enough to live in, protected from bullets and mortar bombs by walls and a low, domed roof of wooden beams and sandbags; but a single shell could wreck it. I had to be careful when walking through the trenches, for they were not deep enough to hide me, and we were under continual fire from snipers and machine guns. I soon became used to keeping my head down, but I hated the shelling. We did most of our sleeping during the day, standing to an hour before dawn and dusk and keeping alert at night in case of an attack. In the early hours of one morning, two days after I took over, my sentries heard noises close to our wire, about twenty yards down the slope in front; we fired a few bursts and the noises ceased. In the morning we saw two khaki-clad bodies entangled in the wire. When we retrieved them that evening we found them to be Canadians from the Mackenzie-Papenac Battalion of the International Brigades. Whether they had come to desert or to probe our defences we never discovered. At nine o'clock on the morning of February 28th I was ordered to withdraw my guns and rejoin the Bandera below; by ten o'clock I had completed the withdrawal. Around noon a '75' shell landed squarely on top of my recent command post, blowing it inside out.

---

[1] *Letters of Private Wheeler.*

CHAPTER NINE

At dusk on the same evening we left the pine-woods of Villanueva for the last time. We marched for eight hours, with only one halt, moving north-westwards along tracks over the Sierra de Cucalon until we reached the small village of Olalla. There were rumours that our High Command was about to launch a great offensive in Aragón in which we were to take part; replacements began to arrive to bring us to full strength, including a captain to take over the machine-gun company—a podgy, middle-aged officer, quiet and soft-spoken, very different from the domineering Almajach.

From Olalla we moved in lorries to Codos, a charming little place in the mountains east of Calatayud. This was a very rich part of Aragón, producing abundance in wine and olives. The sun shone warm on the white almond blossom, announcing the end of winter and the arrival of an early spring; as we drilled in the open in our shirt-sleeves the scented air that filled our lungs made us forget the bitter memories of the winter, and raised our hopes that the end of the war might at last be near. The people were friendly and hospitable. I was billeted with an old peasant and his wife, who gave me an enormous feather bed to sleep in and cooked me some of the best meals I ever had in Spain. They treated me almost like a favourite son, apparently delighted to have an Englishman with them; each evening after supper we sat talking over the fire and drinking a bottle of smooth *anis*, which the old man made himself and matured for many years. When the Bandera left, the old woman wept, and they would accept no payment from me.

Our comfortable time ended abruptly on March 6th, when the lorries came to take us to the front. We passed through the town of Cariñena and continued due east towards Belchite, which the enemy had captured the previous year. We reached the thirteenth kilometre stone at dusk, dismounted from our lorries immediately and moved swiftly off the road into the shelter of thick pine woods. Here we bivouacked for the next two days and nights. The enemy was only a mile or two away, strongly entrenched in fortifications which dominated the area; not only were we forbidden to light fires at night, but we must keep under cover all day. After the usual cold supper of bread, tunny and sardines, we lay down to sleep under the trees.

Next morning we heard the sad news of the sinking of the new Nationalist cruiser *Baleares* by Republican destroyers in the Mediterranean, with the loss of nearly all her crew. This was the first and only Republican success at sea; it showed a remarkable departure from their usual torpid tactics. The destroyers attacked in darkness, in the early hours of the morning, pressed their attack vigorously and, after launching their torpedoes, disengaged without loss. Rumours immediately circulated that they had been commanded by Russians or by Communist ex-officers of the Imperial German Navy; certainly there would be no officers of the old Spanish Navy left to command them. But the Nationalist Press was surely a little naïve when it abused the enemy destroyers for 'fleeing cravenly into the darkness' after discharging their torpedoes.

While Paulino was building me a shelter of earth and brushwood de Mora sent for me to say that he had approved my transfer to Cancela's company. Cancela assigned me to take over his third platoon; Marchán commanded the second and a new officer, Lieutenant Martín, the first. Torres remained as second-in-command of the Company. I had my hands full that day, getting to know the N.C.O.s and men of my new platoon and making myself familiar with their weapons. It was clear that in a very short time we should be in action again, and it was essential that we should feel confidence in each other. I had about thirty men, in two *pelotones*, each commanded by a very capable sergeant. They were a merry, self-confident crowd who seemed to know their jobs and to look forward to the prospect of battle; in addition I had two platoon runners, keen and intelligent lads who were to give me valuable and devoted service in the days ahead. All the rifle companies had been issued with new Fiat light machine-guns —two to each platoon. They were good enough weapons by our standards— light, accurate and giving a fair rate of fire—but they were liable to jam.

The new machine-gun captain asked me to a farewell party in his shelter that evening; it was a spacious structure. Besides the machine-gun officers and myself he had asked a number of others, including Cancela, Arrieta and a young lieutenant called Terceño who was temporarily commanding the 54th Company. De Mora had called a conference of all officers for nine o'clock the following morning. All our talk at first was of the impending attack: this time we should have plenty of support from aircraft and artillery, as well as superiority in numbers; but the enemy positions, we also knew, were extremely strong— considered impregnable by their defenders. The dug-out, lit by a single flickering candle, was filled with an air of tense excitement as we debated our chances of success. Some rash person had ordered a barrel of Cariñena wine, a sweet, heady red wine, not quite so disagreeable as it sounds; under its influence we soon relaxed and forgot our hopes and fears of the immediate future. Our host was determined not to let us go until we had finished the barrel—an impossible task even for so many of us. Much later I remembered getting to my feet with great difficulty, mumbling a slurred good night and then, foolishly, trying to stand to attention and salute. This was fatal. I ended up flat on the floor. Luckily Paulino was waiting outside to haul me to my bed.

My memories of the next week have been impaired, partly by the excitement and exhaustion of those days, partly by the passage of time; but I still remember clearly the aching head and throbbing eye-balls with which I awakened early next morning. However, fires were allowed in daylight and, after a mug of hot coffee, I was able to attend de Mora's conference feeling almost intelligent.

General Franco gave the Republicans no time to recover from their disaster at Teruel. Within a fortnight of the recapture of the town he had regrouped General Dávila's Army of the North in seven Army Corps along a line running from the Pyrenees to Teruel, poised for the greatest offensive of the war. This time the campaign was to be conducted along the blitzkrieg lines advocated by the Germans. Concentrating an overwhelming superiority of aircraft, artillery, tanks and troops, the Nationalists shattered the Republican defences and in less than six weeks swept across Aragón to the borders of Catalonia and the Mediterranean coast; cutting Republican Spain in two, this offensive virtually settled the outcome of the war. There were three phases of campaign: the first, from March 9th to 17th, comprised the breaking of the enemy front south of the River Ebro and the Nationalist advance to Caspe and Alcañiz; the second, from the 22nd of March to the 20th of April, saw the break-through north of the Ebro and the advance to the borders of Catalonia, with the capture of the towns of Lérida, Balaguer and Tremp and the power stations which supplied the industries of Catalonia; the last, which overlapped with the second, brought the Nationalists from Caspe and Alcañiz to the shores of the Mediterranean, south of Tortosa. My story is concerned only with the first phase.

This attack was launched by four Army Corps: on the left, with its left flank on the River Ebro, was the Marroquí Army Corps, commanded by General Yagüe and consisting of the 15th, 5th (Navarre), 13th and 150th Divisions, in that order from north to south. On the left centre with a Corps known as 'Agrupación Garcia Valiño', from the name of its commander; this contained two infantry divisions and General Monasterio's Cavalry Division. On the right centre was the Italian Corps, consisting of two Italian divisions and two mixed divisions. General Aranda's Army Corps of Galicia, with five divisions, formed the right flank of the advance. The 14th and 16th Banderas, under Lieutenant-Colonel Peñaredonda, made up the mobile striking force of the Marroquí Army Corps; for the present we were to operate as part of General Sánchez González's

5th Navarre Division.

At dusk, de Mora explained, we were to move forward to our assault positions, just east of the village of Villanueva del Huerva. The axis of our advance would be the Cariñena-Belchite road. After capturing Belchite we should continue eastward to Azaila, where we should join up with the 15th Division on our left, who would be advancing along the south bank of the Ebro. Our next objective would be Escatrón, after which we should move on the important road junction and enemy headquarters of Caspe. Much of this time we should be operating as motorized infantry in conjunction with tanks. The three rifle companies would take it in turn to lead the Bandera.

The assault would start to-morrow at daylight with an intense bombardment. Our first objective was a hill, known as the *Frontón*, a heavily fortified position of great natural strength. A *Frontón* is a *pelota* court—a Basque game something like fives; this hill was called the *Frontón* because its face rose perpendicularly, like the back of a fives court, dominating the plain across which we should be advancing. If there was any serious enemy resistance left after the bombardment we should have a hard time of it. A screen of tanks would move between one and two hundred yards ahead of us—one section of tanks to each company; a section of tanks consisted of six light German tanks, each carrying two machine-guns, and two of the captured Russian tanks, each mounting a 37 mm. gun; their crews were from the Tank Bandera of the Legion.

* * *

The sun had dropped below the horizon behind us when, at the head of my platoon, I followed the rest of the company out of the pine woods and down a winding track that led into a shadowy ravine. We were all in excellent spirits, partly because we were on the offensive again, partly because of our confidence in our commanders and partly because we believed that we were taking the enemy by surprise. Even so, we had no idea how complete our victory was to be; my own private exaltation sprang from the knowledge that at last I was going to get grips with the enemy under a company commander I liked and trusted unreservedly, and from my happiness in my new command. Some leaders have a genius for inspiring confidence by their very presence, making their subordinates feel themselves capable of achievements or endurance beyond their normal powers; de Mora was one of these, Cancela another, as both had proved and were soon to prove again. My platoon was singing *Mi Barco Velero*, a song they had adopted for their own and a popular song of the period; it had a gay, lilting rhythm, well suited to the quick marching step of the Legion. A clear, full moon came up, washing the sides of the valley in silver light and casting deeper shadows in the depths. Overhead we heard the rising drone of an approaching aircraft. An order came down the line to halt and keep close to the cliffs that rose above the road. The aircraft circled overhead for several minutes, then the pulse of its engine increased as it straightened into a run. In front and to the left of us we saw a series of flashes and heard the detonations of a stick of bombs falling on Villanueva del Huerva. We reached the bottom of the valley and started to climb to the further side. In a little while we emerged into open pasture, with hills on three sides intersected by ravines; in one of these ravines we halted for the night.

I slept well, warmly wrapped in my greatcoat and two blankets, awakening before sunrise with the first paling of the sky. The ground, covered with hoar-frost, was thick with troops, some still asleep, others bustling about or stamping their feet for warmth. Paulino brought me some bread and a few slices of smoked ham, which we ate together, washing them down with draughts of rough red wine from my *bota*. The sun rose in a clear sky, its early warmth giving promise of a perfect day of spring. I felt excited and happy. A runner arrived from Company Headquarters with orders for me to report to Cancela. There I found Torres, Marchán and Martín.

'The bombardment will be starting soon,' began Cancela. 'So I'll give you my orders now. We are the left-hand company of the Bandera today. The Comandante is deploying the Bandera in inverted arrowhead formation for this attack—the 53rd and 54th companies leading, with the 55th in the centre and a little to the rear. I am going to use the same formation for our company. Your platoon, Marchán, will be on the right, yours, Martín, on the left, with Peter's[1] in reserve. Torres and I, with Company Headquarters, will be in between the two leading platoons. Watch me carefully for signals. Above all, when you see me stop, halt your platoons immediately and get down on the ground. Keep your men well spaced out, and see that they keep formation and distance at all time. Don't hesitate to check your men whenever necessary'—he laughed—'it will keep their minds off the bullets!'

Soon after nine o'clock the first squadron of bombers flew over us towards the enemy, and our artillery opened fire with a barrage far more powerful than that which we had witnessed in the Sierra Palomera. The bombardment continued for over two hours with constant relays of aircraft and incessant fire from our batteries; if the enemy had artillery it was silent. Beyond the low ridge of hills in front of us, which hid the enemy from view, we could see columns of smoke and dust drifting upwards.

Shortly before noon we heard the rumble of engines as our tanks moved into position; a few minutes later the advance began. We left the shelter of the hills and began to cross a flat, open plain covered with coarse grass. Less than a mile in front of us I saw, for the first time, the bulk of the *Frontón*—a great black mass of rock rising sheer above the plain; a grey pall of smoke hung over and around it; clouds of earth and stones erupting from it as our guns continued their pounding. I deployed my platoon in open order, with one *pelotón* in advance and to the left of the other, myself and the two runners in the middle. I had plenty to occupy my attention, watching Cancela and seeing that my platoon kept station; it was a while, therefore, before I noticed how meagre was the enemy's fire. Our bombs and shells were no longer falling on the *Frontón*, but small units of our fighters were diving on the position, raking the trenches with the machine-gun fire. About two hundred yards ahead our tanks halted; at the same moment a burst of machine-gun fire passed uncomfortably close. As I saw Cancela halt I ordered my platoon to get down. I saw one of our captured Russian tanks fire three shots from its gun, then move forward; Cancela stood up and waved us on. A few bullets whistled past us and I shouted to my sergeants to keep the men well spread out; someone was hit over to the right—I saw the stretcher-bearers running across. Next moment I was treading on flattened barbed wire, and a line of trenches was gaping a few yards ahead of me; huddled in the bottom and slumped across the further parapet were a few dead bodies; the surviving defenders had fled. I now saw that for the last part of our advance we had been slowly climbing; this was the first line of the *Frontón's* defences. In a few minutes our two leading companies had occupied the whole of the position.

We could not believe that it had been so easy. The 53rd and 54th Companies had less than a dozen casualties between them, of which my company had two, neither of them serious. But when we looked around at the effects of the bombardment we began to understand why we had escaped so lightly; the whole mountainside was blasted into craters; parapets had caved in, trenches were filled with earth and rubble, pill-boxes had collapsed. A few nerve-shattered and tearful prisoners were being given cigarettes by our men before being sent to the rear; they belonged to one of the Republican second-line divisions: 'All the same,' said Cancela, 'if those had been first-class troops we should have suffered heavily.'

Half-an-hour later we formed in column on the Belchite road and continued our advance eastward. Having entered the deserted village of Funedetodos without opposition we halted there for food and rest. This village is the birthplace of Goya; the museum in his house had been gutted by the enemy, but a few of us left our ranks to gaze respectfully at his monument. In our immediate neighbourhood the fighting seemed to have subsided; but the sky was full of aircraft, and from a mile or two away to the south came the sound of intense machine-gun fire and the roll of bursting bombs. We met no more resistance that day. Other troops, who had taken our place in the van of the Division, were sweeping aside such hastily-organized opposition as the enemy could muster. As we marched along the road we saw ahead of us the 'circuses' of our fighters diving in rotation to machine-gun the fleeing Republicans, harrying them incessantly with hand grenades tossed from the cockpits as well as with their guns. Later we heard from prisoners that these grenades, although they caused few casualties, were very demoralizing. In this manner we continued until dark, when we encamped for the night on some high ground beside the road.

Cancela seemed satisfied with our performance that day. 'Of course,' he said, 'you had no chance to prove yourselves in action; but I could see you had your platoons well in hand.'

I awoke with the dawn of another fine, clear day. Before the sun was up we had started our advance along the road. After an hour of marching in columns we bore to the right of the road into open country and deployed in order of battle. Ahead of us lurched a section of our tanks, keeping a constant distance of about a hundred yards between themselves and our foremost files. The other two companies were leading the attack this morning; from our place at the rear it was difficult to see what was going on. Although the country seemed to be flat as a billiard table, no enemy fortifications were visible; however our artillery was firing in support, using high-bursting H.E. as well as percussion fuses, so that we could mark roughly where they were; moreover, our fighter 'circuses' were at work above them. When we approached we ran into small-arms fire; we halted and lay down while our heavier tanks blasted individual strongpoints and the light tanks swept the positions with their machine-guns. A few of our casualties came through to the rear, one or two on stretchers, others walking; among the latter I noticed the Bandera standard-bearer, a tall, fine-looking corporal with long black side-whiskers; he had a bullet in the thigh, but was limping along cheerfully enough, supported on the arm of a comrade, exchanging cracks with his friends in our company.

We remained on the ground for a little more than ten minutes, while the firing in front increased in volume and then subsided. Cancela rose and waved us on at a run. Once again I found myself tripping and stumbling over wire, but the fighting was finished before we reached the trenches. Beyond were several half-ruined shepherds' huts; against their walls about a dozen prisoners were huddled together, while some of our tank crews stood in front of them loading rifles. As I approached there were a series of shots, and the prisoners slumped to the ground.

'My God!' I said to Cancela, feeling slightly sick. 'What do they think they're doing shooting the prisoners?'

Cancela looked at me. 'They're from the International Brigades,' he said grimly.

We were allowed no time to rest. Reforming in column of platoons we struck left to rejoin the Belchite road further east, crossed it and climbed on to a ridge of the Sierra Carbonera. We had eaten nothing all day, and so, when a halt was called to allow the artillery to come into position, we were glad of the chance to swallow some food. Some of us were inhibited from eating by the old theory that if a man were hit in the stomach he would have a better chance of survival if he had eaten nothing; the drawback to this theory is that you cannot fight indefinitely on an empty stomach. My trouble, I found, was rather that as soon as I ever sat down to eat the order would be given for us to move on, and I would have to jettison my food in the scramble to join the platoon.

The spur on which we were halted overlooked the road where it ran through a ravine towards Belchite. Beyond the road rose a steep hill, on the top of which stood an imposing monastery, the sanctuary of the *Virgen del Pueyo*. This was one of the enemy's strong points for the defence of Belchite. The upper slope of the hill was honeycombed with trenches—no hurriedly improvised defences such as we had stormed earlier in the morning, but a well-planned system of fortifications cut deeply into the rock, with a clear field of fire in all directions. The view my glasses gave me was not reassuring.

A mountain battery was climbing the slope behind us to take up position on our left; I caught sight of Spaey, whom I had not seen since the morning of the battle of Villanueva del Rebollar, three weeks ago. After a while he walked over to join us:

'We shall be opening fire on that monastery soon.'

'Well, let's hope you make good shooting,' we answered; 'we've got to take it.'

'I don't think you need worry. By the time the guns and aeroplanes have finished there won't be much resistance left.'

Behind us, from the west, we heard the drone of aircraft. Following the line of the road from Cariñena appeared a squadron of silver twin-engined Junkers. In three flights they turned towards the monastery; when they were almost over it we glimpsed the flashes of sunlight on the falling bombs. Staring through my glasses I saw the whole hilltop erupt in reddish brown smoke, which blanketed the monastery for nearly a minute. The echoes of the explosion had barely ceased reverberating round the hills when we heard another squadron approaching; at the same time, from our ridge and from other heights across the road on our right, battery after battery of medium and field artillery opened fire. For the next ninety minutes our view of the monastery was hidden in a pall of smoke and dust; no sooner had one bomber squadron dropped its load than another would approach the target, while all the time the guns kept up their fire. At the end it seemed impossible that anyone could be left on that hill or, if they were, that they could still be capable of fighting. When the last bomber had turned away to the south and the shells had ceased to fall on the hill, all that we could see of the monastery through the thinning cloud of smoke and dust was a ruin with rubble spilled all round.

From the hills on our right descended a column of infantry, a khaki snake winding across the slopes towards the ravine. A few minutes later we were on our feet, making our way across broken country towards the foot of the monastery hill. Not a shot came from the top as we panted slowly upwards and picked our way through the torn barbed wire. Only the dead remained to great us, sprawled in the trenches and mangled under mountains of brick and stone.

Two of our companies, including the 53rd, were ordered to occupy the ruins for the night; the rest of the Bandera encamped at the foot of the hill. About five o'clock that evening we heard that the town of Belchite was in our hands.

The late defenders of the monastery included, as well as Spanish units, our old adversaries from Villanueva del Rebollar—American and Canadian contingents of the International Brigades. In their flight they had abandoned their personal belongings, including a large quantity of mail from home, some of it unopened. Cancela asked me to look through the letters in English while he and the other officers examined the Spanish. I had barely started to read when he called me back. I found him convulsed with laughter over a letter from a girl in Valencia to her boy-friend, which he insisted on my reading. It was a witty and salacious letter, every sentence alive with bawdy gaiety that was strangely moving in its cheerful allusions to the squalor and discomforts of that suffering city.

'You say you haven't enough to eat at the front,' she had written, 'so hurry back here as soon as you can get leave. At least I can promise you plenty of crumpet.'[2]

Some of the letters I had to examine were more tragically moving; letters from sweethearts, wives and even, in one or two cases, children. It was horrible to feel that many of these men, who spoke my own language and who had come even further from home to fight for a cause in which they believed as deeply as I believed in ours, would never return to enjoy the love that glowed so warmly from the pages I was reading.

'The radio is on,' a girl from Brooklyn had written, 'and I'm writing letters. Yours comes first of course. They are playing the Seventh Symphony. You know how that music brings us together, how often we've heard it together. Please, oh please, come back to me soon.'

The next day, March 11th, was marked by some ugly fighting in which my own carelessness nearly cost me my life. We had been advancing since dawn, after by-passing Belchite; about midday we went into action against a line of trenches and barbed wire similar to those we had stormed the previous morning. The enemy resisted tenaciously and the bare plain across which we were advancing hummed with bullets—most of them, fortunately, above our heads. We were one of the leading companies and my platoon was on the left. About a hundred yards short of the wire the enemy machine-guns pinned us to the ground. As we lay there, gathering ourselves for the final assault while our tanks blasted the position, as hell burst in the air almost directly over my head; the blast seemed to tear at my breeches and I felt a slight pain in my right thigh, like the slightest touch of a hot iron. I looked over at a jagged rent where a piece of shrapnel had ripped through the cloth, leaving a faint graze on the skin. I had time only to note that there were no casualties in the platoon, before I saw that the tanks were moving forward and Cancela was waving me on to the charge. I shouted to my men and, drawing my pistol, leaped over the remains of the enemy wire, closely followed by my two runners. A figure rose up at me out of the trench in front, levelling his rifle and slamming home the bolt. I aimed my pistol and tried to press the trigger; but nothing happened—I had forgotten to release the safety-catch. Even in that second of hypnotized terror as I watched the rifle come to his shoulder there flashed through my brain the bitter message: 'If ever a man deserved to die, you do now! You're no more use in a rifle company than you were in the machine-guns.' At that moment there came two rifle shots, almost simultaneous, from behind me; the man fell back into the trench. My two runners had been wider awake than I.

By now the Bandera had overrun the whole position; legionaries were moving among the trenches, dispatching with rifle butt and bayonet the few remaining defenders. The enemy were German soldiers from the Thälmann Brigade, good soldiers and desperate fighters, since even their homeland was barred to them. They expected no mercy and received none; I felt a sickening disgust as I watched the legionaries probe among the fallen, shooting the wounded as they lay gasping for water. I resolved to speak to Cancela at the first opportunity; I had not come to Spain for this. We had in our Company a German lance-corporal, known as Egon; I never knew his surname, for he was not in my platoon. He was a very young, quiet boy, with a baby face, fresh complexion and innocent light-blue eyes; he was not very popular with his fellows. Reporting for orders I found Cancela interrogating a prisoner; Egon was interpreting. When he had finished Cancela looked away at the legionaries around him, then motioned the prisoner away, saying 'A fusilarle'. Egon's face became suffused with excitement: 'Please let me shoot him, sir,' he begged. 'Please, let me do it.' His eyes were shining and a small droplet of spittle trickled down his chin. Cancela seemed surprised, but he told Egon to take the prisoner away. Trembling with excitement Egon jabbed his rifle into the prisoner's ribs, barking at him in German: 'About turn! Start walking!' They had gone about a dozen paces when the prisoner suddenly bent double and started to run, zigzagging as he went. In that flat country he had no chance. Egon fired two or three shots after him; then the legionaries around him joined in; within a few seconds the fugitive lurched and fell to the ground. Egon ran to him and fired a couple of shots into his head. He seemed a little disappointed.

We spent that night on a desolate, rocky mountainside, so precipitous that it was impossible to find a level place to lie down and sleep. Torres was suffering from acute tonsillitis and the rest of us from sore feet and frayed tempers, inflamed by a biting wind from which there was no cover. I thought it better to defer my discussion with Cancela on the shooting of prisoners to a more favourable occasion.

Such an occasion did not arise the next day, which was the most arduous of the whole offensive; for on that day the Marroquí Army Corps made a spectacular advance on foot of thirty-eight kilometres. Starting from a few miles east of Belchite, the 5th Navarre Division swept though the road junction of Azaila in the early afternoon and reached the south bank of the Ebro at the town of Escatrón late in the evening; by this rapid advance large enemy forces were cut off, with the Ebro at their back, in a pocket between Escatrón and Quinto to the north-west; there they were destroyed at leisure. As the spearhead of the Division, the Bandera covered a full twenty-five miles on foot during the day, marching and fighting from daylight until long after dark with scarcely a pause for rest.

Our manoeuvres followed a familiar pattern: preceded by an advance guard of tanks we marched at a forced pace along the main road; ahead of us flew fighters for reconnaissance and protection. At the first sign of resistance we would deploy across the country in battle order, the tanks extending in line abreast in front of us; if the position was strongly defended there would be a brief artillery preparation before we went into the assault, in the same manner as on previous days. Although we repeated this performance several times that morning and afternoon, our casualties were remarkably light; the speed of our advance had disorganized the enemy, who was throwing in his forces piecemeal in a vain effort to gain time for a stand further east. Only on one occasion did we meet serious opposition—in the morning, at a place between Belchite and Azaila, where the old front line used to run before the Republican offensive against Belchite in August 1937. Here the enemy trenches were deep and well traversed, stoutly reinforced with concrete, well concealed from observation yet commanding an excellent field of fire. They held us up for an hour before we overran them and their garrison of International Brigades.

At about five o'clock we were enjoying a brief rest on the top of a broad escarpment that overlooked the valley of the Ebro. I had taken off my boots and socks and was rubbing my swollen feet with surgical spirit, reveling in its refreshing coolness, when Spaey walked over from his battery.

'Hullo!' I greeted him, 'Your bloody battery dropped some shells pretty close to us this morning.'

'Nonsense! You infantrymen always think it's us when it's really the enemy shelling you.'

'Their artillery has been pretty accurate to-day for a change,' I observed.

'But not very accurate. You can think yourselves lucky they've got no officers. I'm prepared to bet those are sergeants in command of batteries.'

At that moment Colonel Peñaredonda approached with de Mora and two legionaries, escorting a prisoner, a lieutenant of Carabineros who had surrendered after the last engagement; he was a stocky little man with dark, curly hair, whom fear and exhaustion had made into a pathetic figure. The Carabineros, like the Guardia de Asalto, were especially detested by the Nationalists; few of their officers who were taken prisoner survived. Addressing Cancela, de Mora said:

'The colonel wants some men to shoot this prisoner.'

There was a wild scramble around me as a dozen legionaries leaped to their feet, clamouring for the job with an eagerness surprising in men who a moment earlier had seemed exhausted. Even Peñaredonda was startled.

'Quiet, my children, quiet!' He urged in a pained voice. 'There's nothing to get excited about. This is simply a creature who is about to pass over to the other side.' His unctuous tone barely veiled his satisfaction. He turned to de Mora:

'I think we'd better have an officer.' De Mora caught sight of Torres. 'Will you undertake it?' he asked. Poor Torres, still suffering from his tonsils, turned a shade paler.

When the prisoner had made his confession to our padre, Torres pulled himself together and, with obvious reluctance, approached the man; they spoke together for a moment; then they walked slowly towards the edge of the escarpment, the escort following. The prisoner stood with his back to us on the top of the bluff, gazing across the shadowed valley to the further side where the slanting sunlight touched the hills with gold. Torres stepped back, drew his pistol and shot him once through the back of the head.

It was after midnight when we halted beyond Escatrón, turned off the road and encamped for the night on a cliff-top overlooking a small tributary of the Ebro. After a while Cancela returned from a visit to Bandera Headquarters with news that we were to rest all the next day. 'I'll spit the liver of the man who tries to wake me before eight o'clock!' he announced as he sank to the ground.

It was over lunch the next day that I nerved myself to ask Cancela:

'Where do the orders come from that we must shoot all prisoners of the International Brigades?'

'As far as we're concerned, from Colonel Peñaredonda. But we all think the same way ourselves. Look here, Peter,' he went on with sudden vehemence, 'it's all very well for you to talk about International Law and the rights of prisoners! You're not a Spaniard. You haven't seen your country devastated, your family and friends murdered in a civil war that would have ended eighteen months ago but for the intervention of foreigners. I know we have help now from Germans and Italians. But you know as well as I do that this war would have been over by the end of 1936, when we were at the gates of Madrid, but for the International Brigades. At that time we had no foreign help. What is it to us if they do have their ideals? Whether they know it or not, they are simply tools of the Communists and they have come to Spain to destroy our country! What do they care about the ruin they have made here? Why then should we bother about their lives when we catch them? It will take years to put right the harm they've done to Spain!'

He paused for breath, then went on: 'Another thing; I mean no offence to your personally, Peter, but I believe that all Spaniards—even those fighting us— wish that this war could have been settled one way or another by Spaniards alone. We never wanted our country to become a battleground for foreign powers. What do you think would happen to you if you were taken prisoner by the Reds? You'd be lucky if they only shot you.'

Torres's quiet voice interrupted: 'If it comes to that, what chance would any legionary stand if he were to fall into their hands, especially into the hands of the International Brigades? We know what they did to their prisoners at Brunete and Teruel.'

'We realize you can't feel the same as we do,' concluded Cancela, 'but please, Peter, do not speak to me of this again.'

Nevertheless, I knew this was not the policy of the Nationalist High Command, who already had several thousand International Brigade prisoners in a camp at Miranda de Ebro, and who released all of them a few months later. Spanish prisoners, of course, were decently treated by the Nationalists at this stage of the way, with the exception of regular officers of the armed forces, who were regarded, by a curious process of thought, as traitors. Apart from the difficult question whether International Law can be applied to a civil war, I believe that its rules afford no protection to volunteers from non-belligerent countries. For myself, if I were taken prisoner, I expected no mercy.[3]

While we were enjoying our rest on the 13th, other forces were mopping up the numerous large pockets of the enemy isolated by the last few days' advance. Although doubtless necessary—and certainly welcome to us—this delay gave the enemy time to reorganize his defence and give us a nasty shock a few days later.

The following day remains in my memory for one of the most horrible incidents in my experience.

The horror of it is still with me as I write; nor, I fear, will it ever leave me. I can scarcely bear to write of it now. At noon next day we were still resting on our cliff-top when I was ordered to report to Cancela. I found him talking with some legionaries who had brought him a deserter from the International Brigades—an Irishman from Belfast; he had given himself up to one of our patrols down by the river. Cancela wanted me to interrogate him. The man explained that he had been a seamen on a British ship trading to Valencia, where he had got very drunk one night, missed his ship and been picked up by the police. The next thing he knew, he was in Albacete, impressed into the International Brigades. He knew that if he tried to escape in Republican Spain he would certainly be retaken and shot; and so he had bided his time until he reached the front, when he had taken the first opportunity to desert. He had been wandering around for two days before he found our patrol.

I was not absolutely sure that he was telling the truth; but I knew that if I seemed to doubt his story he would be shot, and I was resolved to do everything in my power to save his life. Translating his account to Cancela, I urged that this was indeed a special case; the man was a deserter, not a prisoner, and we should be unwise as well as unjust to shoot him. Moved either by my arguments, or by consideration for my feelings, Cancela agreed to spare him, subject to de Mora's consent; I had better go and see de Mora at once while Cancela would see that the deserter had something to eat. De Mora was sympathetic. 'You seem to have a good case,' he said. 'Unfortunately my orders from Colonel Peñaredonda are to shoot all foreigners. If you can get his consent I'll be delighted to let the man off. You'll find the Colonel over there, on the highest of those hills. Take the prisoner with you, in case there are any questions, and your two runners as escort.'

It was an exhausting walk of nearly a mile with the midday sun blazing on our backs.

'Does it get any hotter in this country?' the deserter asked as we panted up the steep sides of a ravine, the sweat pouring down our faces and backs.

'You haven't seen the half of it yet. Wait another three months,' I answered, wondering grimly whether I should be able to win him even another three hours of life.

I found Colonel Peñaredonda sitting cross-legged with a plate of fried eggs on his knee. He greeted me amiably enough as I stepped forward and saluted; I had taken care to leave my prisoner well out of earshot. I repeated his story, adding my own plea at the end, as I had with Cancela and de Mora. 'I have the fellow here, sir,' I concluded, 'in case you wish to ask him any questions.' The Colonel did not look up from his plate: 'No, Peter,' he said casually, his mouth full of egg, 'I don't want to ask him anything. Just take him away and shoot him.'

I was so astonished that my mouth dropped open; my heart seemed to stop beating. Peñaredonda looked up, his eyes full of hatred:

'Get out!' he snarled. 'You heard what I said.' As I withdrew he shouted to me: 'I warn you, I intend to see that this order is carried out.'

Motioning the prisoner and escort to follow, I started down the hill; I would not walk with them, for I knew that he would question me and I could not bring myself to speak. I decided not to tell him until the last possible moment, so that at least he might be spared the agony of waiting. I even thought of telling him to ty to make a break for it while I distracted the escorts' attention; then I remembered Peñaredonda's parting words and, looking back, saw a pair of legionaries following us at a distance. I was so numb with misery and anger that I didn't notice where I was going until I found myself in front of de Mora once more. When I told him the news he bit his lip:

'Then I'm afraid there's nothing we can do,' he said gently. You had better carry out the execution yourself. Someone has got to do it, and it will be easier for him to have a fellow countryman around. After all, he knows that you tried to save him. Try to get it over quickly.'

It was almost more than I could bear to face the prisoner, where he stood between my two runners. As I approached they dropped back a few paces, leaving us alone; they were good men and understood what I was feeling. I forced myself to look at him. I am sure he knew what I was going to say.

'I've got to shoot you.' A barely audible 'Oh my God!' escaped him.

Briefly I told him how I tried to save him. I asked him if he wanted a priest, or a few minutes by himself, and if there were any messages he wanted me to deliver.

'Nothing,' he whispered, 'please make it quick.'

'That I can promise you. Turn around and start walking straight ahead.'

He held out his hand and looked me in the eyes, saying only: 'Thank you.'

'God bless you!' I murmured.

As he turned his back and walked away I said to my two runners: 'I beg you to aim true. He must not feel anything.' They nodded and raised their rifles. I looked away. The two shots exploded simultaneously.

'On our honour, sir,' the senior of the two said to me, 'he could not have felt a thing.'

I went to examine the body. There was no doubt the death had been instantaneous. When we had buried him I reported to Cancela, who said:

'The Comandante has asked me to give you this message: he wishes you to know that he deeply regrets the shooting of that Englishman; that he considers it a crime, and that the responsibility for it must rest for ever upon the conscience of that—he spat the word—'gentleman! You know, he went so far as to send a pair of legionaries after you to shoot you if you did not immediately carry out his order? That is something we shall none of us forget.' He looked hard at me: 'We are all sorry, Peter.'

I excused myself hurriedly.

I was not left long to my thoughts. In a few minutes a messenger came running from Cancela to tell me that the Bandera was on the move. Two hours later we were assembled beside the main road that led from Escatrón to the important town of Caspe, the last town in Aragón remaining in Republican hands. Here we waited until dusk, when a company of tanks rolled up the road from Escatrón. Behind them came a column of lorries, into which we climbed. It was dark when we started towards Caspe, the tanks moving about half a mile ahead of us. A few minutes later we put out our lights. The driver beside me seemed to think that we were bound for Caspe itself, in a sudden dash to take the enemy by surprise; I doubted we should get so far in our lorries, even at night. It was impossible to see anything of the country, for the night was very black.

After half-an-hour the column came to a halt. I heard the sound of small-arms' fire ahead of us. A minute later bursts of tracer fire flew over us from high ground on our right. This was the first time I had been under fire from tracer; I was fascinated to watch the little red bulbs, each seeming to approach ever so slowly, then suddenly accelerating to fly past with a very frightening hiss. I began to wish that someone would order us off the lorries. I heard our tanks moving across towards the enemy positions and saw the flash of tracer from their guns. In half-an-hour the engagement was over and we were on the move again. There was another brief action a mile or two further on, which held us up for a quarter-of-an-hour, while we stayed in our trucks. We finally halted near the hamlet of Chiprana, about eighteen kilometres from where we had started. Leaving our lorries, we climbed to the top of the hills overlooking the road, where we spent a cold and uncomfortable night, alert for possible counter attacks.

We made steady progress next morning, moving well ahead of the 5th Division. We met no serious opposition but came under a good deal of artillery fire in the afternoon, most of it from '75s'. Towards evening we halted on the fringes of the thick olive groves that cover the approaches to Caspe. The sun was setting when a runner from Bandera Headquarters hurried up to me with orders to report at once to the Major. I found de Mora with his company commanders on the top of a knoll overlooking a wide vale, from which a silvery-green sea of olives swept upwards to a distant hill. Briskly he gave me my orders:

'Yours is the leading platoon of the leading company to-night. I want you to make a reconnaissance through those olives ahead of us and try to find out where the enemy are located. Put out scouts in front, but don't let your men get scattered in that close country. Get moving as quickly as you can.' Calling the platoon to attention, I briefly outlined our mission, issued my orders and detailed a pair of scouts to move fifty yards ahead; I took the rest at a trot down the valley. We had hardly started to move through the olives when we were fired on by a machine-gun from the hill in front. As the bullets slapped against the trees I felt a sharp stinging pain across my ribs; realizing that it was only a flesh wound and that nobody else was hit, I looked around quickly for cover. In front of us was a ditch with an earth bank, one of many that intersected the plantations. I ordered the platoon into the ditch while I tried to fix the position of the machine-gun through my glasses; but I could not find it in the falling light. Unwilling to waste time I gave the order to advance, hoping that the gloom would cover us as we went deeper into the trees. Suddenly we came upon a railway, a single track running at right angles to our advance; about twenty yards to the right was a level-crossing where the main road from Escatrón ran over the line. As I halted before crossing the exposed piece of track my senior sergeant caught my arm:

'Listen, sir!' He jerked his thumb in the direction of the road.

From behind us I heard the deep rumble of heavy engines coming up the road towards the crossing.

'We're ahead of our own tanks, sir,' said the sergeant, looking worried.

For a moment I failed to grasp the significance of what he had said. Then I realized that the tanks, seeing us ahead of them, would certainly take us for the enemy; in the half-light they could not see our uniforms, and they must suppose themselves to be the most forward of our troops. This was one of those moments, with which the textbooks deal so light-heartedly, when the young officer must use his initiative. The decision was taken out of my hands by the sergeant himself; bulling out a white handkerchief he ran to the level crossing, planted himself in the middle of the road, and started to wave it, shouting through a cupped hand at the leading tank. This must have had a nervous gunner; I was running to join him when there was a bright flash and a sharp explosion; the sergeant staggered to the side of the road with his hands to his face. A few seconds later the tank lumbered into view, with its turret open and the officer peering out of tis top. When he saw us he halted, horrified at his mistake. At that moment Cancela came to tell me to discontinue the reconnaissance and rejoin the company with my platoon. The sergeant was carried back to the medical officers, who patched him up and sent him off to hospital; miraculously he had escaped serious injury, although he had a nasty gash in the side of the face. I was going to miss him badly. His *pelotón* was taken over by a tall, red-haired Portuguese corporal called Mateu, a good enough soldier but lacking the sergeant's experience.

The Company crossed the railway in extended order and began to move at a rapid pace through the olives that covered the gently rising slope beyond. We were no longer under fire, but I found it an exacting task to keep touch with Cancela on my right in the thick country and gathering darkness; our feet sank heavily into the earth, we fell into ditches and stumbled up banks, sweating and cursing in a frenzied effort to keep pace. The graze on my ribs smarted and irked me where my clothes pulled on the caked blood. I tried to console myself with the thought that it was better to be one of the heroic wounded than one of the glorious dead; but even so, I found my temper running very short. I had no idea where the rest of the Bandera was, nor even in which direction we were advancing. As far as I was concerned, the military situation was, in official language, 'obscure'.

Quite suddenly we halted in the last of the fading light. Ahead of us the hill rose sharply and steeply to a conical mound, falling away gradually to our right in regular, unbroken lines of olives. A hundred yards or so on our left ran a road, roughly parallel with the line of our advance; we could hear tanks moving along it. One of the rifle companies was sent to occupy the mound, supported by Colomer's machine-gun platoon. We stayed where we were, near de Mora, ready for instant action. It seemed that we had run into heavy opposition and would not take Caspe without a fight.

When we were settled I went to Bandera Headquarters to get one of the doctors to dress the graze on my side. I found them in a small hut with the Padre and de Mora; the latter was lying down, looking very tired. Back with the Company I forced myself to eat something, and then lay down to sleep. But I found sleeping as difficult as eating. The air was charged with tension and uncertainty. The night was full of the sounds of impending battle: explosions and bursts of machine-gun fire from over the hill, and the rumble of tanks along the road on our left. At first I was confident that the tanks were ours; but soon afterwards I was disturbed to hear the sound of engines coming down the road from the direction of Caspe. A few minutes later the last of my complacency was shattered by a series of sharp reports, followed immediately by the hiss and explosion of shells among the surrounding olives. The tanks were hostile; moreover they were shooting at us. At first we lay where we were, hoping the bombardment would subside; on the contrary, it increased rapidly in volume, shells raining on the ground around us or bursting in the branches overhead. I heard the clamour of Colomer's machine-guns from the mound, and the thud of grenades. Cancela shouted to the Company to stand to; I felt better on my feet. The shelling continued for half an hour; then it died almost as suddenly as it had started, to be succeeded by a silence almost unnerving in contrast. I doubt if any of us slept for the rest of that night.

We were on our feet again before dawn. De Mora ordered the Company to take up a position over on the right and prepare for a strong enemy counter-attack. Our delay on the 13th and 14th had given the Republicans time to pull the bulk of their retreating forces into Caspe; these they had strengthened with four International Brigades and part of a fifth. Pushed far ahead of the 5th Division, our two Banderas and supporting tanks were now thrown back on the defensive in face of vastly superior numbers; furthermore, the enemy controlled the high ground. Until substantial reinforcements could arrive we should be batting, in the language of Mr. Naunton Wayne, on a very sticky wicket.

In the first faint grey light we moved to our new positions, crossing without incident one very exposed piece of open grounds, bare of olives or other cover. Cancela posted my platoon on the left, Martín's on the right and Marchán's in the centre; at first he had planned to keep mine in reserve, but with the length of the front we had to hold and the danger of enemy infiltration on the left, he felt he could no longer afford the luxury of any reserve but that of his own headquarters. Our orders, Cancela explained, were to hold our positions at all costs; rather than retreat we must die where we stood. Remembering the open ground across which our ammunition supplies would have to reach us, I wondered if we should be able to achieve even that usefully.

As the sun rose we heard the first sounds of battle over on our left, where the rest of the Bandera was engaged. I was relieved to note that the enemy seemed to be very short of artillery; apart from the 37 millimetres of tanks I could hear none.

In trying to describe the action that followed I am at a disadvantage which anybody who has been an infantry subaltern in battle will appreciate: I had little idea of what was happening anywhere but in my own immediate vicinity, and not always a clear idea of that; moreover, my mind was so fully occupied at the time that, even while I was in hospital immediately afterwards, I found it difficult to recollect the sequence of events.

De Mora could not spare us any machine-guns, and so we must depend on our own Fiats and rifles. I was thankful that the olives at least made it difficult for the enemy to use mortars.

Taking advantage of the cover afforded by the banks and ditches, I disposed my platoon with a view to giving the maximum depth to my defence. 'Fire at anything you see moving to your front,' Cancela had said. there was, of course, no time to cut away the olives that blocked our field of fire, giving excellent cover to an attacker. I awaited the enemy's assault, trying to dissemble my anxiety from the men. I did not have long to think about it. One moment we were waiting, the men crouched behind their weapons, myself scanning the olive groves through my glasses: the next, bullets were hissing through the trees, slashing the trunks, spattering earth from the bank in front of us. I heard Marchán's guns go into action a second before my own. All we could see of the enemy was an occasional glimpse of a crouched figure darting from one tree to another. For a while we held them off; but at the end of twenty minutes, when the firing died down, I had lost half a dozen men and we knew the enemy were appreciably closer.

I sent a runner to Cancela with an account of the action; he returned with orders for me to report in person. I found the Captain looking grave.

'There's a hill just above you on your right,' he said, pointing it out to me. 'Take one of our *pelotones*, get up there as quick as you can and hold it at all costs—at all costs.' he repeated.

I was getting to know that phrase pretty well. I ran back to my platoon, made a quick readjustment of my plan of defence, and ordered Corporal Mateu to follow me with his *pelotón* to the top of the hill. There was a small piece of open ground in front of the foot of the hill. As we ran across it a sharp burst of fire came from the left; I felt a searing pain across the front of my throat; a bullet had torn a shallow furrow through the flesh, but I had no time to think about it as we scrambled panting up the hillside. On the top was a small space of open ground before the olives began again on the farther edge; hurrying across it we dug in on the other side. When I returned to Cancela to report my dispositions, he said:

'Go and get that wound dressed.'

I hesitated. It had bled profusely, making a picturesque mess on the front of my jacket, but it was causing me no trouble; I felt that this was scarcely the time to bother with trivialities.

'Don't argue,' he said, 'the sooner you go the sooner you'll be back.' And so I went, running all the way.

Bandera headquarters was under heavy fire from the enemy tanks. It seemed the fuses of the shells were adjusted to explode immediately on impact, so that many of the burst in the trees on striking a branch or even a twig, producing an alarming effect and causing a number of casualties. The sound of fighting seemed to come from all sides. De Mora was looking a little worried. I noticed the Subteniente sitting by himself, huddled despondently beneath an olive tree, peering through the collar of his greatcoat; he looked like an old, mournful, red-faced sheep. Paulino greeted me with a look of friendly concern.

'You again!' laughed Doctor Larrea when I came up to him. I apologized for bothering him because I could see that he and Ruiz had their hands full, with the wounded pouring in from all companies. De Mora, standing near, looked up.

'I think you ought to go to hospital,' he said, 'those throat wounds can be very dangerous.'

I had not the face to follow up this suggestion and ran back to rejoin Cancela. I found the battle had broken out again; I could hear the sound of continuous small-arms fire from ahead and from the right where Marchán and Martín were closely engaged. As I arrived a runner hurried across from Martín with the news that he was under severe pressure, heavily outnumbered, and in danger of being outflanked.

'He's got to stay there,' said Cancela. Sounds of firing came from the hill which I had recently occupied. Cancela told me to take the rest of my platoon up there to join Mateu.

'The position on the left can look after itself; but that hill is vital. We ought to have occupied it before. For God's sake hold on to it, Peter!'

For some reason the enemy had ceased to press his attack on the left, so that my *pelotón* was not engaged when I reached it. We climbed to the top of the hill without difficulty and took up firing positions. Mateu was glad to see us; with his limited firepower he had been unable to stop the enemy closing in. I cursed the thickly-planted olives which prevented my seeing where the enemy were, or at what point they were likely to launch their main attack; their fire seemed to come from straight ahead and from the right, saturating us in a deluge of bullets that was carrying off my men at a frightening rate.

During one of the intervals I found Cancela beside me, come himself to see the situation. I told him quietly that if the enemy were in the strength that I believed them to be, I did not see how we could avoid being overrun. He nodded gravely:

'This is a classic Legion situation, Peter, but don't be dismayed.' He raised his voice in a laugh for everyone to hear: 'We'll enjoy our drinks more in Zargoza when we look back on this day.'

'Well,' I said, 'I certainly hope the girls will look better than they did the last time I was there.' Our poor sallies were acknowledged by a few grins from the men. Suddenly one of them attracted our attention, pointing over to the left, where we saw a figure crawling painfully on his stomach across a piece of open ground, trying to reach the shelter of some trees.

'Shall we shoot, sir?' he asked.

We studied him for a moment through our glasses, then Cancela said firmly: 'He's wounded. Leave him alone.'

He walked back down the hill, leaving me to make my final arrangements to meet the assault which I knew could not be long delayed. Both my Fiats were still in action and I reckoned I had enough ammunition and grenades; on the other hand I had already lost half my men, including one of my runners. However, the rest were in good heart and I knew they would stand by me. I resolved that, before we were finally overrun, I would pull my force back to the edge of the hill and make my last stand there, where we could at least deny the position to the enemy. There was a small ditch which would give us some protection. I warned my sergeant and Corporal Mateu of my intention.

'They're on the move again!' cried the sergeant as a fresh hail of bullets started to fly among us. This would be the final assault. While we poured our full volume of fire into the attackers—or what we could see of them—the legionaries tearing at the bolts of their rifles, slamming them back and shooting as fast as they could, the Fiat gunners firing in long steady bursts, I ran, crouching, from one *pelotón* to the other, checking the fire to see that we were not shooting too high and trying desperately to forecast the point of the enemy's principal thrust. But from what I could make out they were converging on both sides in equal and overwhelming strength. They were getting terribly close to us. The explosions of grenades were added to the crackle of small arms fire. Realizing that if we were going to disengage we must do so at once, I gave the order to retire; in a few seconds we had covered the twenty yards to the edge of the hill. We were now ready for what I reflected grimly was, literally, a 'last ditch' stand. I sent my runner to warn Cancela.

Across the clearing we saw the gaps in the olives fill with figures. I noticed one of them steady himself against a tree and take aim, I thought at me; I fired twice with my pistol and he disappeared. I gave the order to fix bayonets. I remember being fascinated by the sight of the diminutive legionary beside me working feverishly to get his bayonet onto the boss of his rifle, his little monkey face puckered with anxiety, the tassel of his forage cap bobbing up and down like an agitated yo-yo. We were a pitiful remnant, a bare dozen; around us the ground was strewn with the bodies of our comrades. In a few moments— minutes at most—the enemy would close and that would be the end. As I unwound the tape from a grenade and slung it across the clearing I understood that at last I was face to face with death; that there was nothing I could do about it. With that realization there came over me an extraordinary sense of freedom and a release from care. A few yards in front of me I caught sight of the red and yellow colours of a Nationalist flag which had been carried by one of our *pelotones*; it was on the ground beneath the dead body of its bearer. Running forward—I realize now, of course, that this was the most puerile dramatics—I seized the flag and ran back with it; calling encouragement to my men, I waved it in a wide arc. Whether this nonsense had any moral effect I am unable to say: a second or two later there was a soft thud beside me, an anguished shout of warning from my runner—'*Cuidado mí Alférez* !—and a violent explosion.

I was knocked clean backwards clean off my feet to roll over and over down the hill, ending up in a heap in front of Cancela, who, with Torres, was on his way to visit us. I pulled myself up, dazed and shaking, to feel the blood pouring down my left arm. I began to climb back, but Cancela reached the top before me; taking one look at the situation he shouted: 'Down the hill, all of you!'

I feared we should be shot down as we ran, but the enemy was slow to press his advantage. We halted about a hundred yards beyond the foot of the hill, behind an earth bank among the olives, where we found Cancela's headquarters.

Nearly a year later I learnt that our adversaries this day were a British battalion of the International Brigades; Captain Don Davidson, my informant and one of its Company Commanders, told me that their own casualties were very heavy.

Although embarrassed by the enemy's capture of the hill, with the dominating position it gave them, Cancela was determined to hold his ground, covering de Mora's right flank. After pulling the remnants of Marchán's and Martín's platoons, which were in danger of being cut off, he awaited the enemy's next move. But the latter made no attempt to advance further, and confided himself to raking us with small-arms fire. In the end it was our own artillery that forced us from our new positions, coming into action now for the first time; I suppose it had just arrived. A battery of six 77 mm. dual purpose anti-aircraft guns began to fire at the enemy on the hill. Unfortunately, three shells in every salvo landed in our midst. After what we had been through we were enraged as well as unnerved each time we heard the guns fire to know that within a few seconds we were likely to be disemboweled or maimed by one of our own shells; pressing my face into the earth and shrinking as the blast of the explosion swept over me, I cursed a fate that had delivered me from an honourable if uncomfortable death at the hands of the enemy, only to consign me to ignominious and messy annihilation by my own guns. After a grim ten minutes, during which time we had as many casualties, Cancela took us back another hundred yards, where life seemed peaceful in comparison, with only the enemy's bullets to worry us. Soon even these abated, and we reckoned that the guns, with their high rate of fire, must be giving the enemy as bad a time as they had given us.

About twenty minutes later we had our first really happy moment of the day: a section of our tanks appeared through the olives behind us, negotiating the difficult country with remarkable agility.

'It looks as if the worst is over,' said Cancela. He turned to me: 'Now go and get that arm looked at.'

I was glad enough to obey; the blood had clotted and the arm was stiff and painful. I moved warily through the olives, having no wish to be knocked out at this stage of the battle by a sniper's bullet. I came to the edge of the open ground we had crossed early that morning; among the trees on the other side I saw Lieutenant Terceño, who shouted to me not to linger while crossing it; I saw what he meant when a couple of bullets sang past my head as I hurried over. The tanks were still shelling Bandera headquarters, where Larrea and Ruiz were working calmly and efficiently, while the Padre was busy among the rows of wounded on the ground. De Mora looked strained and grim, but he cheered up a bit when I told him about our tanks. The Subteniente was wailing that he had been hit in the chest by a shell fragment that was hurting him horribly. When the girl *practicanta* had cut away the sleeve of my jacket and shirt, prattling happily to me the whole time, Larrea examined the wound; there were no bones broken, but splinters of metal had lodged in my forearm and above the elbow. He looked at me with his hands on his hips:

'This time, damn it, you really are going to hospital! I haven't enough lint and bandages to keep on wrapping up a bloody great bean-pole like you.'

When he had dressed the arm and put it in a rough sling he wrote out a hospitalization order, which he handed to me:

'You'll find a casualty clearing centre somewhere back down the road; just go on walking till you find it.'

De Mora added: 'Be careful for the first part of the way; it's dangerously exposed to fire.'

Accompanied by Paulino, who, I was delighted to see, and hung on to my wine *bota*, I walked away from the battle. We went very carefully at first, for Paulino told me that several casualties had been hit again as they were being carried back, and a stretcher-bearer had been killed. For the first half-mile bullets flew over us, but afterwards we were pretty safe. About three-quarters of a mile back we passed a culvert where the railway ran over a sunken track. Here Colonel Peñaredonda had established his command post, though he alone knew what control he could exercise at such distance. He greeted me with effusive cordiality:

'Hi Mr. Peter! What's it like up there?'

'Arduous, sir,' I repeated sourly. 'You could see it better from up the road.' And I passed on.

Soon afterwards we came to the main road, where we met a column of cavalry, who hailed us gaily; they were part of General Monasterio's division, just arrived from Alcañiz. With a light heart I realized that the agony of the Bandera was over. A mile further we came to a tent, marked with a red cross, in a small grove of oaks; in a field beside it a battery of 10.5 cm. field guns was in action. I gave my hospitalization order to the medical officer in charge, who told me that I should have to wait some time before an ambulance could evacuate me —he indicated the rows of wounded lying around; I had better make myself as comfortable as I could in the meantime. Paulino spread a blanket for me at the edge of the trees. I fell asleep immediately, undisturbed by the firing of the guns fifty yards away.

In the hospital train at Zaragoza, where the ambulance dropped me late in the evening, I found myself sharing a compartment with Antonio Marchán. In the turmoil of the battle I had neither seen him nor given much thought to the fortunes of his platoon; but I had gathered from Cancela that he had done very well. He had become a casualty soon after me, with a grenade wound in the hand; it was more painful than mine but did not seem to damp his gypsy spirits. Two days later we were reveling in hot baths and clean, comfortable beds in the General Hospital at Bilbao.

The day after we were wounded Caspe fell to an assault from three directions by overwhelming Nationalist forces. The International Brigades, particularly the 14th (British), had fought a gallant and determined action, inflicting terrible casualties on the 16th Bandera and ourselves; our own company had barely twenty men left, out of the hundred and ten with which we had started the battle.

---

[1] I was always known in the Bandera by my Christian name, the double consonant at the end of my surname being difficult for Spaniards to pronounce.

[2] The Spanish idiom was *No te faltará conejo.*

[3] Captain Don Davidson, an English officer of the International Brigades whom I met subsequently, confirmed that I should certainly have been shot if captured.

CHAPTER TEN

After three days in hospital my wound ceased to throb and I felt a great deal better. I knew my brother was still in Gibraltar and I was anxious to see him before his ship left for England. The Commandant of the hospital in Bilbao was sympathetic, although he was doubtful if I was yet fit for so long a journey, especially as I should have to hitch-hike; but I convinced him that with my uniform and my arm in a sling I should have no trouble getting lifts, and with Paulino to look after me I should come to no harm. He only insisted that I report to the Red Cross Hospital in Seville for treatment on the way. We reached Seville in two days, riding some of the way in luxury in the car of a Divisional General, which I had stopped on the road outside Burgos. After a night in the Red Cross Hospital, where I had my arm dressed, I made the rest of my journey to Algeciras in a very uncomfortable and dilapidated old bus, which lumbered across country along appalling roads for eight hours; I reached the Rena Christina Hotel in the evening, feeling that the Commandant in Bilbao might have been right.

A telephone call to Gibraltar brough my brother to Algeciras the next day and Charles Owen, his observer, with him. They had borrowed a car in Gibraltar, in which we drove to Seville and, on the way back, to Jerez, where we were taken over the *bodegas* of the Marqués del Mérito—a delicious but exacting orgy lasting more than two hours. Our host was the Marqués nephew, whom I had known in San Sebastian. This young man, much to his grief, was unfit for military service; instead he had worked for the S.I.M., or Military Intelligence, where one of his jobs had been to keep tabs on me. The Nationalists were no more spy-conscious during the Civil War than the British were during the last war, or than the Americans have been since. My position as an infantry subaltern was not one where I could have been very useful as a spy; but the S.I.M. probably thought that any lone foreigner would bear watching. In fact it never occurred to me to offer my services to the British Intelligence authorities, even if I had known how to do so; certainly they never approached me—I suppose I was considered too irresponsible.

After saying good-bye to Neil and Owen I returned to Seville, where I entered the Red Cross Hospital as an in-patient; not only did I need some rest after the past few days, but I felt that I had tried the patience of medical authorities far enough. In the hospital the medical attention was adequate, the nursing conscientious rather than skilful, the food plentiful and excellent; but there was little opportunity for rest. In the first place, I was in a ward with fifteen other officers of about my own age and, like myself, only lightly wounded; secondly, it was now Holy Week, when the processions went on all night and no one seemed to mind how long we stayed out, provided we were back in time for our treatment in the morning. On Easter Sunday there was the usual grand bull-fight, the first of the season. Cancela used to tell me that since he had gone to war he no longer enjoyed watching bull-fights; that the reality of his own escapes from death blunted for him the thrill of watching those of the matadors. I could not agree with him; to my mind the exhilaration derives as much from the flow of colour and grace of movement of cape and body, the grandeur and tragedy of the culmination, and the brilliance of the whole magnificent spectacle, as from the crude physical excitement of watching me risk their lives.

Towards the end of April I was discharged from the Red Cross Hospital with a week's sick leave, which I decided to spend in San Sebastian. Through the good offices of Captain Burckhardt of the German Condor Legion, whom Neil and I had met in Algeciras, I was given a seat in a Junkers 53 transport aircraft as far as Burgos; I hitch-hiked the rest of the way. While I was in San Sebastian I paid a visit to Biarritz to see my friends, the O'Malley Keyes. It was a foolish thing to do: the Spanish authorities made no objection, but as soon as I arrived in France I realized that I was going to have difficulty in getting out again; officers of the Non-Intervention Commission were patrolling the frontier and it was made clear to me that I stood no chance of obtaining a French exit visa to return to Spain. However, at a dinner party one evening at Bar Basque at San Jean-de-Luz a friend pointed out that a simple way was to walk up the disused funicular that climbed La Rhûne, a prominent mountain nearby, along the top of which ran the frontier.

'Plenty of picnickers walk up there to spend the day,' he explained. 'When you get to the top you should be able to find an unguarded spot where you can slip across. Anyway, it's worth taking the chance.'

I agreed, and he promised to drop me in his car at the foot of the funicular next morning.

The Bar Basque at this time must have been one of the liveliest spots in Europe: a gathering place of play-boys and play-girls, journalists, black-marketeers and conspirators of every nationality and political complexion. It seemed to pivot on the sinister but intriguing personality of a Mittel-European barman known as Otto, whose pale face, light eyes and thin lips had been schooled over the years into expressionless immobility; he made it his business to know everybody, and everything about everybody. I remembered meeting Esmond Romilly there, with whom I had been at school at Wellington; although a charming young man of great intelligence, initiative and personal courage, he had early acquired unpopularity with the school authorities for editing, in collaboration with his elder brother, Giles, a subversive newspaper, entitled *Out of Bounds*. When the Spanish war broke out he joined the Republicans. On this occasion I asked him to have a drink, with no other motive than the wish for a friendly chat; he accepted, but kept looking furtively around the bar, hissing in apology: 'This place is full of Fascists!'

On a perfect morning of early summer I left my friend's car at the foot of La Rhûne and started to walk along the track leading to the funicular. In an old machine-gun ammunition case, which did not look as suspicious as it sounds, I carried my uniform, intending to put it on as soon as I crossed the frontier. I had not climbed more than two hundred yards up the railway when I heard a shout and, turning, saw a gendarme coming after me. I waited for him with what I hoped was a smile of polite attention. When he arrived, puffing but amiable, I explained that I was an English tourist out for a day's picnic on the mountain; I indicated my ammunition case, saying that it contained a bottle of wine and my lunch. He beamed and wished me *bon apetit*. I went on my way, a bit out of breath myself. It was a monotonous as well as tiring climb along the sleepers; La Rhûne is about three thousand feet high. Fearing that there might be a guard post in the building at the head of the funicular, I left the track a quarter-of-a-mile short of it and cut across the side of the mountain to the top. A little way down the farther side was a thick belt of woods, already coming into leaf. I imagined that the frontier would run along the crest, but in any case I ought to be safe once I had reached the trees. Trying not to hurry, I began to walk across the crest with as nonchalant an air as I could manage although my heart was pounding uncomfortably. I heard a shout from the funicular building a few hundred yards to my right; pretending not to hear, I walked steadily without turning my head or hurrying my pace. I heard a couple of shots. But by now I was walking down the farther side, among large rocks which I hoped would give me some shelter. I dived into a narrow gully, ran down it for a hundred yards, paused a moment to get my breath, and scrambled over a small spur to drop down the other side to the shelter of the woods. I did not linger there, but hastened downhill for another quarter-of-a-mile, where I struck a small track leading further to the south. Now at last I reckoned I must be in Spain; however, I decided to take no chances and to keep on my civilian clothes until I was quite certain.

When I had cooled off and felt calmer I started to walk down the track. I had gone about half-a-mile when, round a corner, I walked into a Spanish soldier, his rifle slung on his shoulder, his jaws moving rhythmically as he plodded up the hill.

'Good afternoon,' I said. 'I am Alférez Peter Kemp, of the 14th Bandera of the Legion, returning from leave in France. I should be grateful if you would escort me to your guard post, where I could change into my uniform and perhaps get transport into San Sebastian.'

The soldier looked at me in astonishment, his jaw dropping open to reveal a bolus of well-chewed bread. After a moment he nodded and turned on his heel, beckoning me to follow. Half-an-hour later I was drinking a beaker of *chacolí* with the officer in charge of the frontier post of Vera.

At the General Mola hospital in San Sebastian, where I had to report for my final examination before rejoining the Bandera, the doctors found that the wound on my upper arm showed signs of festering. In consequence, it was not until the middle of May that I was allowed to return to duty.

I had no idea where I should find the Bandera after all the operations that had taken place since my departure, but Zaragoza seemed the best place to inquire. There I met an English girl, Pip Scott-Ellis, who had been serving as a nurse with the Nationalist armies since the previous autumn; she had come to Spain with no knowledge of the language, had passed the Red Cross examinations in Spanish within a few months of her arrival and had worked in field hospitals throughout the battle of Teruel and the offensive south of the Ebro. During the latter she had been attached to the Marroquí Army Corps and, with a Spanish friend, Consuelo Montemar, had worked in a hospital at Escatrón under heavy fire from artillery across the Ebro; both girls had been proposed for the *Medalla Militar* for their gallantry during these bombardments.

I found the Bandera resting in the village of Villanova de Alpicat, a few miles from Lérida, just inside the borders of Catalonia. Any regrets I may have felt for the end of my leave were immediately dispelled by the warmth and kindness of my reception by de Mora and my brother officers. Marchán had already returned; and so with my arrival the Company had all its old officers back; but among the other ranks there were many new faces, replacing our losses at Caspe. Colonel Peñaredonda was no longer with us, having been posted to another command. Cancela told me that shortly after I left him our tanks had stormed the hill in line abreast with every gun blazing; when he reached the top the scene of carnage was indescribable. The '77s' had done most of the damage and the tanks had completed the work, so that the company took possession of the hill without another casualty. He had found the flag lying where I had dropped it, the pole broken clean off by the explosion of the grenade that had blown me off the hill; he gave me the flag as a souvenir. Since the fall of Caspe the Bandera had not been in action.

Villanova de Alpicat was a pleasant little village in flat country intersected by canals and irrigation ditches. We had horses and plenty of leisure for riding, good food and plenty of wine. But I had a strong impression that the sympathies of the villagers were not with us, although they were polite enough to our faces. Separatism and Anarchism were the strongest political forces in Catalonia; I felt that these people would not be sorry to see the village change hands.

Towards the end of May we found ourselves in the line again. In this sector the front followed the course of the Segre, a river that flows past Lérida in a south-westerly direction to join the Ebro about half-way between that town and Caspe; twelve miles below Lérida the Nationalists had established a bridgehead across the river at the village of Serós, where the river flows through a deep ravine about three hundred yards wide. throughout the months of June and July this bridgehead was garrisoned by the 14th Bandera. It was an unhealthy and uncomfortable position, consisting of a semi-circle of trenches about half a mile in diameter and nearly the same in depth. It was connected with the ruined village of Serós on the west bank by a narrow iron bridge, which was under constant artillery fire. Our trenches ran along high ground, which rose steeply from the river bank; near the bridge there was a small piece of ground at river level, on which stood a damaged house that served as Bandera Headquarters. Of our three rifle companies two occupied the trenches, the third being disposed around Bandera Headquarters in reserve.

The Republicans were entrenched on three sides of us, at distances of between one and two hundred yards; they were second-line troops of inferior quality and poor morale, but their situation enabled them to shell and mortar us from three directions, inflicting a small but steady drain of casualties. Sometimes it was more unpleasant for the company in reserve than for those in the trenches; enemy artillery was persistent in its efforts to destroy Bandera Headquarters, and although they never succeeded, owing to the steep angle of fire, it was unnerving to be Orderly Officer during a bombardment and have to sit unprotected beside the field telephone while shells rained close around. Otherwise our worst enemies were the flies, the bad water and the heat. I have never seen so many flies before or since; they hung above us in great black clouds, covered our food, polluted our drink and swarmed all over our faces. It says something for the qualities of my brother-officers that during those two months there were no quarrels among us and we managed to have a great deal of fun together.

On the 23rd July my company was occupying the trenches on the left flank of the bridgehead, a hundred yards from the enemy. It was a day of intense heat. During the morning I had mortared the opposing trenches at Cancela's request, trying to silence a troublesome machine-gun. I lunched as usual with the other officers of the Company in Cancela's dugout. Afterwards I remained behind to discuss an operation he wanted me to undertake after dark—to lead a patrol against an enemy working party which we had heard the previous night in no-man's-land in front of us. While we were talking the enemy started to mortar our position—I suppose in retaliation for my effort in the morning. Their trenches were so close we could hear the thuds of the discharges long before the grenades burst; they were using 50 mm. mortars, not the more lethal 81 mm. I excused myself in order to go and see that all my men were taking shelter; then I returned to Cancela's dug-out. He was lying on his bed, and I sat down on a packing-case by the table in the middle of the floor just inside the entrance. I had started to explain my plan, using my hands for gestures, as one does when speaking Spanish, when a grenade burst in the opening beside me. I barely heard the explosion: I was conscious of it only as a roaring in my ears, a hammer blow on the left side of my face and a sickening dizziness as I fell to the floor. My mouth seemed to fill with a sea of pebbles; as it fell open the sea resolved into a deluge of blood and the pebbles into fragments of my back teeth; twice more the floor welled up into my mouth to pour in a widening pool across the floor. I watched with a detached bewilderment, changing to near-panic. 'Oh God!' I prayed, 'don't let me die like this, in terror!' I took a grip on myself, remembering how someone once said to me, 'You're never dead till you think you are'. Cancela, on the bed, was unhurt; he provided a comic interlude by standing over me, exclaiming in tones of sincere and horrified concern:

'Are you hit, Peter? Tell me, are you hit? He pulled himself together; faintly through the singing in my ears I heard his strong voice calling for stretcher-bearers. Slowly I rolled over my back, then painfully raised my head to examine my wounds; my mouth and throat felt numb and soggy, I could not speak, my jaw hung loose—I realized it was shattered; there was a bloody gash across each hand, another at the top of my right arm and something at the back of my head. Cancela examined my body and assured me that the haemorrhage was not internal. Heartened by this news and filled with exhilaration that follows shock and precedes collapse, I motioned away the stretcher-bearers and walked three or four hundred yards down to the Bandera Headquarters. On the way I stopped to rest: leaning against the parapet I looked out north-eastwards along the shimmering band of the river to the old stone citadel of Lérida dancing in the heat haze. Somehow the sight of that harsh and alien landscape drove into my fuddled mind the firm resolve that I would not die there, far away from my home.

At Bandera Headquarters Larrea and Ruiz were busy with other casualties from the bombardment; but as soon as they saw me they shouted to an orderly to lay me on a mattress and make me comfortable. They had their hands full, and it was nearly half-an-hour before they could attend to me. I lay on the mattress, my head propped up on a haversack and greatcoat, watching the black clusters of flies settle on the wounds in my hands and feeling the movement of their buzzing through my jaw; I watched them with interest, even fascination, as though from a long way off. By the time Ruiz came to look at me the flies were congealed into the wounds; he worked on me quickly but with surprising gentleness, cleaning and bandaging while he talked to me about the wonderful time I was going to have in San Sebastian when I was well again. Larrea came to help him, and then they tried to cheer me by a discussion of the joys of leave and love of a cool climate. I was soon to hear what they really thought. After giving me injections of anti-tetanus and anti-gangrene serum and a shot of morphia, they went away to arrange the evacuation of the wounded. After a while I heard them whispering; they probably thought I was asleep, but in fact I seemed to hear everything with increasing clarity:

'It's no good sending Peter back,' one of them said, 'he won't live more than a few hours.'

In my mind flooded that view of the Segre and the ruined citadel of Lérida, filling me with the determination to overcome this death that threatened me. Slowly I raised myself on one elbow; painfully I turned my head, caught their gaze and held it. Larrea smiled:

'Send him in the first ambulance.'

*　　*　　*

The war was over before I saw the Bandera again. In July 1939, I visited them in a village near Madrid to say good-bye for the last time. I was on my way to England, the threat and excitement of another war hanging over me; my former comrades, with years of peace ahead of them, were already falling under the spell of that post-war reaction, called by C.E. Montague 'Disenchantment', which spread throughout England in the twenties and Spain the forties. Now that the stimulus of imminent battle was over, routine training and discipline seemed to have lost much of their purpose. The temporary officers were awaiting demobilization and the uncertainty of civilian life; the regulars could look forward only to the monotony and slow promotion of peacetime soldiering. Now, too, they had time to mourn the good friends they had lost in action—the Bandera had been heavily engaged in bitter fighting in the Pyrenees at the beginning of the year. Antonio Marchán was dead, half his face blown off by a grenade thrown from a trench which he was storming at the head of his platoon. Arrieta was killed by a stray bullet a moment after he had dispatched a prisoner with his pistol.

I last saw de Mora in Madrid in the spring of 1951, when he was a lieutenant-colonel; he had commanded a battalion of the Blue Division in Russia —an experience he seemed to have enjoyed. Cancela, he told me, was a major in an infantry battalion in the Canary Islands. Larrea, whom I saw at the same time, was also a major.

'When I sent you off in that ambulance from Serós,' Larrea told me, 'I didn't expect you to live very long.'

* * *

During the weeks that followed I was to experience something of the self-sacrificing generosity that is part of the Spanish nature. In the ambulance that took me to the hospital at Fraga—a ten-mile journey over rough roads pitted with shell-holes—a gunner lieutenant with his left arm shattered by a shell splinter stood over me, bracing his body with his foot against a stretcher on the other side, holding me on to my own stretcher with his remaining arm to prevent me being shaken out by the bumps; there were six of us serious casualties in the ambulance with only one attendant.

In the hospital at Fraga, where I arrived late at night, I met with a stroke of luck that may have been decisive: the medical officer on duty was Captain Tomás Zerolo, one of the most brilliant surgeons in Spain; a Canary Islander by birth, he had taken his degrees in London. Hearing him talk to me in English raised my morale immediately. I had not once lost consciousness since being hit. Now Zerolo explained that he must operate immediately, to clean the wounds and remove fragments of metal that had lodged in them; but, for medical reasons which I could not understand, he dared not give me an anesthetic. He offered me some brandy instead, but my throat was so burnt by white-hot metal from the mortar bomb that I could not bear the thought of alcohol. While he probed the wounds and cut away the burnt and infected flesh, he helped to take my mind off the pain by talking quietly and incessantly of England and the things he loved in London—the roses at Regent's Park, the sweep of the Thames from Chiswick to Greenwich, Ferraro's food at the Berkeley and his favourite night-clubs. When he had finished he bound my jaw together so skillfully that the broken bones eventually knitted of their own accord.

I remained conscious, unable to sleep, all that night, the next day and the following night. Each time I felt the approach of oblivion I would be jerked awake as though by a violent explosion. On the morning of the third day Zerolo came to my bedside with a long face:

'I'm sorry old boy, but I've got to send you to Zaragoza right away. I hate to do it, but I've just had orders to clear this hospital immediately for a heavy intake of casualties.' He tucked an envelope into the pocket of my shirt:

'This is for your doctors in Zaragoza; it explains that there are still pieces of metal in your hands and jaw. See that he understands.'

I was past caring. I did not know that the Battle of the Ebro had begun that morning—the last desperate Republican offensive—and that in a week every hospital in Aragón would be over-flowing with the wounded. Many months later Zerolo told me that he had not expected me to survive the move; I know that his skill on that first evening was decisive.[1]

It was a grim journey: two hours on a stretcher inside a hot and stuffy ambulance, driving at high speed along a road pitted with shell-holes, where every bump sent a spasm of agony through my jaw. I remember little of my first days in the General Hospital in Zaragoza, because at last I began to lose consciousness for long periods of time. I have a vivid picture of the chief dental surgeon, a cross little man with steel-rimmed glasses and a grey goatee beard, who, after probing my mouth for a few minutes, asked how he could be expected to operate on anyone whose throat was so badly burnt. He seemed to think it was all my fault. Severe urticaria from Larrea's serums added to the pain of my wounds and the discomfort of the heat—it was agony to swallow even saliva, and I dreaded the liquid meals that were forced down my throat. Most of all I dreaded the arrival of the dressing trolley each morning; there was a deep hole in the joint of each of my thumbs, into which they would pour neat surgical spirit. Usually I fainted. I was, however, lucky in the nurse who looked after me, an angel of skill and kindness who never seemed to sleep, for at whatever hour of day or night I rang my bell she was always there to help me.

During my conscious periods I used to have visits from two of my friends: a retired American general, Henry Reilly, a red-faced, white-haired, warm-hearted old man who lived near Paris and was visiting Nationalist Spain as an observer; and Eileen O'Brien, a small, purposeful young woman who represented an organization called the Irish Christian Front. I had met Miss O'Brien in

Salamanca the previous September, General Reilly on my last visit to Zaragoza. I could not speak at all, but was happy to listen to them and the news they brough me of the world outside my tiny, whitewashed room. I remember how my spirits would rise at the sight of the General's burly figure staggering into my room beneath a crate of beer—though it was agony for me to drink it—his friendly red face pouring with sweat and his breath coming in short gasps as he panted his indignation against the Spanish Government, who had just issued an edict forbidding civilians to shed their jackets in public; this was published in the newspapers with a preamble full of humourless pomposity of which the Nationalist Government was fond: only Zulus (why pick on them, we wondered) and similar savages, it announced, went about naked; in a civilized country, such as Spain, gentlemen must appear decently clad in jacket and tie—presumably also trousers, though these were not mentioned.

Soon the hospital filled with wounded from the Ebro. A young Requeté officer from Navarre with a mangled leg was brought into my room. He was in terrible pain, his face green and waxy with sweat. Unlike me, he never complained of his wound, but expressed himself delighted to be sharing a room with an Englishman who had come to fight for the cause of Spain. I woke up one day after a long period of oblivion to find that he had gone. Eileen O'Brien told me the reason; the hospital was overcrowded, with fresh casualties pouring in; one of us two had to be moved to another hospital further away. I was unconscious when the order came, but the Requeté contended that, as an English volunteer, I must have priority over him; although he was in no better state than I to travel, he insisted on going. Deeply moved, I begged Eileen to find him and thank him for me. She shook her head:

'I can't. He died on the way.'

*　　*　　*

At the end of the first week in August I was moved to General Mola Hospital in San Sebastian, which was to be my home for the next three months. Despite the rigours of the journey the climate of San Sebastian was a wonderful relief after the heat of Zaragoza; because it was a base hospital the medical attention was very much better. For the first week I took little interest in my surroundings; although I was no longer in acute danger, I was still in considerable pain and could only sleep after heavy doses of morphia, which I was not denied. I was fortunate in coming under the care of three distinguished doctors: the Catalan doctor Soler, a dental surgeon called Scherman and the famous Irish-American plastic surgeon, Eastman Sheean. Sheean had run his own hospital for the British

Army in the First World War, after which he had gone to America, where he had a fashionable and lucrative practice lifting the faces of the ageing rich; but his hobby was travelling round Europe, treating wounded ex-Servicemen without payment; just before coming to Spain he had paid a visit to Turkey for this purpose. He took wonderful care of me, and, when I was better, accompanied me on long walks to help me to recover my strength. The nursing in Mola Hospital was supervised by nuns, devoted and kindly souls whose indifference to the principles of asepsis nearly drove Sheean mad; they had an irritating habit of waking me in the middle of the night, when I had barely managed to fall asleep, to ask if I would like a cup of coffee. The routine nursing was done by enchanting women who, before the war, would never have been permitted by their families to go out without a chaperone; the effect of their charm and beauty on our morale made up for any deficiencies in their knowledge or skill.

At the end of August Scherman told me that he would have to operate on my jaw to remove the broken and septic fragments of teeth, bone and metal that still remained there; he warned me that it would be a painful business because, for some reason that I did not understand, he would not be able to give me any effective anaesthetic. The day before the operation I had a visit from Michael Weaver and George Sheffield, who had been staying with the Hennesseys in Cognac; they brought with them a bottle of Three Star brandy. Next morning, when I was wheeled down to the operating theatre, I took the bottle with me and asked Scherman if I might use it in place of the anesthetic he couldn't give me.

'Certainly! I might even have a nip with you.'

I started with an enormous swig, he with a very small one to encourage me; then he set to work. Whenever the pain became too much for me I signaled him to stop and took a long pull at the brandy. In this way I finished the bottle, feeling comparatively little pain during the operation, although I felt a great deal when the effect of the brandy had worn off. I was quite proud of myself until I remembered that this was the manner in which operations were usually performed before the last century.

A few days later I was moved from the large ward where I had been since my arrival, to a small room with two beds. As I entered it for the first time I was greeted by a shout from the other bed: 'Why, Goddammit, you old bastard!' and saw my friend, Goggi von Hartmann. He had a bullet in the arm—the nineth or tenth wound of his life—which had damaged the main nerve; but he seemed to rise above it. After a lengthy and painful operation, with only local anesthetics, he found it difficult to sleep, even with morphia; he would therefore swear horribly, when awakened in the night by the light being switched on, to find a smiling nun offering him a cup of coffee. We besought the nuns to abandon the practice, but with the obstinacy of the truly pious they persisted—for three nights. On the third night, no sooner had I been awakened with the light in my eyes than I was startled by a couple of deafening reports in quick succession from Hartmann's bed; there was a pungent smell of cordite as the room was plunged into darkness; a shower of splintered glass fell to the floor, followed immediately by a sharp scream and the clatter of breaking cups.

'Next time,' von Hartmann shouted as the door banged behind the fleeing nun, 'I shoot *you*, not the light!'

We made a good recovery from our operations, gaining strength rapidly. By the end of the first week of September we were already on our feet; we began to go around the town, visiting Chicote's every evening and often dining out afterwards. It may seem surprising that hospital discipline allowed us such latitude; but the theory seemed to be that the freedom would benefit our morale without seriously endangering our recovery. For myself, I found that a few glasses of gin or whisky deadened the pain in my throat, making it easier for me to swallow the soft foods that were all that I could manage; from this it was a very short step to drinking far too much. 'You be careful,' said Scherman to me, 'or you'll get yourself a red nose and become a dull fellow.' Von Hartmann throve on the treatment, sometimes staying out all night and slipping back to the hospital just in time for breakfast. One morning he ran straight into the Mother Superior in the entrance hall. Without batting an eyelid he opened the conversation with a cheerful but respectful: 'Good morning, Reverend Mother! I'm just back from early Mass.' The good woman beamed at him:

'Ah Captain, if only you could persuade some of the other boys to follow your example!'

I was less amused one evening a few days later when I had gone to bed early: von Hartmann came in at midnight looking morose and dangerous.

'I have had a fight with two officers of the Legion. They are coming here to kill me.'

'Well they won't get very far,' I said, 'the guards will stop them.'

He shook his head as he finished undressing:

'They will come. But they will get a big surprise when they come in here.'

He cocked his automatic and released the safety catch.

'Now,' he said, climbing into bed, 'I have my hand on this all night.' And he had, too; the barrel, where it lay on the pillow, pointed straight at my head.

The Munich crisis came upon us in the middle of September, filling me with particular alarm as I considered the difficulty of my own position. There was general certainty among the Nationalists that, if war were to break out, the French would immediately attack Franco; unable to leave hospital, enlisted for the duration of the Civil War in the Nationalist Army, I was threatened with a very delicate situation, which at best could only land me in a Nationalist concentration camp. Whatever the merits of the Munich settlement, it was for me, personally, an unmitigated blessing. My Nationalist friends evidently considered it was the same for them; I have never been stood so many drinks as I was in Chicote's the night we heard that the immediate danger of war had been averted. Curiously enough, at the end of the crisis the general opinion in Nationalist Spain seemed to be, not that British prestige had suffered a severe blow, but rather that by her initiative Britain had assumed the leadership of Europe.

Early in October I applied for convalescent leave to England; it was clear that I should not be fit for active service for at least another three or four months, and I saw no reason why I should not convalesce as well in England as in Spain. The application would have to be approved by the Generalissimo, and so I went to Burgos to try and pull a few strings there. I was lucky enough to get an interview with the Colonel commanding Medical Services at G.H.Q., who was most sympathetic and undertook to forward my application immediately, together with his own recommendation; I also met with the Duke of Piñahermosa, one of General Franco's A.D.C.s, who promised to speak personally to the great man. Three weeks later I received news that I had been granted two months' leave in England, dating from the day I crossed the Spanish frontier. At the end of November I arrived home.

*　*　*

I never doubted that my application for home leave would be granted, once it came to the personal attention of General Franco. Abused by his enemies, criticized by his allies and even by his friends, he was nevertheless, like all good commanders, devoted to the interests of his subordinates, especially the officers of the Foreign Legion which he had helped to found. The following July, when I was passing through Burgos on my way to England, having obtained my discharge from the Foreign Legion, I was informed by the Duke of Piñahermosa that the Generalissimo wished to see me.

When I had passed through the enormous gates of his headquarters, receiving an impressive salute from the Moorish guard, walked along a curving drive and climbed a flight of stone steps, I was shown into a long, dim ante-room, full of heavy, black furniture. After a lengthy wait, for there were several people before me, Piñahermosa escorted me through a door to a small sitting-room, with another door leading out of it. Knocking on this further door he disappeared, leaving me to seat myself on a small sofa by the window.

Five minutes later the door opened to admit a small, tubby figure, dwarfed by the broad scarlet sash and pendulant gold tassels of a full general. As he came towards me with short, brisk steps I sprang to my feet and saluted:

'*A sus ordines, mi General* !'

He told me to sit beside him; then, inkling his dark sombre face towards me and putting his hand on my knee to emphasize his words, he began to speak in one of the quietest voices I have ever heard. He talked for half-an-hour, practically without intermission. He had always admired the English, he said, especially their system of education with its emphasis on self-discipline, breeding the spirit of adventure that had made so small a country the ruler of so great an empire. He regarded the British Empire as perhaps the greatest bulwark against Communism in the world; but he doubted that the British were fully alive to the Communist danger. Whenever any of his friends returned to Spain from a visit to England he made a point of examining them on all aspects of English life: political, social, and economic. It seemed to him that our Universities in particular—perhaps because of their commendable anxiety to preserve intellectual freedom—were paying too little attention to the spread of subversive influences among our youth.

Throughout this interview his tone was informal and friendly, neither didactic nor condescending; sensitive, no doubt, to the embarrassment I should feel if I had to express my own views, he invited no comment. At the end he rose, shook hands gravely, thanked me for my services and wished me luck.

'What will you do now?' he asked.

'Join the British Army for this coming war, I suppose, your Excellency.'

He cocked his head, then gave a wintry smile:

'I don't think there will be a war.'

I wonder what he really thought.

* * *

In England I was plunged into a political as well as a social mêlée. The former involved me in such various activities as writing for *The Times* and for monthly reviews, addressing Members of Parliament in a committee room of the House of Commons and speaking at a meeting in Northampton in company with disillusioned ex-members of the International Brigades. I was astonished by the initiative and vitality of Republican propaganda in Spain—fortified, of course, by the growing fear of Germany; certainly the Republicans seemed to have the ear of Fleet Street, where the Nationalist voice was only the faintest of squeaks. I found myself involved in bitter and often painful controversies with some of my best friends; for the Spanish Civil War aroused in ordinary Englishmen an intensity of interest and partisan feeling unusual in people notoriously indifferent to the affairs of other countries. On top of these activities a series of parties with friends in London and with my brother and sister-in-law at Portsmouth scarcely helped my convalescence. My mother did her best to look after me; Sir Arnold Wilson asked me to stay at Much Hadham, where he tried to make me rest, and Archie James put his comfortable house near Brackley at my disposal for rest or writing. Nevertheless, when my leave was due to expire at the end of January I was far from well. Fortunately for me, the Duke of Alba, the Nationalist Representative in London, had observed this himself. He sent for me to say that he had caused my leave to be extended for another two months and forbade me to return earlier. It was typical of that great man that he took such trouble over the welfare of someone who could have been no use or interest to him.

When eventually I was able to return to Spain the Civil War was over. The Battle of Ebro, which had caused the Nationalists some anxious moments and severe casualties, ended on November 16th with the withdrawal of the beaten remnant of the Republican Armies. Two days before Christmas the Nationalists began their offensives against Catalonia; on January 26th they entered Barcelona. Rejecting all peace overtures, whether directly from the Republicans or through the intermediacy of foreign powers, General Franco launched the last offensive of the war on March 26th, 1939; two days later his troops entered Madrid. He was the master of Spain.

---

[1] I was sad to read the news of his death in *The Times*, early in 1956.

ACKNOWLEDGEMENTS

I would like to express my appreciation of the kindness of the Oxford University Press and Messrs. Jonathan Cape in allowing me to reprint extracts from their respective publications, *Stalin* by Dr Isaac Deutscher, and *Spain* by Salvador de Madariaga.

My particular thanks are due to the following friends: Tom Burns and Gavin Maxwell, without whose encouragement and patient help I should never have begun this book; John Marks, Collin Brooks, and Archibald Lyall for their careful reading of my MS. and for much valuable advice; Mrs Michael Hurt and Mrs John Hanbury-Tracy, who, together with my wife, corrected my proofs while I was in Budapest; and Vane Ivanović, aboard whose ships I have done most of my writing.

P.K.

January 4th, 1957

ABOUT THE AUTHOR

Peter Kemp was an English soldier and writer. Educated at Wellington College and Trinity College in Cambridge, Kemp was preparing for a career as a lawyer before, alarmed by the spread of Communism, he volunteered to assist the Nationalists during the Spanish Civil War. Kemp saw extensive combat in both the Requetés militia and later the Spanish Foreign Legion. After the Civil War ended, Kemp was recruited as an agent for the British Special Operations Executive, taking part in numerous commando raids and other irregular warfare activities in France, Albania, Poland, and several colonial territories throughout the Pacific during and after the Second World War. After that war ended, he worked an insurance salesman and international journalist, continuing his life of distinction and adventure. He passed away on October 30, 1993.